W9-CMJ-569

a thousand moons on a thousand rivers

Modern Chinese Literature from Taiwan

hsiao li-hung

translated by michelle wu

a thousand moons

a thousand moons

columbia university press new york

on a thousand rivers

Columbia University Press wishes to express its appreciation for assistance given by the Chiang Ching-kuo Foundation for International Scholarly Exchange and Council for Cultural Affairs in the preparation of the translation and in the publication of this series.

COLUMBIA UNIVERSITY PRESS
Publishers Since 1893
New York   Chichester, West Sussex

Library of Congress Cataloging-in-Publication Data
Hsiao, Li-hung.
[Ch'ien chiang yu shui ch'ien chiang yüeh. English]
A thousand moons on a thousand rivers / Hsiao Li-hung ;
translated by Michelle Wu.
p. cm. — (Modern Chinese literature from Taiwan)
ISBN 0–231–11792–2
1. Hsiao, Li-hung—Translations into English. I. Wu, Michelle M., 1970–
II. Title. III. Series.
PL2862.I3177C4813 2000
895.1'352—DC21   99–28441

Casebound editions of Columbia University Press books are printed on permanent and durable acid-free paper.
Printed in the United States of America
Designed by Linda Secondari
c 10 9 8 7 6 5 4 3 2

contents

foreword

PANG-YUAN CHI

I am often asked to speak about Taiwan to Westerners who do not read Chinese. Each time I feel compelled to talk about Taiwan's remarkable literary accomplishments, which I consider to be as important as her economic miracle and development of a multiparty democracy. Through this literature, one can see the true face of Taiwan and hear the voices of the people living here. But we have had until recently very few translations of Chinese literature from Taiwan into English.

One of the books that I have most wanted to see translated into English is *A Thousand Moons on a Thousand Rivers*, which is an innocent, almost naive love story set in a Taiwan that has faded away. The book was an instant best-seller when it was published in 1981. The Chinese-language edition has already gone through more than sixty printings, and its readers span all age groups. The middle-aged feel a sense of nostalgia when they read about the romances and family relationships described in the novel. The younger generation, living in this age of sexual liberation, harbor a kind of suspicious yearning for the "till death do us part" love depicted in the book.

Some critics have commented that the book reads like a fairy tale, and doubt the existence of the kind of innocent and platonic love described in the novel. All readers and critics, however, have nothing but praise for Hsiao Li-hung's lyrical language. The extended family in this little coastal town in southern Taiwan live a charmed existence, fully in tune with the sea and the changing seasons. Hsiao Li-hung merges simple yet powerful dialogue with scholarly and popular allusions, puns, folk songs, and Buddhist chants and maxims to portray life in southern Taiwan during the 1970s when the cohesive agricultural society was in the midst of transforming itself into an alienated industrial society. With a delicate and refined literary flair, she brings the people of that time to life with strong and genuine emotion.

Zhenguan, the main female character in the novel, has been born and raised in the small coastal town. Daxin, her male counterpart, comes from the city of Taipei and leaves Taiwan after graduation from college to study abroad. Since childhood, Daxin has visited Zhenguan's hometown, often during festivals. He is a city boy, full of curiosity and a longing for the rustic pleasures of country life. He is fascinated by traditions such as the ancestral worship during the Lunar New Year, the riddle-solving during the Lantern Festival, the noontime water and the rice dumplings prepared for the Dragonboat Festival, and the story behind the special rice balls for the Lovers' Festival. These celebrations, together with detailed descriptions of local scenery and life, add charm to the romance of these two kindred souls.

It is not difficult to understand why some critics have discredited the book, saying that it indulgently describes the beauty of country scenery, the warm sentiments among family members and neighbors, and the innocent romance between two young people without mentioning the harsher and sadder aspects of life in Taiwan. I would argue, however, that many writers of love stories have concentrated on the positive. When Shakespeare wrote *Romeo and Juliet,* he did not dwell on the deadly plague sweeping through Europe at that time, but rather focused on the romantic and tragic love story that only has room for the two protagonists.

In order to find out what readers of the current generation think of this book, I visited many discussion groups on the Internet between 1996 and 1998. It was an exciting experience to reach across such an expanse of time, during which great changes have taken place in Taiwan. Most readers admit to having been deeply impressed by the character of First Aunt, a Buddhist nun who plays an important role in the story, but they are puzzled by the outcome of the relationship between Zhenguan and Daxin. Almost all say that the book evoked nostalgic recollections of childhoods spent in their grandparents' small hometowns. These two themes—of one-sided, unfulfilled love experienced by two generations, and childhood memories of home—are intricately intertwined.

The novel is really a book describing admiration. With quiet dignity, First Aunt, a traditional Chinese woman, succumbs to her fate to be a Buddhist nun in a most "virtuous" fashion, so that readers come to respect rather than pity her. The relationship between Zhenguan and Daxin can actually be read as a young woman's quiet admiration of a "perfect" man. Daxin comes across as talented and almost ideal—he excels in the fierce competition to get into the best university; he pursues his dream to become a scientist; he is well versed in classical and modern poetry; he is familiar with Chinese knight-errant novels; he carves ornate stone chops; he writes beautiful letters with flower petals folded within; and he is appreciative of the beauty of nature, demonstrating superb taste as he praises the sea and the moon. He is the man that many women are waiting for. Daxin's charisma is all the more attractive when framed by the old courtyard gates of Zhenguan's family compound. The forlorn love story can inspire and console only when set against the changing seasons in the seaside town. As the novel develops, Hsiao Li-hung also strives to expound the enlightening and healing power of Buddhism. The Buddhist temple where First Aunt takes up residence as a nun, with its zenlike silence and ringing temple bells, emphasizes the fatalistic coupling of pain and joy, and the coming together and separation that is inherent in life.

A Thousand Moons on a Thousand Rivers is a singular book. Compared with mainstream novels of violence and sensational sex, and books preoccupied with grotesque absurdities and eerie and unthinkable calamities, this novel may seem to lack intensity. But its slow and riverlike movement has its merits and may contribute to a balanced understanding of what Taiwan has really been like, imparted through its literature.

The English translation of this book must have been a long and difficult process, as the text is strewn with puns, folk songs, local dialects, classical poetry, Buddhist maxims, and local sentiments, all of which defy Western logic. The translator, Michelle Min-chia Wu, has successfully overcome these many obstacles and produced a translation that will be sure to move English readers as much as the original has countless Chinese readers.

I would like to extend my appreciation to Nancy Du, also a promising young translator, who helped proofread the first manuscript of this translation and offered many valuable suggestions. Many thanks to Ms. Connie Hsu Swenson for her gracious, time-consuming, and painstaking editing, which has helped make the book more fluent for English readers. I also thank Ms. Jennifer Crewe and her staff at Columbia University Press for their patience in seeing this project through. Special thanks to Taiwan's Chiang Ching-kuo Foundation for International Scholarly Exchange and the Council for Cultural Affairs, which generously supported the translation and publication of this book.

—Pang-yuan Chi

Professor Emeritus, National Taiwan University

Editor-in-Chief, *Chinese PEN*

a thousand moons on a thousand rivers

one

I

Zhenguan was born between Great Snow and Winter Solstice.[1] The midwife had predicted that the baby would arrive in late October. By late November, however, Zhenguan's mother was still walking around with a swollen belly. People would tell her, "Shuihong, overdue babies are supposed to be more intelligent; you are surely going to give birth to a scholar!" Her mother was of calm disposition, and such comments aroused neither surprise nor elation. She would reply, unaffected, "Who knows? It's all up to nature, we are what we are. . . . Who knows?" Zhenguan wasn't born until the eve of Winter Solstice. They couldn't tell yet whether the baby girl was gifted or not, but the fact was that she had hidden in her mother's womb for a little over eleven months.

When Zhenguan grew a bit older, adults would tease, "Little

Zhenguan, most people are born in ten months' time; why did you take so long, making your poor mother suffer more than other mothers?" At first, Zhenguan didn't know what to say, and she took the question very seriously. She pestered her mother, pressing for an answer. Finally fed up with Zhenguan's persistence, her mother suggested, "Why don't you tell them: I chose to be born just in time to savor the rice balls that families eat for Winter Solstice." Armed with a satisfactory reply, Zhenguan learned to respond quickly, often surprising the adults. Her third aunt even said, "Our little Zhenguan is certainly smarter than other six- or seven-year-olds. After all, she did hide in her mother's belly for almost one year!"

Eventually Zhenguan came to believe that she had indeed been born at just the right time. One day, while playing a game of shuttlecock with her cousin, Zhenguan and Yinchan tied with twenty-six consecutive kicks each. But Yinchan insisted that she was the winner, saying, "Since we have the same number of kicks, we should go by age. And since you're one year older than me, you lose!"

"Didn't I say that it's a tie? I'm six years old too!" Zhenguan laughed.

Yinchan snickered. "Counting backward or forward?"

"Six is six, no matter how you count it!"

Yinchan picked up the shuttlecock and dragged Zhenguan to the back garden. "All right, let's go ask somebody—maybe Grandpa or Grandma. If anyone says that you're six years old, then I lose!"

Zhenguan's third aunt and uncle lived in the back garden. In early summer, when magnolia and jasmine flowers came into full bloom, their room would be filled with breezes perfumed by sweet blossoms. The womenfolk occasionally went there to play cards. The two little girls entered the room, one following the other. When Zhenguan caught sight of her mother, she demanded, "Mom, how old am I?"

The grown-ups all turned around, surprised. Only Zhenguan's mother, instructing Zhenguan's first aunt at a game of cards, seemed unperturbed. Zhenguan sat down to await a reply, when her second aunt proclaimed, "Little Zhenguan was born in the year of the ox.[2] That makes her seven this year!" Suddenly deflated, Zhenguan fell silent. Yinchan went at once to her side, giving her a consoling pat on the hand. "But as Zhenguan was saying: since we are both in the same class at school, why am I six years old?"

"Yinchan was born in the year of the tiger."

"What difference does that make?" Zhenguan's question made everyone laugh. Even her mother smiled and said, "What's with you today, making such a fuss over nothing?"

Second Aunt got the trump card, and everyone shuffled their deck for a new game. Touching Zhenguan's shoulder gently, her first aunt said, "Little Zhenguan, let me explain. Your age is determined by the calendar. The year of the ox comes first, so naturally, you're one year older than those born in the year of the tiger!"

This time Zhenguan got right to the point. "But Auntie, there's only a month's difference between the two of us. Yinchan came forty-two days after me."

Now it was Third Aunt's turn to speak. As she gathered her winnings, she laughed. "If we all counted the way you do, there would be chaos in the world! Don't you know that a child born before the new year—even one born on New Year's Eve—is a year older than a child born on New Year's Day?"

Zhenguan was speechless for a moment.

Her third aunt continued, "When you grow up, you will be grateful for not being born in the year of the tiger, for it is not a very auspicious sign. Those who are born in the year of the tiger have to stay away when there is a wedding in the family. And think of it this way: you get to enjoy the Winter Solstice rice balls first! Have you forgotten? You should be happy to be one year older, if only for the sake of the rice balls!"

Everyone laughed and Zhenguan blushed all the way to her ears, saying, "But I didn't really get to taste the rice balls . . ." Before she could finish, someone summoned her from the doorway; as she turned around to leave, she heard her amused third aunt remark to her mother, "Listen to your daughter. She's blaming the rice balls for making her one year older!"

II

Contrary to expectation, Zhenguan did not particularly stand out during her six years of elementary school. Although she certainly did not fall behind her peers, she didn't excel either. Upon graduation, she ranked an unremarkable seventh in the class, and when she received her report card, her mother wasn't very pleased at all. She scolded Zhenguan, but Zhenguan's grandfather jumped to her defense. "Shuihong," he said to his daughter, "you're not being fair. Think about this: your fifth uncle was an intelligent man who made it all the way through medical school at Tokyo Imperial University. But guess what? He ranked twentieth in his high school class! The age-old adage tells us that big roosters learn to crow later; likewise, roosters that learn to crow first do not necessarily grow into big ones.

How can you judge Zhenguan by her grades from elementary school?"

Her mother was quiet as Grandpa continued. "Listen to me: you can't expect the same of daughters and sons. Girls are not cut out for studying as hard as boys. Any learned person knows that girls are the future mothers of the world; it's good that they learn to read and write, and to know right from wrong. The way that I see it, however, those who excel in school are too often ignorant of virtues. It would be a big mistake to push Zhenguan to pursue good grades at the expense of her womanly morality!"

Zhenguan's ears perked up at her grandfather's words: "If a son is bad, only one person, one family, is affected. But a daughter is bestowed with the solemn responsibility of raising the next generation. A daughter's virtue, therefore, bears a direct impact on the human root, the human seed. If a bad daughter marries into another family she may give birth to a bunch of impudent brats . . . and then what would become of this world?"

Grandpa's explanation made sense to Zhenguan. In fact, she reasoned to herself, she had seen two unruly boys fighting in the neighborhood alley just that morning. He continued, "Your grandfather used to say: only women of virtue give birth to noble sons. He also said that a good wife at home keeps men from committing atrocities. It is self-evident that daughters are far more precious than sons, and we must be especially careful to guide them well."

"Yes, Father, you're right."

"Now, after Zhenguan gets through her joint entrance examinations, have her come to me every day to study the *Thousand-Word Classic*."[3]

Zhenguan did not feel confident about her performance on the joint entrance exams for junior high school. Nevertheless, she felt relieved when they were over, as if a heavy burden had been lifted from her shoulders. She had, after all, studied hard for six years, and her parents should be pleased. But more than anything else, she was excited to begin her studies with Grandpa, who would teach her about the *Women's Book of Family Etiquette* and the *Book of Maxims*.[4]

Grandpa had twenty grandchildren, young and old. All of his children had families, with the exception of Zhenguan's fifth uncle, who was still single. Zhenguan's first uncle had been drafted into the Japanese army and sent to Southeast Asia during World War II.[5] Decades passed with no news of him. His wife, who never remarried, lived with their two sons, Yinshan and Yinchuan. Zhenguan's second and third uncles had two boys and two girls each: Yincheng, Yinhe, Yinyue, Yingui, Yinan, Yinding, Yinchan, and Yincharn. Her fourth uncle had a girl and a boy, Yinxing and Yinxiang. Grandpa's grandchildren all loved to visit him, so it was always festive at his house.

After she began her studies with Grandpa, Zhenguan came to know the first few verses of the *Book of Maxims* by heart: "Lie not to heaven. Desecrate not the earth. Deceive not the sovereign. Disobey not your parents." But when reciting the lines, she always had to start from the very beginning, for if she were asked to recall the text from somewhere in the middle, she would be completely lost.

Once Grandpa asked each of his pupils to memorize a different passage. Yinyue started: "Defy not your teachers. Deceive not the Almighty. Insult not your brother. Spoil not your children." Yingui followed: "Abuse not your friends. Hurt not your neighbors. Alienate not your family. Exaggerate not your words." Next came Yinchan: "Take not any shortcut. Discard not your books. Neglect not your manners. Forget not your promises." Yinchan recited her passage: "Manipulate not your power. Flaunt not your riches. Blame not your poverty. Trample not the underprivileged." But Zhenguan was so busy mumbling under her breath, repeating from the first line again and again, that she forgot to stand up for her turn!

When they progressed to the *Thousand-Word Classic,* the verses became more complicated and ever more difficult to remember. Weeks later, Zhenguan was still stuck on the same passage: "Echoes resound in hollow valleys, modest hearts learn to listen. Bad causes accumulate bile, good deeds accumulate good will. A foot of jade is no treasure, an inch of time is far more precious."

And yet, the more the children studied, the clearer their minds became. As the words took on resonance, the wisdom of the texts began to reveal itself. Zhenguan fell in love with the immaculate order of things embodied in these classics.

When they got to the *Three-Character Classic,*[6] they really had to start concentrating . . . from "as a child, during one's childhood, love one's teachers, learn one's manners," to "in growing up, set one's priorities, first be filial, then accumulate knowledge, learn to count, learn to read" and "dogs patrol nightly, roosters crow daily, carelessness in learning becomes you not, silkworms spit silk, bees make honey, one's not learning makes one inferior, learn when young, walk when grown, benefit the nation, good for citizens, build a reputation, make parents proud, reputation comes first, fortune comes later."

After every recitation, Zhenguan felt like a different person, her body and soul cleansed and refreshed by the very act of reading the simple text.

III

The summer days were long and hot, so Zhenguan's grandfather conducted the study sessions in the morning. After lunch, everyone would sit together to enjoy a bowl of iced sweet soup. When it came to eating, Zhenguan was extremely slow. She was always the last one to put down her spoon. Those who didn't know her well might suspect that she had already had seconds. Her cousins took to calling her Miss Nine Servings. Yinchan and her other cousins laughed. "While other people have one serving, you have nine!"

"Me, nine servings? Have you ever seen me eat that much? I don't like this nickname; give me another one. Oh, I know! During last night's story-telling under the tree, Grand-Uncle was explaining how the Tang Dynasty was founded. All right then, I want to be Xu Maokung!"[7]

"I want to be Qin Shubao!"[8]

"I want to be Cheng Yaojin!"[9]

"But Yu Chigong has a dark face! I don't look like him!"[10]

"So what? We're just playing make-believe!"

At five, Yinxiang was too young to participate, so he stood by the side and watched the other children. Yinding was the only person without a part, and yet he refused to play Li Shimin, the emperor.

"How are we going to play without anyone as Li Shimin?"

"Okay, who wants the role? I can trade with him!"

Yinchan could not help but blurt out, "Ha, are you stupid or something? Li Shimin was the emperor, and you're turning down the chance to be king!"

Yinding rolled his calflike eyes and retorted, "What do you know? Daddy says that only the most foolish people want to become emperors; second in line are those want to be bosses, and then those who want to become fathers. . . . Now who's the stupid one?"

Yinchuan finally proposed, "Let's play something else so that Yinchan and the other girls can join us too; how about hide-and-seek? The more the merrier!"

They usually played hide-and-seek in the courtyard in front of the salt shop at the end of the alley, where a number of bunyan trees with long whiskers that swept the ground kept it shady and cool. From the courtyard they could see the fish ponds and grass shacks of the back harbor. The only drawback was the coffin shop that faced the courtyard, filled with piles of painted and unpainted slabs of wood that, whether colored bright red or not, were frightening to behold.

The children agreed to play hide-and-seek. Almost everyone, except big cousin Yinshan, was there. Zhenguan wanted to join them at first, but strangely enough, she had been having bad dreams about the coffin shop for several nights in a row, and for the past two days she'd had to run past the courtyard.

"Why don't you want to play?"

"Me? Uh . . . I'm sleepy."

Everyone went along, even little Yinxiang. Zhenguan, left with nothing better to do, wandered into Grandma's room. Her grandmother's bed, the old-fashioned type firmly rooted in the floor with thick wooden nails, was large enough to accommodate many people. Zhenguan lay down next to her grandmother and tossed and turned for a while, only to discover that she wasn't drowsy at all. Grandma was fast asleep, though, and Zhenguan didn't want to wake her, so she stood up, put on her shoes, and walked toward the back garden.

Of all Grandma's daughters, only Second Aunt lived at

home. Her husband had died young, leaving her with a six-month-old baby. Now, with Cousin Huian already seventeen going on eighteen and attending high school in Tainan, Second Aunt was alone and had decided to return home. All of this suddenly occurred to Zhenguan as she stepped into the room and caught sight of her first and second aunts.

So that was why her mother and aunts came here so often! They played cards all afternoon, with wins and losses of no more than five dollars. What kept them there? They were really trying to keep their widowed sister company, to help her pass the time. No wonder her grandfather didn't put a stop to their "gambling."

Her second aunt saw her and laughed. "Good, little Zhenguan is here. Whenever she comes, fortune turns in my favor!"

Her third aunt smiled. "So, Zhenguan has become the money lady! But she was born with an opportunistic heart; she looks down on people and lends a hand only to the winners, not the losers!" The others were chuckling even before she had finished her sentence. Zhenguan, embarrassed, rubbed her eyes and asked incredulously, "Third Auntie, are you really losing?"

Everyone laughed. "Don't take her seriously! Just check her pockets, they're filled with money! She'll only need your help to count it all!"

The conversation gradually turned to Zhenguan's studies. Second Aunt asked about how Zhenguan had fared on the provincial junior high school entrance exams.

"Why don't you ask her?" her mother replied.

"I'm not sure, but my teacher predicted that I should pass," Zhenguan answered. The women all looked pleased, but her mother said, "If she really does make the mark, then we'll be in trouble! She'll suffer from motion sickness if she has to commute to the city; but if she stays in the school dormitory, she'll miss home. After all, she's only thirteen years old!"

"Why doesn't she try the local junior high school?" Second Aunt proposed. "Then she and Yinchan could keep each other company."

"Her homeroom teacher came to see me on his bicycle several times, and he urged me to register her for the exams, saying that it would be a pity for her to go to the local junior high school. He said he could guarantee that she'd make it into the provincial girls' junior high school!"

There was a pause, and then her first aunt said, "Doesn't Zhenguan have an uncle in Jiayi City?"

"He moved there the year she was born, so she hasn't had a chance to meet him yet."

Zhenguan listened as they talked, but before long, she had dozed off. When she was a little girl, she used to go to see plays with the adults but ended up falling asleep every time. No one knew why she slept so much. She almost always had to be carried out of the theater by her mother or her aunts, the midnight breezes caressing her face as she drifted, half-awake, half-asleep. The adults would cover her head with a scarf, gently trying to wake her by patting her face, fearing that the little child's soul would be left behind in the theater, unable to find its way back home.

It was time for dinner when Zhenguan awoke. The card game had broken up, and her mother had already gone home to prepare the evening meal. The neighbors all envied her mother for living so close, with her parents and her in-laws only a short walk apart. Seeing the dining room ablaze with light, Zhenguan quickly washed her face and went inside. At Grandpa's house, the men, the women, the young, and the old all sat at different tables. However, the food served at every table was the same. The old traditions did not change, and they had been observed for countless generations.

Zhenguan remembered once, when Yinchan tried to sit at Yinding's table, Third Aunt insisted that she return to the girls' table immediately. Later, Zhenguan heard her mother say, "Girls are girls. They should stand properly when standing, and sit properly when sitting. If one runs from place to place, or changes seats when dining, she will end up marrying into two different households!"

Zhenguan met Yinyue at the entrance to the dining room and asked, "Has dinner started yet? Where are you going?"

Yinyue caught her by the elbow and said, "The game of hide-and-seek is not over yet. Big Brother has been out searching for a long time already, and still no news. . . . How can anyone sit down to eat?"

Zhenguan grabbed Yinyue's hand and said, "Come, let's find out what's going on!" She saw Yinxing, Yinchan, and the others crying as they came toward her. Yinchan was a very spirited girl who never shed a tear after a spanking, who never admitted defeat. To see even her in this state, who wouldn't be alarmed?

"What's the matter?"

"What happened?"

No answer to all the questions. Zhenguan and Yinyue entered the dining room quietly and, getting no response from the adults, approached Yinchan. Zhenguan tugged at her sleeve and asked, "Yinchan, what's wrong?" The wild and unruly Yinchan burst into tears.

Zhenguan's third uncle turned to Yinding. "What's the matter? Didn't Yinshan go out to find you? Where is he?"

Yinding mumbled, "Big Brother told us to come home first. He and Second Brother and Third Brother are going to look for—"

It was at that moment that everyone noticed Yinxiang was missing.

"Where's Yinxiang?"

The boys seemed dumbstruck, and the girls started to wail. Dropping the bowl of soup in her hands, Zhenguan's fourth aunt grabbed Yinchan by the arm and demanded, "What happened? Tell your auntie!"

Yinchan swiped at her tears, but as she looked up, more fell down her cheeks. "We were playing hide-and-seek, and now we can't find little Yinxiang."

"Have you looked everywhere?"

"Yes, but we couldn't find him. We didn't dare come back, but Big Brother . . ."

As everyone scrambled to join in the search, the coffin shop carpenter came rushing toward them in a panic. He said to Grandpa, "Oh dear, how can I put this—your little grandson . . . oh God! He climbed into one of our ready-made coffins while we were napping, and—"

Four or five voices asked in unison, "Where is he?"

"We only found out just now, when someone came to the shop and wanted to see the merchandise. He had been in there for too long and suffocated, he wasn't breathing. Our boss carried him to the hospital at once, running barefoot, without even putting his shoes on. His wife asked me to come tell you . . . you had best be on your way."

Within minutes, all the adults had left the room. Zhenguan was going to follow, when First Aunt stopped suddenly on her way out: her two sons, Yinshan and Yinchuan, had returned amid the chaos.

"Come here!" she called out to Yinchuan. Zhenguan had never seen her aunt so angry before.

Yinchuan walked toward his mother deliberately, step by step, and knelt down before her. "Ma . . ."

"Tell me, how old are you?"

Yinchuan was silent.

"You're the oldest of the lot," First Aunt shouted. "When you take your younger cousins out, it is your responsibility to return all of them home safely. Now—with Yinxiang . . . how can you ever face Grandpa, Grandma, Fourth Aunt and Uncle?" She burst into tears. "And you still have the audacity to come back! I have no face left to show the others. I might as well beat you to death right now, to pay for your little cousin's life!"

"Ma—"

"Auntie—"

Yinshan had crouched down over his brother, and Zhenguan and Yinyue tried to hold their aunt back. But she was very stubborn, and she had a heavy hand. Seeing that she was already reaching for the bamboo whip, the two girls urged Yincheng, "Go fetch Grandpa, hurry!" But Yincheng, like Yinshan, bent beside his cousins, refusing to budge. So Zhenguan grabbed Yinyue's hand, saying, "Let's go to the clinic. Maybe Yinxiang is all right after all, and Yinchuan will be spared a spanking!"

IV

Zhenguan's fourth aunt hadn't eaten for two days. Two days ago, she had still been able to weep with grief, "Yinxiang! My poor baby . . . gone!" Later, though, she lost her voice, and her wail turned into a hoarse whimper. Morning and night, Zhenguan wept too when she heard her aunt's pitiful cries.

On this day, the seventh day of the seventh lunar month, all the families would steam glutinous rice and make rice balls, as offerings to Qi-xing Niang-niang.[11]

Zhenguan lay on her bed, now on her stomach, now on her back, head spinning. Everybody was busy at the stove in the kitchen, and Fourth Aunt was probably in her room. Was there no one there to comfort her? At this thought, Zhenguan nearly sprang up in alarm. But then it occurred to her: what could she say to Fourth Aunt? Would she be able to do anything but cling to a corner of her skirt and weep along?

"Get up! Get up, lazybones!" Yinchan appeared in voice and person at the same time; she sat down next to Zhenguan and said, "Everyone is making rice balls. If you don't join in, you won't get any to eat!"

Zhenguan ignored her. Yinchan laughed. "Come on, you'd better come help out. Second Aunt says that you make the roundest rice balls, but Yingui and the others won't buy it. They want to challenge you!" Zhenguan moved a little but still wouldn't get up.

"What's wrong?"

"Where's Fourth Aunt?" Zhenguan demanded.

The light in Yinchan's face went out at once. "She was in the kitchen at first, but they persuaded her to go back to her room. I think it hurts her even to swallow."

Zhenguan turned around and covered her face with her hands.

She remembered the day Yinxiang turned one month old. She was still in third grade, and as she passed by Grandpa's house on her way home from school, Third Aunt called out to her and asked her inside. And there, sitting on the edge of the bed, she ate two large bowls of glutinous rice. She remembered that day so clearly: Fourth Aunt had on a crimson red dress as she carried the baby in, with a big smile on her face. The baby's bracelets and hat decorations all glittered with gold. A necklace with a small golden gourd pendant hung around its neck.

She had asked Fourth Aunt's permission to hold the baby, and as she gently took the child from his mother's arms, her fifth uncle came in, laughing. "Well well, take a look here! A little kitten is trying to snatch a mouse bigger than she is!"

As Zhenguan indulged herself in these memories, another cousin came in shouting, "Come to the front hall! We have guests from Taipei!"

Yinchan could not imagine who might be visiting.

"It's Fourth Aunt's sister-in-law and nephew." And like a scout, she was off again.

Zhenguan scrambled off the bed and groped around for her slippers. Yinchan had already rushed out the door. The two of them, one close on the heels of the other, were running to the courtyard when Yinchan came to an abrupt halt.

"What's the matter?" Zhenguan followed Yinchan's gaze and understood immediately. Fourth Aunt's nephew was a high school student about fifteen or sixteen years old!

They slowed down and turned back toward the kitchen, where everyone was busy at the stove. There wasn't much they could do to help, although all their female cousins were gathered in the room next to the kitchen kneading rice balls between their palms. When the bamboo trays were filled with rice balls, they would be passed on to the kitchen. As the two girls entered the room, Yinchan said jokingly, "Okay, Zhenguan's here, who wants to challenge her to a competition of rice-ball making?"

Zhenguan nudged her. "Shut up, I'm here to eat."

"It's not your turn yet, we have to offer the rice balls to Qi-niang-ma first," Yinchan said.

They both sat down and began rolling the glutinous rice dough into little balls. The rice balls for July 7 differed from those made for Winter Solstice. Winter Solstice rice balls could be either salty or sweet, with meat or sugar fillings; they could even be dyed partially red. The rice balls for July 7, however, must be pure white. First they were kneaded into round balls, and later, marked with indentations made with the index finger.

"What are the dents for?" When she was a little girl, Zhen-guan would ask this question over and over, but she always got the same response from the adults: "To hold the tears of the spinner-girl." Because the answer was given laughingly, Zhen-guan was suspicious; but indeed it was true that for as long as she could remember, it had always drizzled on the eve of July 7. The rain was the spinner-girl's tears.

Why did the spinner-girl weep so much? For this question the grown-ups all had different answers: "The spinner-girl has-n't seen the cow-herder for an entire year, so tears of happiness gush forth when they meet," "The cow-herder hasn't done his dishes for one whole year, so the spinner-girl has many to wash," "Zhenguan, the rain is the spinner-girl's dishwater!" ("But why doesn't the cow-herder wash his own dishes?") "Silly girl, men don't wash dishes!"

The dent on the rice ball is actually a very shallow, symbol-ic one. But, ruminating about the legend, Zhenguan forgot to pull her finger back and pressed hard instead, poking a big hole in the rice ball. Everyone laughed.

"Wow, what is that?"

"Zhenguan has made a water basin!"

"It's large enough to hold both the spinner-girl's tears and her dishwater!"

Zhenguan laughed along with them. At this point, the first batch of rice balls was being brought into the room next to the kitchen; Grandma followed the procession of food into the room. Zhenguan was about to do the same when she saw the high school student beside her.

"Daxin, don't be shy, they are all your uncle's nephews and nieces," said Grandma.

The boy nodded but sat timidly at the side of the table. Grandma turned around to get a bowl of glutinous rice from her daughter-in-law and placed it before him, saying, "Eat up! Your aunt is not feeling very well, and your mother will want to spend more time with her."

"I know." The boy accepted the bowl of rice but didn't take a bite.

The rice balls were all ready, and the girls started carrying the bamboo trays from the kitchen. Zhenguan tugged at Yinchan's sleeve and said, "Don't we have to sprinkle chrysanthemum petals on the glutinous rice offered to Qi-niang-ma? Come, let's go gather some in the back garden!"

two

I

It was fishing season, and everyone in the family went to bed as early as possible. Zhenguan, Yinchan, and her sister usually slept with Grandma, and by seven or eight o'clock all would retire for the night. But tonight it was already nine-thirty, and the girls were still wide awake, asking their grandmother to tell them some of the many stories she always had tucked away.

"Zhan Dien left home to do business and made a fortune. When he returned, his father-in-law, blinded by greed, devised a plan to kill Zhan Dien and even forced his daughter to marry someone else. Zhan Dien's wife was a virtuous woman and a filial daughter. Caught in such a predicament, she had no choice but to write up a petition accusing her own father of murdering her husband. . . .

"Zhou Cheng came to Taiwan to do business, and he took in a concubine named Amien. His wife Yuenu waited in vain for him back home and finally decided to cross the Taiwan Strait from Fujian Province to seek out her husband. Amien pretended to treat her husband's first wife well but in the dead of night secretly poisoned her soup of pig's stomach and lotus seeds. . . ."

Zhenguan wanted to continue listening but was afraid to. She used to be scared senseless by Hugupo, the child-eating tiger that could transform itself into an old woman, and now she trembled at the thought of the ghosts of Zhan Dien and Yuenu. Yinchan and her sister fell asleep soon after listening to Grandma's stories, but Zhenguan kept tossing and turning. She finally nudged her grandmother awake. "Grandma, are you asleep?"

"Mmm . . ."

"Grandma, what if the ghosts appear?"

Grandma opened her eyes, blinking slowly, and smiled. "Silly girl, why not tell yourself, I'm going to get up early tomorrow so I can feast on delicious morsels of fish?"

Hearing her grandmother's words made Zhenguan feel silly. Indeed, with so many pleasant things to think about, why dwell on ghosts? Feeling that the wrinkles in her heart had been ironed out, she yawned and was nearing slumber when she suddenly remembered with a start. "Grandma, will you wake me at one o'clock?"

"In the middle of the night? Are you going out to steal chickens?" Grandma laughed.

"Of course not," Zhenguan replied. "I want to go to the fishponds with Uncle and the others!"

Her grandmother responded with a grunt and was soon asleep.

At midnight Zhenguan was roused by a quick succession of chopping sounds. She awoke to find the backyard flooded with light. The womenfolk were preparing snacks for the men to eat if they got hungry at the fishponds. Yinchan and her sister were still fast asleep, but Grandma was nowhere to be seen. Zhenguan rubbed her eyes and picked up the wooden pail on the shelf to fetch water for washing up. She ran into Daxin, Yinshan, and the others in the courtyard.

Everyone greeted her with a warm "good morning" except for Yincheng, who couldn't pass up a chance to make fun of her. "Ha, you're up too? The last four or five days that we've returned with the fish and nets, you've still been in dreamland! And now you want to join us? If everyone were to wake up at the hour you do, the fish market wouldn't open until late afternoon or evening!" Zhenguan walked to the water basin without answering. Had there been no witnesses, she would definitely have splashed water on him.

The water basin was made of cement and lined with stones. Half of it was outside the kitchen and half of it within, so water could be retrieved from both sides. Zhenguan bent down to grasp the water ladle, but her hand caught only midnight air heavy with dew. Peeking into the basin, she found that Yincheng, one step ahead of her, had already grabbed the ladle from inside the kitchen.

Zhenguan had no choice but to await her turn. Standing there, looking down again into the water basin, she discovered that the white shimmer inside was the reflection of moonlight. The slanting beams of the moon shone past the rooftops and dipped, cold, into the bottom of the water basin. The moon seemed to Zhenguan closer than she had ever seen it before. It was a moment of clarity.

After washing up, everyone had a bite to eat. As they were leaving, Yinyue and Yingui caught up with them.

"Zhenguan, wait up."

The fishmongers, workmen, and uncles had already started on their way. Zhenguan glanced at Yinshan and the others and suggested, "Why don't you guys go first, we'll catch up later."

Yinshan, always the responsible one, said, "No, we'll all wait—the two of you hurry up!"

The sisters scurried to get ready, and Zhenguan added, "Don't worry about eating anything right now—Yincheng has food with him!"

The children all reached the front gate ten minutes later, but the entourage of men was nowhere to be seen. Six pairs of feet broke into a run. The early morning breeze was so cool that one would never have guessed it was the middle of July. Everything glistened in the waning moonlight, and the street lamps seemed to stretch toward infinity. Zhenguan looked ahead, feeling as if she were filled with a luminous glow.

Outside the village, with a turn to the right, a narrow path meandered along the bank. Flanking it were eighty or ninety hectares of fishponds, one linked to the other. The children formed a procession. Yinshan let the girls take the lead: Yinyue was first, followed by Yingui and Zhenguan. Next came the boys, Daxin and Yincheng, with Yinshan at the end, making sure that everyone was accounted for.

Listening to the rhythm of her own footsteps, Zhenguan thought about how their great-grandfathers had come to settle here, developing this expanse of land and building narrow embankments like the one on which they now walked.

Yinshan explained to Daxin, the visitor from Taipei: "These fishponds cover an area of almost one hundred hectares. They all connect to the Huwei River, which in turn flows into the sea. . . . The fishing lanterns of Huwei are one of the eight scenic attractions of Budai Harbor."

Then Yincheng recounted the ownership of each pond. "These belong to Fifth Great-Uncle. His family doesn't live here anymore, so he has entrusted the care of his fishponds to others. And this property belongs to Third Great-Uncle. And this is the Lis' property, and the Huangs'. . . . Zhenguan's family's is to the north, see where the fishing lanterns are hung?" But Yincheng wasn't content to merely explain things; he had to point here and there as well, which caused him to spill the soup in his food pail.

"What's the matter with you?" Yinyue scolded, taking the food pail from his hands to examine its contents. Most of the soup was still intact, but she didn't feel confident about returning it to her brother. She moved back in the procession to follow Zhenguan.

Walking along the embankment, Zhenguan admired the beauty of the pools of water. The moon was mirrored on the surface of each fishpond, and the water shimmered in its light. A thousand moons reflected on a thousand rivers. What a sight to behold. . . . In the distance, lanterns hanging from the thatched fishing huts lit up the night. Adorning heaven and earth so touchingly, so magnificently, it was no wonder that they had become the best of the eight sights of Budai Harbor!

Yincheng was still babbling on. Yinyue warned him, "You'd better talk less and watch your step more; otherwise, you're going to slip and fall to the bottom of the fishpond!"

"I'm not going to slip!" Yincheng retorted. "Grandpa and Uncle can run on the embankment without even looking!"

Just then, a night watchman making his rounds passed by.

He approached the children, shining a flashlight into their faces, but retreated apologetically as soon as he recognized them. At that moment Zhenguan realized that she didn't want to go to the provincial high school and wished instead that she would flunk the middle school examinations. She suddenly felt a strong bond to her hometown, where everyone knew, or was related to, everyone else. Even those who didn't know your name knew your parents'! All at once, she didn't want to leave the warmth of this familiar place. If she were to go to Jiayi, she would certainly be homesick and cry every night.

Her heart beat faster at the thought, and quickening her pace to match, she said, "Grandpa and the others are not the only ones who can walk the embankment with their eyes closed!" Yinyue, trying to keep up and to keep her balance at the same time, found it difficult to carry the food pail, which she returned to Yincheng. As he caught it in his hand, he said to Zhenguan jokingly, "Ha, copycat!"

"Who am I copying?"

Yinshan laughed. "Daxin already used your metaphor. He lives in the West District of Taipei, and he said that he could make his way around his neighborhood in the dark!"

Bickering and teasing, they soon arrived at their destination. The fishpond was surrounded with people. Zhenguan looked on as her uncles leaped in to pull back the nets or remained on the embankment to give orders. She felt embarrassed to be standing there, neither sweating nor helping, so she grabbed Yingui's hand and retreated to the thatched hut.

With twenty or thirty people working together, there were shining torches and flashlights everywhere. But Zhenguan discovered as she entered the hut that most of the light was actually coming from the moon. Not only did the moonlight gleam on the rubble on the ground, it also shone on Daxin's standing figure. Illuminated by its clarity and caressed by the delicate breeze, Zhenguan felt as if she were wearing a gown of pale moonlight herself.

The first haul of fish was the most abundant. The fishmongers flung the nets, and the fish leaped and struggled, piled one on top of the other by the thousand. The smaller fish at the bottom could sometimes escape through the mesh and return to familiar waters. They didn't want to leave their home, just as Zhenguan dreaded leaving hers! Two or three fish had made it halfway through the netting, but because their bodies were larger than their heads, they became stuck.

Zhenguan lay back on a bed of straw, feeling sorry for the fish. She had intended only to rest but actually drifted into slumber. When Yinyue nudged her awake, her eyes opened to a vast expanse of sky and moist air. The thick fog around her was like the genesis of the world. Before the first dawn, heaven and earth banished all pretense and became newborn infants. Zhenguan supposed that she was lucky to have been born a daughter of the harbor. These thoughts formed as the first sea breezes caressed her, but she kept them to herself.

II

They had milkfish for many days in a row. The table was laden with dishes prepared in so many different ways: fish porridge, crispy fried fish, fish soup, roasted fish, poached fish, baked fish. . . . It was a treat for Daxin in particular because, as Zhenguan had been told, urbanites rarely have the opportunity to feast on so many fish dishes. Of course, inexperienced as he was, Daxin suffered a number of fish bones caught in his throat. Third Aunt was able to extract the bones with her chopsticks the first couple of times, but on one occasion a fish bone lodged itself so deeply that it disappeared from sight. Chopsticks and rice balls were of no help at all. Daxin, a big boy, sat in the living room as tears welled up in his eyes. The adults were panicky, and even Zhenguan felt sorry for him.

Zhenguan recalled the many times she had eaten fish since she was a child and an idea came to her. She rushed home. Her mother caught sight of her and said cheerfully, "Your report card has arrived. You're just in time to see it!" As she handed it to her daughter, she added, "The results of the examination will be posted in the papers tomorrow. Why don't you go to school and show your grades to your teacher? He will be thrilled!"

Zhenguan glanced at her score indifferently. "I'm going to get some malt sugar from Auntie Zhong-yi first. Fourth Aunt's nephew has a fish bone stuck in his throat."

She walked through the backyard and went into the bakery down the alley. She found some malt sugar there, a soft glob perched upon a bamboo stick, and went directly to Grandpa's without going home first, fearing that the malt sugar would drip to the ground. Back at her grandparents' house, everyone was still running around, frantically seeking remedies for Daxin.

Zhenguan was too timid to approach Daxin directly, so she handed the malt sugar to Yinan in the chaos. Minutes later Daxin stood up, happily proclaiming his recovery. Later no one could recall who fetched the malt sugar. Daxin said it was Yinan who asked him to swallow it, but Yinan couldn't remember who had handed it to him. Questioned again and again, he finally shouted, "What does it matter? He's okay now! Let's just say it fell from the sky!"

From then on Daxin stayed away from fish and developed a taste for boneless clams and freshwater mussels. Every day, he would venture out to the fishponds with the boys, carrying bamboo baskets to catch "red mouths," meaty clams with thin shells that liked to hide in the mud, emerging at dusk to drink water.

Ten days passed, and Daxin's face tanned under the sun. He discovered that the secret of catching red mouths is to plunge your hand in wherever you see something resembling a keyhole along the banks. Just as he was becoming an expert, his mother packed them up to go home. "Please stay a while longer, just a few more weeks," everyone urged. "After August and September, hairy crabs are abundant on the beaches and by the ponds. These crabs are tiny, but they are filled with *xie-huang*!"[1]

Daxin's mother protested, "October is still two months away! We've been here for more than a month already, and Daxin's father is beginning to complain."

"At least wait until Mid-Autumn Festival. There are so many festivities then, and all the boats in the harbor carry people out to sea to enjoy the sight of the full moon."

Daxin seemed tempted, but his mother said, "That won't do! Daxin's father has been urging us to return, and school is going to start soon!"

"Well, Daxin's uncle can take him back to Taipei first," Zhenguan's grandmother suggested. "But it is so rare that you get to come home that you should at least stay a while longer."

"Next time, next time. . . . I'll come back again, I promise! Dear cousins, visit us in Taipei whenever you can!"

After checking the schedule, mother and son decided to take the early train the next morning. Zhenguan thought they would retire to bed early, but her grandfather was telling stories in the courtyard, describing the military conquests of the legendary Tang Dynasty general Xue Rengui. Zhenguan found herself a seat and discovered Daxin sitting in front of her. The audience was enchanted with the tales of magic and wonder spun from Grandpa's mouth. Daxin turned and whispered to Yinan, "Too bad I'm not going to be here for the next episode tomorrow night."

As always, Fourth Aunt passed around iced dessert. Zhenguan was reaching out for a serving when Daxin's words registered in her mind. She almost dropped the bowl as she thought of her own imminent departure from home, sealed in the registration notice for school that had arrived by mail that morning.

three

I

The years passed. Zhenguan was nineteen, fresh out of high school, coming home to prepare for her university entrance examinations. Jiayi City had transformed her from a little girl into a young lady. Six entire years she had spent there, but as she tried to summon her memories, they came to her unreal and hazy, as if through a smoke screen.

Every time she went home it became harder to leave. She felt great reluctance at each tearful departure, and her grandmother would say that she resembled an orphan about to return to her wicked stepmother.

How could such a nostalgic person bear to leave home?

Zhenguan knew herself well and, as a result, did not take the idea of university too seriously. Jiayi had been far enough away from home. Taipei, to her, seemed almost at the end of the earth! The university exams were only a month away, but Zhenguan remained unconcerned. She studied off and on, half-heartedly. When Fourth Aunt offered to have Daxin tutor her, Zhenguan shook her head. Fourth Aunt thought her niece was too embarrassed to accept any help, but Zhenguan made her intentions clear: "Fourth Aunt, the truth is that I do not have my heart set on going to college. You'll understand when the test results are announced. If you were to ask Daxin to tutor me and I failed the exams just the same, he would feel guilty for not doing a good job, and he wouldn't have the face to see us again. I certainly don't want that to happen—it wouldn't be fair to him, would it?"

This made sense to Fourth Aunt, who did not bring up the issue again.

Although Zhenguan and Daxin were both born in the year of the ox, Daxin's birthdate enabled him to start school in the fall term, so he was always a year ahead of Zhenguan in his studies. Daxin was now a proud freshman at the country's highest institute of learning: National Taiwan University, famed for a campus full of azalea blossoms in the springtime. Apparently he had not even been required to take the joint entrance exams, for his outstanding scholastic achievement won him honorary admission to the university straight after graduation from the island's top Boys' High School. Furthermore, he was admitted into the Department of Chemistry, his first choice. His ambition was to win another Nobel Prize for the Republic of China. It was said that all the girls wanted to be his lab partner. . . .

Fourth Aunt talked endlessly about Daxin, and yet it was difficult for Zhenguan to piece together a complete picture. She could glean only fragments of what he must be like.

Later Fourth Aunt gave birth to another boy, a baby even heftier than Yinxiang, the child she had lost in that accident years ago. In Zhenguan's eyes, this child seemed to grow up in no time at all, as if he were inflating like a balloon, because she got to see him only every two or three months when she returned home.

Sometimes when Fourth Aunt was through talking about Daxin, she would wave her baby's hand and say, "When Yinxi grows up, he's going to be just as smart as his cousin Daxin, isn't he?" Yinxi would gurgle and then wobble back and forth, seeking a place to bury his face. Such occasions would always remind Zhenguan of how Fourth Aunt had lost her baby son, and she came to believe that all wounds must heal. Otherwise, how could anyone survive a lifetime of eighty, ninety years?

Fifth Uncle, Yinshan, and Yincheng had all gotten married. Yinchuan, Yinan, and the others were either in college or completing their compulsory military service. They did not get together often anymore. As for the girls, some worked at the fishery, some at the waterworks, and others at the farmers' association. They all had to wake up early for work, and to chat, they could come together only at dinnertime in the evenings. The thick, tight bond that kept them together as children had become a thing of the past.

Zhenguan missed home during the years she was away. She took care of her own meals, licked her own wounds when she was ill, and suffered terribly from homesickness. She remembered the day she first returned. It was drizzling when the train pulled into the station, and Third Aunt and Mother were waiting for her under an umbrella. Her mother was wearing a pea-green dress with a sailor's collar, and Zhenguan caught sight of her familiar figure before she saw her face. The only thought in her mind at that moment was: I will never leave home again.

They stopped over at her grandfather's first and then went to Third Aunt's, where they talked until evening, the room all abuzz. Zhenguan's eyes were rimmed with tears all the while.

Soon the girls came back from work, one after the other. Yinyue and Yingui held Zhenguan's hand, not knowing what to say. Yinchan, who came in after them, could only whisper, "You're . . . finally home!" Zhenguan let go of the sisters' hands to take Yinchan's. She opened her mouth, but no sound emerged from her lips.

She realized that Yinchan was mistaken, for when had she ever really left home? Now that she was with her family again, she felt as if she had never gone away at all. No, she had never really left! It seemed that just yesterday they were saying good-bye to each other at the door, and today, together again! The six years in between disappeared without a trace; little Zhenguan went to Jiayi to attend school, but the real Zhenguan had stayed behind. Her heart and soul had always been firmly anchored in her hometown.

Zhenguan came to realize: happy are those who never have to leave home! When she was in elementary school, she noticed that the farmers living nearby chose to be buried in a corner of their own farmland when they died. Generation after generation, year after year, they remained close to their hearts and homes, even in the afterlife.

Later, her Western Civilization textbook lay open before her, but Zhenguan's mind was still there, with the farmers. Her motivation to study for university dwindled further. She had been reading in the backyard "arm's-length" cottage these days. Nobody in the house made a sound or even dared cough for fear of distracting her. Yesterday when Yinxi cried, Fourth Aunt said, "Your elder cousin is studying. If you're going to cry, go outside!"

The cottage was even cooler than Third Aunt's room. Her grandfather usually took his afternoon naps here. For her sake, however, the old man had even vacated his napping bed. So many expectations, and such a dilemma: should she or shouldn't she take the exams?

The arm's-length cottage came by its name because its eaves were a little lower than on most houses, and a tall, grown man could easily reach up and touch the roof. When Zhenguan was three years old, her third uncle raised her to the rooftop. She climbed around there in glee and in no time at all had crawled to the ridge, refusing to come down, no matter how the others beckoned. Her six-foot-tall uncle stood red-faced and anxious, not knowing what to do. It was her third aunt who finally found a ladder, and her fifth uncle who carried her down from the cottage.

And then, when she was five . . . Fifth Uncle was but seventeen or eighteen. One day he volunteered to feed her. Since there were bones in the fish and bones in the meat, he decided to feed her the fishballs in the soup. She still had her baby teeth and had not yet learned to chew; she knew only that she should open her mouth when food was in sight. Fifth Uncle stuffed the fishballs and rice into her mouth, piece by piece, until Zhenguan could no longer keep her mouth open and started to wail.

It turned out that she hadn't been chewing at all. The fishballs bounced onto the floor, and as her fifth uncle leaned down to pick them up, he counted five, six, seven of them. He inspected Zhenguan's mouth, puzzled: how could such a small mouth hold so many fishballs?

Grandmother scolded him. "Are you trying to kill her? If she were to choke to death, how would you return a daughter to your brother-in-law? You're single, you know!"

II

Zhenguan was close to the uncles on her mother's side, but she dreaded her father like the devil. He worked at the salt mines, which she used to pass by on her way to school. Behind the offices, there was an air raid shelter built during the Japanese occupation, and in the yard, purple and red pansies. Yinchan would always insist on picking these flowers on the sly for their grandmother but once, while the two of them were busy collecting bouquets, Zhenguan's father and the deputy director of the salt mines came walking out of the office. . . .

The adults didn't say a word, but no one could ever persuade Zhenguan to step near the salt mines again. She was ashamed to have embarrassed her father in front of an outsider. From then on, when her father came to visit Grandma, she would do everything possible to hide from him. She would volunteer to watch over the fishponds, or to go fishing, or even to help Third Uncle grind ink in his studio all afternoon, anything to stay out of her father's sight.

They watched over the fishponds to keep the egrets away. June was a wet month, which meant that July would be scorching hot. Only mad dogs would venture outdoors in such sweltering heat. Egrets, however, loved to come out at this time of the year. At dawn and dusk they hovered over the fishponds and feasted on the fish until they were full. Targeting their prey, they would circle the skies and swoop down to secure their catch.

The guardians of the fishponds had to move fast, swinging bamboo clappers and making whooping sounds at the egrets before they could descend. The startled birds would fly up into the skies again, casting spiteful looks at their assailants. Another way to scare the egrets away was to light firecrackers. The gunpowder, however, would fall into the ponds and pollute the water, so most people opted for the clappers, made of the best bamboo, the thicker the better. The bamboo was cut into three-foot-long poles; one third of each was cut into cross-sections and hollowed out. When the bamboo pole was swung around, the hollows would emit a loud *whoosh*.

The sound was harmless to human ears, but it scared the egrets senseless. Judging by the way that they swooped down on fish at the ponds, one might surmise that they were fierce and strong. But they feared the mere sound of the bamboo clappers. Maybe what Grandpa said was true: the evil have no guts!

Fishing reminded Zhenguan of earthworms. She never really learned how to fish because she was afraid of the squiggling worms that were used as bait. When she was young, she wanted to help her fourth uncle fish, but while attempting to net small shrimp from the fishpond, she slipped and fell into the water. Fourth Uncle carried home a little girl caked in mud; no one could recognize her, and milkfish jumped out of her soggy pockets.

Compared to these episodes, ink-grinding did not seem particularly exciting. But because it was done in the service of Third Uncle, this small act took on special significance. . . . The world does not lack strong men who can lift heavy weights, nor does it lack scholars versed in all manner of intellectual pursuits. Few, however, are well equipped with both physical strength and literary talent. Zhenguan's third uncle was one such man. Since childhood, Zhenguan had viewed him as a kind of Tarzan, one person who possessed the strength of ten. Everyone sought out his help on all kinds of occasions, from fishing expeditions to temple meetings. When others failed, he would be summoned, for he was capable of bearing the most burdensome of loads, physical and metaphorical alike.

Later, after she learned how to read at school, Zhenguan saw her third uncle's calligraphy engraved on the temple pillar, a couplet describing the beauty of the temple facing Budai Harbor. It read: "Here on the shores of the Tiger Tail River, may the deities of this temple bless all of humanity. Miracles are performed when Heaven consents, and the sea gleams with celestial light."

Ten-year-old Zhenguan stood at the temple gate, before the colorful portraits of the temple guardian gods, and tears glittered in her eyes. The ocean stretched out, moving yet still, almost from beneath her feet. Third Uncle's temple poem sounded in her mind and rang in her soul. Lifting her eyes, she sensed that she was born not just of her parents, but of the huge expanse of water as well. She was a child of the Tiger Tail River that flowed into the sea, and like a female warrior in the kung fu novels, she had a gleaming sword flung across her back. With that sword, she would traverse far and wide under the stars and the moon.

For the next three years, Zhenguan was caught up in this world of kung fu novels. Such chivalry and adventure and grand romance had long become a thing of the past, but she came to know the tenets of the kung fu masters by heart: they must never fight out of spite; they must do their utmost to help loyal government officials, filial sons, virtuous women, and martyrs, even when it meant sacrificing their lives. . . . Zhenguan would recite the passage over and over again, reveling in the glory of each word. It was the valiant spirit embodied in these novels that kept her up nights on end, lost in the pages.

And this was what brought Daxin to mind.

When he was in seventh grade, going on eighth, he came back to visit Grandma with his mother, and the boys brought out all their kung fu novels and comic books to impress their visitor. Daxin read all day and throughout the night in the arm's-length cottage, skipping meals. The lamp there was always on, under a mosquito netting with white cloud motifs hanging over the bed; Daxin had even burned two holes in the mosquito netting. The first hole was covered up by Fourth Aunt with a piece of gauze, but her needlework was so fine and intricate that there was hardly any trace of a patch at all. Daxin was going to report the second hole as well, but Yinan decided to darn it himself and enlisted Zhenguan's assistance. "Zhenguan, be a good soul, give us a hand."

Yinan had found a piece of gauze with the right texture but the wrong color. He had cut it out unevenly, and his needlework was clumsy. Zhenguan inspected the repair and blurted out, "You're only drawing attention to the hole!"

She immediately regretted her outburst. Yinan's handiwork was indeed awkward, but she shouldn't have embarrassed him in front of their guest. Feeling guilty, she did her best to make amends by fixing up the patchwork. When she was done, she walked away without looking at Daxin.

That night, she tossed and turned restlessly, unable to sleep.

Dozing off on occasion, she would wake again to study the clock, which didn't seem to be ticking at all. Patience, patience! At daybreak she could finally apologize. . . . Zhenguan understood now what her grandfather meant when he said: "One can sleep well and eat well when he is wronged by others; but if he is the one to wrong another, he will find it difficult to do either."

It is always one's conscience that prevents bygones from being bygones.

When she saw Daxin the next day, she could hardly open her mouth to speak, but he seemed not the least bit bothered and immediately put her at ease. She had not realized it at the time, but a couple of years later, when she finally trusted her own judgment, she would come to understand that Daxin was genuinely kind and sincere by nature.

That night, Zhenguan's thoughts roamed as she dozed off. She was startled awake by something burning and let out a scream when she saw that the lamp had fallen against the mosquito netting. In a rush to save the net, Zhenguan burned her hands. It only then occurred to her that she should have put out the lamp earlier, before fire became a threat.

four

1

A hole had been burned in the mosquito netting!

Zhenguan later covered it with a piece of red satin, one of the little round patches that her grandmother cut out and kept on her boudoir to use as plasters for ointments when she had dizzy spells or headaches, pasting them to her temples.

Now the adults had no doubts: Zhenguan was literally burning the midnight oil, studying for her exams! They were proud of her but also concerned for her health, and to keep up her stamina, they would bring her dried ginseng pieces wrapped up in old calendar paper when they visited. Zhenguan didn't chew on the ginseng, instead putting it into a glass jar that filled up in a matter of weeks. Zhenguan thought: If this supply keeps up, I'll be able to open up a ginseng shop soon! One day, Yincheng's new wife walked in. Zhenguan knew that she was there to deliver more ginseng. But she brought a whiff of something strange with her as well.

"I beg you, return all this ginseng to Grandma. I have too much already!"

"Forget it." The bride smiled. "Grandmother will only send me back. And if she knew that you still had leftovers from last time, she'd really be upset!"

Zhenguan could see that she had no choice. "What's in the other packet?" she asked.

"Guess!"

Zhenguan sniffed but could not tell what it was. "Perfume?"

"No, no."

The fragrance had permeated the cottage, something strangely familiar that she couldn't quite identify. The bride didn't want to give her sister-in-law a hard time and was about to open up the package, but Zhenguan stopped her, saying, "Wait, I don't need to see it. I've known this scent since I was a child. I can name it."

Eaglewood, sandalwood, musk . . . ? What was this secret scent?

The two women looked at each other and laughed as Zhenguan finally gave in. "Okay, tell me! I'm dying of curiosity!"

The bride opened up the small red packet, revealing a clump of dark powder wrapped in red cellophane paper. Zhenguan looked perplexed.

The bride laughed, explaining, "It's root of the Chinese scholar tree mixed with other spices, used for—"

"Of course, for sachets! Dragonboat Festival is just around the corner!"

The custom of making fragrant sachets for Dragonboat Festival had existed for generations; not even Grandma could remember its origins. It must have come to Taiwan from southern China hundreds of years ago. Every fifth month of the lunar year since she was six years old, the day before rice dumplings wrapped in bamboo leaves were to be eaten, Zhenguan would seek out any new brides in the neighborhood to ask for the fragrant sachets they would make especially for the occasion. The brides would come to the door with lacquered boxes, smiling as they passed out colorful, beautifully embroidered sachets shaped like monkeys, tigers, eggplants, pumpkins, and roosters.

Zhenguan would go from one house to the next, trying to collect as many fragrant sachets to dangle from her clothes as she could. Sometimes she gathered so many that there weren't enough buttons to hang them on. In fourth grade, she stopped wearing all the sachets when the boys made fun of her. But she continued to visit the brides, asking for fragrant sachets and hiding them in her pockets or in her schoolbag.

She eventually lost or misplaced most of the sachets she had collected over the years; all that remained now were a yellow tiger and a purple eggplant. The tiger sachet, sewn of yellow satin, was the size of a longan fruit. Stripes were etched on its back and feet; its eyes were two spots of shining black. It seemed a very clever tiger, so lifelike that even the boys fell in love with it; they almost snatched it away! The eggplant was constructed painstakingly of an exquisite satin that gave off a faint purple sheen; the green stem gave it a fresh-from-the-garden look. Zhenguan cherished these sachets and kept them in her mother's wooden box. She had grown up with their fragrance.

In her grandmother's day, all newlywed women followed the local tradition of making fragrant sachets to distribute to children in the neighborhood. It was even observed, more or less, by her mother's generation. Now, however, the custom was fading into history. Brides no longer knew how to sew, or perhaps had little patience for such pastimes, and assigned the task to their mothers and sisters or old women who were paid to do it.

So when Zhenguan learned that her new sister-in-law planned to sew two hundred fragrant sachets herself, she was filled with excitement. In the past, her mother and aunts would brag about the beautiful sachets they had made when they were brides, and Zhenguan would ask, "Why didn't you give me one?"

The adults would laugh. "Where were you then?"

And she would retort, "Well, I hadn't been born yet. But you could have saved me one anyway!"

They laughed at her childish talk but later asked each other why, indeed, they had not saved any of their sachets for posterity.

To be brave and confident enough to embroider her own sachets, her new sister-in-law must be proud of her needlework. Zhenguan proclaimed, "All right, then, here's your first order: I want more than a few!"

The bride laughed. "Aren't you too old for this? Sachets are for little children!"

"Says who? Have you bought the fabric for the sachets yet? I'll go to the textile store with you!"

"I have the material already. It's kind of late to go shopping for fabric now!"

Looking up into the face of this bride before her, Zhenguan felt as if she were a child again. She asked excitedly, "What patterns do you have? Do you have monkeys? Do you have roosters?"

"Of course! Mice, oxen, tigers, rabbits, all the signs of the Chinese zodiac."

II

On the day of Dragonboat Festival, when the sun reached its peak in the sky, every household would set out earthen urns and fill them with water drawn from wells. According to legend, the "noontime water" would never spoil and could be used to cure diarrhea, stomachaches, all kinds of physical ailments. It was also said that if calamus and bunyan leaves were soaked in the noontime water, it could be used to wash the face and body, after which the skin would be radiant, clean, and clear.

Early in the morning, Zhenguan awoke to the sound of water splashing in earthen pots. Ladles were scraped across the bottom of the urns to scoop up every last drop. The sound was not particularly pleasant, but for Zhenguan, it was the sound of her childhood, the sound of her life; it was to her like music. She was young at heart; festivals always filled her with such joy!

She breathed deeply, and the aroma of steamed rice dumplings from the kitchen filled her lungs. Her aunts and sisters-in-law must have worked late into the night, wrapping rice and other condiments with bamboo leaves. As she shuffled toward the kitchen in her slippers, Zhenguan's stomach rumbled.

She heard the distinctive scraping sound: the water basin must be empty. Around the corner, Yinyue laughed. "There's still some water in that pail for you to wash your face. . . . By the way, Yincheng was making fun of you. He told us that you, already an adult, were still begging for sachets from his wife!"

Zhenguan splashed water on her face as she countered, "As if he doesn't want any! Wasn't he the one who was always asking for the tigers, leaving only monkeys and pumpkins for me?" She choked abruptly on the water, which spouted from her nostrils as if from a nozzle. Yinyue patted her on the back and was passing her a towel when the bride herself came by and announced, "Great Fifth Grand-Uncle is here. Grandpa wants everyone to greet him in the front hall."

Zhenguan wiped her face. Who could that be? she wondered. Was it the father of Fifth Great-Uncle, a doctor in the city of Tainan? No, that couldn't be, for Fifth Great-Uncle was her grandfather's brother, and Great-Grandfather had passed away already. His photograph and spiritual tablet were placed on the family altar. So who was this man? And then it occurred to her that Great Fifth Grand-Uncle was in fact Fifth Great-Uncle himself! So many names and titles, so much confusion!

Women were expected to be humble because they were of lower status in the traditional family hierarchy. Zhenguan often forgot all the protocols expected of her, but the new bride had impeccable etiquette and always demonstrated her respect for elder members of the family. She was born in the year of the mouse and was just one year older than Zhenguan; and yet, she was responsible for running such a large household! Zhenguan felt a sense of deep admiration for her sister-in-law. Her every move since joining the family reminded Zhenguan of the saying: "She practiced womanly virtues as the pious live by holy books." And this is the best way that a daughter can ever repay her parents, for all those who observe the bride will praise her father and mother.

The young women appeared as a group before Fifth Great-Uncle, but he couldn't remember all of their names at once; after all, they hadn't seen each other for some time. He did, however, recognize Zhenguan: "Oh, so you're the daughter who stayed in her mother's womb for twelve months!"

Zhenguan listened and soon came to understand the purpose of Fifth Great-Uncle's visit: he was here to claim his share of the family's property. Great-Grandfather had left twenty-five hectares of fishponds for his children, and the three brothers received eight hectares each. The remaining hectare was to be divided equally among the three brothers, but since Fifth Great-Uncle had married a woman from Tainan and ran a medical clinic there, Grandfather and Third Great-Uncle administered his share jointly on his behalf. But now that Fifth Great-Uncle was getting older, he had become more self-interested and calculating. Zhenguan heard him remark, "The ancestral house is not registered under my name, and First Brother and Third Brother have always lived here. Because I had to buy my own house in Tainan, the remaining hectare should be mine!"

These unkind and unfriendly words were not fit for the ears of the grandchildren, so Zhenguan's grandmother asked them all to leave the room. Zhenguan was only too happy to retreat to the kitchen to feast on the sticky rice dumplings wrapped in bamboo leaves.

Her cousins always laughed at her "rice dumpling tummy." From the first batch of rice dumplings steamed on the fourth day of the fifth lunar month, until the last batch had disappeared from the house seven or eight days later, she could eat them for breakfast, lunch, and dinner. Licking the grease off her fingers, she returned to the cottage to study in peace and quiet. A glance at her wristwatch, however, reminded her that it was time for the noontime water. She scurried to the backyard to find her cousins and sisters-in-law fetching water pails.

"Hey, why didn't anyone summon me?" Zhenguan demanded.

"Your job is to study now. We can manage!" her two sisters-in-law said.

Yinchan added, "We didn't think you'd want to carry water. But since you're here, give us a hand!" She passed a pail to Zhenguan.

Bucket in hand, Zhenguan felt a surge of excitement. She hadn't done this in a long time! She walked to the side of the well, lowered the pail, tilted it a bit, and watched the water flow in. When she felt the weight of the water against the palm of her hand, she started to pull the pail up, slowly, one foot, half a foot, taking in the rope; and when the bucket appeared at the rim of the well, she looked into the clear water and exclaimed in glee, "Oh! Noontime water, noontime water!"

And they repeated the process again and again until all the water vessels were filled to the brim. Zhenguan was helping the bride soak calamus when she jumped up suddenly and said, "I have to go to the front hall. I'll be right back!" She had just remembered seeing a small red blister on Fifth Great-Uncle's forehead, and she wanted to remind her grandfather to recommend that Fifth Great-Uncle wash his face in the noontime water.

The front hall was extraordinarily quiet. Oh no, Zhenguan thought, Fifth Great-Uncle must already have left! As she approached the window, she heard Third Great-Uncle saying, "How could Ayien say something like this in his ripe old age! Doesn't he remember how many hectares the family had to sell to send him to medical school in Japan?"

Grandpa didn't respond, and Third Great-Uncle continued, "We're brothers, of the same flesh and blood. If he wants that hectare we can give it to him. But to have said such cruel words . . . ! It's clear that he has no brotherly regard for us."

Zhenguan could tell that her grandfather had just let out a big sigh. He said softly, "There are but the three of us, brothers of the same legacy. Every time we meet, we've all aged more. But he is the youngest, so we might as well let him have his way. We are brothers but once this lifetime."

five

I

Lights out at ten o'clock, rise and shine at the crack of dawn. So it went. But last night Zhenguan stayed up past midnight reading Bambi comic books, so this morning, when the rooster crowed, she was still in bed, unable to move, like a rusty old machine. Only after three rounds of the rooster's crowing did Zhenguan finally force her eyes open. It was already five o'clock. She had to get up—the sun would soon be rising!

She grabbed a towel and washed her face. Usually she could still catch glimpses of the moon and stars when she awoke, but today the sky was already a pale white, the color of fish scales. The heavenly bodies were still faintly visible, but only like paper cutouts in the misty white fog.

A glimmer of light and the sound of splashing water came from the kitchen. Yincheng's wife was up, washing rice to make rice congee for breakfast. Walking toward the backyard, Zhenguan found the gate doors open: Grandpa and her uncles must already be on their way out to sea. She suddenly remembered the sight of fishponds in the morning mist, the image still fresh in her mind. She wanted to see it again and was about to slip out the gate when Yincheng's bride greeted her. "The rice congee is ready. Why don't you have a bowl before you leave?"

Zhenguan stopped to smile. "Please do set aside a bowl for me and let it cool. I'll be right back, I'm just going to take a short walk."

She followed the narrow path that wound past the herbal jelly shop. During the summer, they could sell up to three or four thousand buckets! Every time Zhenguan walked by, she could smell the warm scent of herbal jelly cooking over the fire. The path then led to the harbor. A certain household had piled little hills of rice chaff on the side of the road, and two old women dressed in black were chatting as they washed chamber pots.

As Zhenguan was passing by them, she slowed her pace so that she could eavesdrop on the latest morning news.

"He stole his parents' money in the middle of the night and fled!"

"What a shame, what a shame! To be such a scoundrel at seventeen!"

"Exactly! To be rotten to the core before he's even an adult. Do you remember last winter? The local police found him rolling around in the hay with the Wang family daughter."

"What a disgrace!"

"And now the Shih family daughter is pregnant with that rascal's child! The old saying is true: one mustn't mingle with the wrong sort, for it will only breed malice."

"That good-for-nothing, no one's going to cry over his dead body!"

Zhenguan walked away, feeling disappointed. She thought she'd hear some interesting news, but it turned out to be only the usual gossip about her third great uncle's family. Third Great Uncle had two sons. The elderly parents doted on the younger son and his wife, but this daughter-in-law, Achou, was aggressive and rebellious. She had begun clamoring for her husband's share of the family wealth not long after she married into the household. Once they moved out into their own house, there was nothing but constant complaining about her children. She had three daughters and one precious son, Pinghui, who had been a scoundrel since childhood. He constantly got into trouble, causing his mother much heartache and pain.

Zhenguan's good mood was soured, and she decided to head back home.

She did not find a bowl of rice congee waiting for her on the table. She entered the kitchen just as Yinchan was leaving. "Looking for your rice congee? It was already cold, so I was told to eat it up!"

Zhenguan laughed. "The sky must be falling. How come you're up so early?"

"It's not by choice," Yinchan replied. "I was awakened at daybreak by the barking of the dogs. Pinghui had stolen something from home, and his mother was running after him, trying to smack him. They fought all the way here—"

Before she had finished her sentence, they heard sounds of bickering from the front hall. Zhenguan could tell it was Achou. "You're going to torture me until I die, aren't you? There's no lid over the sea, why don't you just jump in?"

Other voices tried to calm her down. "What's done is done," they said. "You can beat him to death, but it's not going to do any good."

Achou wailed, "It's not that I haven't disciplined him; and I can't bring myself to beat him to death. But he doesn't fear the rod, even if it hurts him!"

The ruckus went on for some time, and finally Pinghui was escorted home by his father. Grandma urged Achou to stay, though, saying, "Come, child, I would like to have a little chat with you."

As they entered the inner chamber of Grandma's room, Grandma asked Zhenguan, "Will you go to the kitchen to see if there is anything to eat? They've been at each other's throats since midnight, and your aunt is probably hungry!"

Achou's eyes filled with tears. "Grandma, how can I keep anything down?"

When Zhenguan came back from the kitchen with food, her aunt was sitting on the side of the bed, complaining about everything. "I must have killed or looted in my previous life to have given birth to such a son! He's here to make me pay for my sins!"

Zhenguan quietly filled up a bowl of rice congee for her aunt as she listened to Grandma, who said, "Achou, our ancestors told us long ago that there are no cures for malicious wives or rebellious sons." Two rows of tears flowed down Achou's cheeks before Grandma had even finished her words.

Zhenguan thought that Achou must be feeling embarrassed and ashamed, even though Grandma did not mean to reprimand her. It was clear for all to see: Achou was a malicious wife. Coveting her husband's share of the family fortune, she tore the family apart, alienated the parents, separated the brothers; not only did she disregard her duties as daughter-in-law, but she also severed the filial ties between parents and son.

A malicious wife could be the downfall of even the most worldly and intelligent people!

Seeing Achou's tears, Grandma said quickly, "I'm not implying anything. You're a smart girl, and there's no need for me to beat around the bush."

"Grandmother, I know that good medicine is always bitter," Achou wept.

"You're right, it is." Taking Achou's hand, she said, "Achou, life is a two-way street. Think things over, you have a good head on your shoulders! Think about how Pinghui was raised!" Achou became quiet as Grandma continued, "Bringing up a son takes a tremendous amount of time and energy. Not to mention the ten-month pregnancy. Think about his birth, his coming of age, and the ten, twenty years in between. You're lucky if all goes well, but remember how you felt when he ran a high fever or had a bad cough? The kind of worrying that he put you through? You've survived it all. . . . If Pinghui were to suddenly move away with his wife and child and fall out of touch with you, how would you feel?"

Achou began to sob loudly. Grandma gave her a pat on the shoulder. "If you'd had to leave home to make a living, then what you did might have been justified by necessity. But today, your in-laws are both alive, and you live in the same village. Your behavior really is unacceptable."

Achou cried all the more pitifully. Zhenguan had to find her a handkerchief to wipe away her tears. It was quite some time before Achou stopped sobbing. "Grandma, I know how wrong I've been . . ." she almost choked on her words again.

"Owning up is wise. Now don't give it any more thought. Stay for lunch, and then go visit your mother-in-law. She's still looking forward to seeing you."

Achou lowered her head. "Grandma, will you come with me when I apologize to my mother-in-law? I want to tell her that I will pack everything up and move back on an auspicious date."

Grandma was so happy that her eyes crinkled at the corners with a broad smile. "Achou, I am so glad that you've gotten your priorities straightened out. When I was a daughter-in-law, Pinghui's grandparents told me: if one lacks filial piety, one's offspring will come to no good, for filial sons and grandchildren are one's own making. If you treat your in-laws well, heaven will reward you."

Achou gave Grandma's words some thought before asking, "But Grandma, what am I to do about Pinghui? I don't know how to discipline him anymore. They say that if you spoil the pigs, your pantry will be full, but if your spoil your son, you will be left with nothing. I certainly don't spoil him, and yet he has brought me only heartache and pain!"

"That will all eventually pass," Grandma laughed. "When parents say they are angry with their children, it is only ever temporary. Once you're over it, your son will recover. Good daughters-in-law give birth to respectable sons and are destined to enjoy filial piety; there will be no reason for anger then!"

II

The exam was but a few days away. Zhenguan did not appear unusually nervous, but one couldn't say that she was entirely indifferent either. Not even she herself could tell what was really going on inside her head.

Everyone in the family attended to her needs and catered to

her whims. Knowing that she had a liking for rice noodles, they would serve her all kinds of noodle dishes: sweet and cold, hot and spicy. . . . Zhenguan also feasted on bowl after bowl of sweet lotus root paste, made from a lotus root powder that was a family specialty of Yincheng's in-laws; his bride would always bring some of it back with her after visiting her parents. Zhenguan had not known before that such a delicacy existed. The lotus root powder was first mixed with cold water and blended until smooth; boiling hot water was then poured into the mixture, transforming it into a transparent ruby-colored paste that resembled jelly. When Zhenguan savored it, she felt the refreshing coolness of the lotus flower banishing the oppressive heat of summer.

The girls knew that they could taste this delicacy at Zhenguan's, so after work they would all crowd into the cottage, which soon became the place to go for a bite to eat. Yincheng's bride even picked fresh snake gourds from the garden to make soup for the girls. One day at dusk, the cottage was again packed with family sitting on long benches and stools. Everyone had a bowl of sweet-potato congee in their hands. As they were eating, Yincheng came inside.

"Ah, why are you all hiding here? There must be something tasty!"

The girls made space for him, and Yincheng laughed. "Most brides try to please their husbands, but mine seems to be busy making you girls happy!"

"Haven't you heard that sisters-in-law reign supreme?" Yinchan asked.

Yincheng laughed even more heartily. "No, I haven't!"

Yinchan explained, "When a daughter gets married the mother always reminds her: when in the mountains, listen to the birds; when in the house, read people's faces. As a daughter-in-law, you must know your etiquette; if your sister-in-law hasn't yet extended her chopsticks to pick up her food, don't venture to extend yours. How can your bride have time for you?"

Yincheng feigned a solemn expression. "If you do indeed reign supreme, I'll have to seek out my mother-in-law to reason with her!"

Hearing her brother's words, Yinyue scolded Yinchan, "Now look what you've done." And to Yincheng she said, "How can you take her seriously? Doesn't your wife treat you well enough? You greedy pig, what more do you want?"

Before Yincheng could say anything, Yinchan laughed. "Don't worry, he's just joking around. They might put on a show in public, but in reality their hearts and even their livers are connected—"

"Whose hearts and livers are connected?"

All of them turned at the voice. The question came from a neighbor who was standing at the door, head poking around.

"Auntie, do come in and take a seat!"

"No, thank you," the woman declined. She called out to Yinyue, "Please do come outside for a moment, I have something to tell you!" Yinyue followed her out the door and the two talked in muted voices for quite some time. Yinyue returned to the cottage after the woman left.

Zhenguan noticed how Yincheng's expression had changed. "What did she want?"

Yinyue paused. "She said that Uncle Aqi, who lives in the back alley, was stealing snake gourds from our garden."

Yincheng frowned. "Bad melons are full of seeds, and malicious people are full of gossip; don't you girls listen to that woman!" To his wife he said, "Keep the gate in the backyard closed in the future to prevent such womenfolk from charging in; they like to wag their tongues, engaging in idle talk. We don't want the girls in this house to come under her influence!"

The bride kept quiet as the sisters objected, "But if she wants to, she can come in through any gate; and if the gates are closed, she can still knock on the door!"

"Don't let her in even if she knocks!"

The girls were indignant. "We were not brought up to be so impolite! And besides, we are sensible people. Why would we want to be like her anyway? Give us some credit!" Despite their protests, they knew in their hearts that Yincheng was only looking out for them. Tongue-wagging was certainly not a womanly virtue.

After the meal, everyone left to tend to their own business. Zhenguan sat at her desk, thinking about the unusual day she'd had. The truth was that she had actually witnessed Uncle Aqi stealing the gourds! That morning, she had decided to survey the fishponds with her grandfather. On their way home, they stopped dead in their tracks, for there, behind the half-closed door, they saw Uncle Aqi with a knife, cutting gourds from the trellis. He did not see them, and Zhenguan did not know what to do: advance or retreat? Torn, she hesitated with breath bated for a few tense moments before she was pulled back by her grandfather. He held her hand tightly as he led her out of the back alley and onto the main street.

It dawned on Zhenguan that Grandpa's intention to hide from Uncle Aqi was stronger than the thief's intention to hide from his misdeed. Zhenguan took this to be an indication of her grandfather's magnanimity: he must have wanted to spare Uncle Aqi the embarrassment of being caught in the act. But what she did not understand was that people in the elders' generation would rather starve to death than steal, and they would rather die than snitch.

Uncle Aqi was gone by the time Grandpa and Zhenguan circled around through the front gate. Zhenguan was about to return to the cottage when her grandfather asked her, "Did you see what happened?"

"Yes, Grandpa."

"Don't give it another moment's thought, it's nothing. As you should well know, he committed no wrong. . . . And remember, don't mention this to anyone!"

"Yes, Grandpa." She nodded, not really understanding.

But now, as she remembered the face of their gossiping neighbor and the expression on her grandfather's face as he warned her, she suddenly realized what she had failed to grasp before. She sat up, extracted her diary from the stack of books on her desk, and began to write.

Greed is a vice, of course, but poverty isn't. Grandpa did not think Uncle Aqi was wrong because of the compassion he felt for him, knowing that he had to put food on the table for a family of ten. Uncle Aqi was a salt farmer, and salt farmers depended on the weather for their livelihood. When it rained, their hearts were also drenched in bitter water.

She was going to remember this. Someday, as a mother or grandmother, she would pass the story on to the next generation, so that they might come to grasp the magnanimity of their forefathers. At that moment she suddenly remembered a line from the *Basic Annals* of the *Records of the Grand Historian*: "Defend sincerity and constancy, believe in honesty and loyalty, fill the world with virtue, and live up to the good name of one's ancestors."

six

I

One night Zhenguan had a strange dream about her father. He was dressed in his usual suit but was abnormally quiet. Just as Zhenguan was about to call out to him, she was awakened abruptly by a shove. She sat up, looked at Yinchan, who was sleeping beside her, and remembered. . . .

That night Yinchan had had the idea of fixing up something for them to eat before going to bed. So she went to the kitchen and found some sweet potatoes, which she chopped into thin slices and cooked in a clear broth. The broth, pure and sweet, did not contain any rice, and the sweet potatoes were fresh from the garden. One bowl was not enough for Zhenguan.

They had snacked late into the night, so Yinchan decided to stay in Zhenguan's room. Zhenguan felt nostalgic for the days when they used to bunk together as children, and the two fell asleep cramped on the same bed. Yinchan was a notoriously restless sleeper. The girls all called her a tumblebug, because by midnight her feet would be on her pillow and her head at the foot of the bed.

Zhenguan glanced at the alarm clock. It was five-thirty, and she hadn't heard the rooster crow that morning. Tomorrow was the day of the big exam, so she was entitled to sleep in today, even until the sun reached high into the sky! She rearranged her pillow and was about to sink again into sweet slumber when she heard a distinct but fleeting sound.

Zhenguan was tempted to run to the door and lift the bolt to see where it had come from, but instead, she sat transfixed at the edge of her bed. Though her body was still sluggish, her mind was alert. In the clear and cold dawn, the sound cut through her like a pair of sharp, icy knives; she felt as if her heart had been carved in two. Ah, who was playing that bamboo flute?

She nudged Yinchan. "Get up, listen—such an extraordinary sound."

Yinchan rubbed her eyes and mumbled groggily, "They're castrating the pigs! What's the big fuss?" And with that, she immediately slumped back to sleep. Zhenguan lay back down, laughing at herself. Indeed, she had heard this sound many times since she was a child. Why did it sound strange to her ears all of a sudden? Awake now, Zhenguan no longer felt like sleeping. She was just about to get up and turn on the lights when there was a sudden commotion outside the door.

"Who's there?" She had never heard such heavy pounding on her door before.

"Zhenguan, it's me."

"I'm coming . . ." Zhenguan fastened her robe and opened the door. Third Aunt slipped in quickly.

Ordinarily Third Aunt was properly dressed and impeccably groomed whenever she had to appear before her parents-in-law. Even in the faint glimmer of morning light in the cottage, though, Zhenguan was surprised to see that Third Aunt was uncharacteristically unkempt, her hair unbrushed and her face unwashed.

"Auntie—"

"Change into something white; your third uncle is waiting for you outside. Hurry, the car is still running."

Although Zhenguan didn't have any idea what was happening, she followed orders, hastily putting on a white blouse as her aunt handed her a wet towel to wipe her face.

It was only then that Zhenguan noticed her aunt's red eyes. "What—?"

"Don't ask, I don't know how to put it. Quickly now, you'll understand when you get to the front door. Your uncle will explain to you on the way. I'll follow with Yinyue shortly."

Zhenguan walked to the front door, only to be met by complete chaos. What on earth had happened? Seven or eight cars were parked at the front gate: cars from the salt mines and cars from the police station. Second Aunt, Fourth Uncle, and the others climbed into the cars, one after the other; Zhenguan was seated with her third uncle. Uncle and niece sat in silence, not exchanging a word. Zhenguan was anxious to ask questions but wasn't sure she was ready to hear the answers; hands on her knees, she tried to maintain her composure. She felt a bulge inside the pocket of her skirt and, tugging, pulled out a white handkerchief with red dots. Even in the rush, her third aunt had managed to tuck in a handkerchief for her.

She ran her hands over the handkerchief, and suddenly she knew. Covering her mouth, Zhenguan started to cry.

Third Uncle patted her on the back and murmured, "Zhenguan, Zhenguan . . ."

She said nothing. She simply couldn't.

"You know your father was a volunteer fireman. . . ."

Big drops of tears fell from Zhenguan's eyes, uncontrollably. "Where is Papa, where is he now?" she choked out. It took her a long time to form these words because her lips were trembling violently.

Third Uncle hesitated, but Zhenguan persisted. "Uncle, tell me where we are going!"

"Chiayi Hospital."

"Is Papa all right?"

"They say that the fire truck toppled over while it was speeding. I don't know the details."

At that moment, the driver turned to look at her, and in his eyes, she saw the pity that someone might harbor toward an orphan. Zhenguan's tears fell again. If she had been able to foresee such an event, she would never have gone to study in Chiayi; she would have stayed home to attend high school nearby, like Yinchan had. If she had known that this would happen, she would never have moved to live with Grandpa.

They had been father and daughter for such a short time. Her days of calling him Papa were so few and so numbered. Third Uncle was already in his forties, but his father was still alive and well. Even Grandma, who was going on seventy, had a father with a nimble gait and a head full of silver hair. How lucky were those whose fathers were still alive . . . and how suddenly she had come to envy them!

Cries of lament filled the Provincial Hospital of Chiayi. With her third uncle leading her, she passed one ward after the other: internal medicine, pediatrics, surgery . . . until they arrived at a small room in the back corner. Zhenguan ran toward her two aunts and, all of a sudden, saw her father on the bed.

"Papa!" With a desperate cry, Zhenguan flew past everyone and knelt before her father's body. She hardly recognized her mother, who looked as if all her bones had been dismantled, her arms and legs slumped into a heap of a torso. Her two brothers stood wailing at the side. She believed that if her father could wake up at this moment, he would not have the heart to leave them like this.

At some point her cousins arrived. They stood by her side, weeping. When they tried to help her to her feet, Zhenguan refused to budge. Second Aunt whispered in Zhenguan's ear, "Your mother has passed out three times already; don't make it any worse for her. Go to her side and help console her."

Zhenguan stood up, but before she could reach her mother, there was some commotion, and she saw her mother collapse into First Aunt's arms. She had fainted again.

II

The funeral procession moved slowly.

A shaman led the way, chanting, calling back the spirit of the dead. The night wind blew out his strange Taoist gown of scarlet, fringed with black and embroidered with silk threads. Zhenguan's two brothers walked in front, holding their father's spiritual tablet in their hands, their heads bowed. Zhenguan and her grandmother sat in the rickshaw following the procession. The wind kept drying Zhenguan's tears, but her eyes, like inexhaustible wells, only produced more.

Let the tears flow!

Zhenguan thought of her father, who had never really enjoyed life. He'd raised her, but she never had a chance to repay him. Her mother and aunts always remembered to save the tastiest cakes and pastries for Grandpa, who had a mouthful of gold and silver fillings as a result. But Zhenguan never got the opportunity to please her father and make him happy. There might be remedies for other regrets, but for this there were none. She had been deprived of her chance to be filial.

Ancient books tell of filial offspring who cry until their eyes bleed upon losing their parents. Zhenguan used to feel that such accounts were surely exaggerated. But now she understood. She could cry a river or until her tears turned to blood, and she would still feel the pain of her father's death. Words were inadequate to describe the anguish.

Through a veil of tears, Zhenguan watched as the funeral procession moved out across the dark wilderness. A thought struck her: Surely Father's soul must be following them, wanting to find his way home.

"Tien-en, come back! Come back with us!"

"Tien-en, turn around, come back to the house!"

Everyone in the procession echoed her grandmother's plea.

"Papa, come back, Papa!" Zhenguan cried out between sobs, her face and neck wet with tears.

The road was terribly uneven. Was her mother suffering from motion sickness in the car that trailed behind? The cars swayed with the curves of the road as they approached home, not far off amid the darkness and glittering lights. The black shadows of ironwood trees and the yellowish halo of street lamps made for a surreal combination.

Back home, the moonlight still shone over the water. But now Zhenguan was alone, without a father. The thought brought more tears to her eyes, tears that she felt would never be contained. They all stopped at Zhenguan's house. Yinshan and his wife had arrived to prepare a meal for the mourners. Zhenguan's mother was bone-tired, but she mustered enough strength to ask everyone to eat. Most of the guests washed up but could only look at the food, finding it difficult to swallow anything at all.

The menfolk left late that night, one after the other. But most of the womenfolk stayed, saying that they wanted to keep Zhenguan and her mother company. In fact they stayed to keep vigil over Zhenguan's mother, for fear that she would take her own life. Zhenguan, Yinyue, and Yinchan fetched pillows and sheets from the closets, laying out makeshift beds in each room. When the beds ran out, some women just slept on the floor. In no time at all, the house was filled with people lying here and there. Some tossed and turned all night, some sat up and talked, some were reminded of their own suffering and wept until dawn. Zhenguan's widowed aunts shed big tears, which she could almost hear falling, falling.

The murmur of voices did not cease even when morning broke. Zhenguan had not slept at all, and her eyes felt sore from blinking. As the rooster crowed, Zhenguan suddenly remembered: this was her big day. Her father was supposed to escort her to the examination, but now her world had been shattered, and the exam didn't seem to matter anymore. So she'd spent the last six years of her life preparing for an exam that she wasn't going to take! It seemed as if life were playing a cruel trick on her!

Zhenguan shut her eyes tightly, wishing that she could fall asleep and awake to find that it had all been a dream. Even her tears would be tears she had dreamt. She would close her eyes, and tomorrow, when the sun rose, she would still be the proud Zhenguan with a father!

seven

I

A hundred days after the death of Zhenguan's father, her widowed second aunt came to stay with the family. Zhenguan's mother and her sister would keep each other company day in and day out. Zhenguan hadn't been born yet the year Second Aunt's husband died, and his death was something that no one ever talked about. Second Aunt's only son was attending medical school in Kaohsiung, southern Taiwan's largest city. He would fetch his mother to live with him when he started a family of his own.

Yinyue and her sisters would stop by on their way to work and greet their two aunts. They also dropped in on Zhenguan to chat a bit. One day, Yinchan arrived only after the girls had already come and gone. "Your alarm clock must be broken!" Zhenguan joked.

"I got up at six o'clock this morning," Yinchan defended herself. "But somehow the time just slipped away. By the way, Fourth Aunt asked me to tell you to visit Grandpa whenever you can!"

Grandpa's house was but two hundred meters away. Zhenguan had been visiting less frequently during the past three months, and she did still drop by every once in a while, but this was the first time that Fourth Aunt had sent someone to formally tell her to visit more often.

"Has something happened?"

Yinchan seemed puzzled. "No, not that I know of. If there were anything going on, I would know about it! Grandma has probably prepared something nice for you to eat. I'd better get going, or I'll be late for work!"

Zhenguan watched her ride off on her bicycle, swift as the wind, and she turned back to join her mother and aunt for breakfast. After washing the dishes, she informed them that she was going to Grandpa's. As she reached her grandfather's front gate, she saw an old woman dressed in black walking out with a wooden bucket. Zhenguan recognized her as the old woman who went from kitchen to kitchen collecting leftover rice-washing water to feed to the pigs.

The old woman noticed that Zhenguan was wearing a white mourning band. "You must be Shuihong's daughter?" she asked.

"Yes, I am."

The old woman set down her bucket, took Zhenguan's hand, and scrutinized her face, saying, "You look so much like your father . . ." Zhenguan could feel the old woman's fingers trembling. "Your father was the kindest man that I have ever known," she said.

Zhenguan did not know how to respond. She bowed her head, then looked up to see tears flowing down the folds of the old woman's wrinkled skin. Zhenguan wiped them away for her but was unable to withhold her own. The old woman paused for some time before speaking again. "Your younger brother is attending the First Boys' High School in Tainan, isn't he? I've heard that he gets really good grades! It's too bad that your father didn't have the opportunity to bask in the glory of his son's achievements."

Seeing that Zhenguan's eyes were both red, she said, "Oh, look what I've done—it's all my fault!"

"No, no—" Zhenguan quickly dried her tears.

"Is your second aunt living with your family now?"

"Yes, Second Aunt has come to stay with us."

The old woman sighed. "She has had a harsh life, widowed when she was only a little older than twenty. Her husband was a hulk of a man, six feet tall and close to a hundred kilograms, strong as a tiger. But he left this world just like that! Life can be so fragile!"

After the old woman walked away, Zhenguan stood at the front gate for a little while longer, trying to regain her composure. She crossed the front hall and wandered into the courtyard, where Fourth Aunt greeted her. "So you're finally here! Grandma was just talking about you last night."

"Yes, let me check on her."

"Just a moment," Fourth Aunt stopped her. "She was up all night with a headache and didn't fall asleep until four or five this morning. Come to my room first, I have a letter for you." Zhenguan did not know what her auntie was talking about and was confused even when the letter was placed in her hands.

"What is this?"

It was a plain white envelope, and the handwriting was unfamiliar. But no, it *was* familiar; in fact, it looked like her own! It was as if she had written herself a letter!

"Strange, isn't it? And no stamp, either!"

"It is from Daxin," Fourth Aunt said as she turned to shut her closet door. "He enclosed it in a letter addressed to me."

So it was from the boy who'd had a fish bone stuck in his throat! The boy who burned the mosquito net while reading Chinese kung fu novels! Why was his handwriting so much like her own? Zhenguan fiddled with the letter in her hand, not knowing quite what to do with it.

"Aren't you going to open it up?" Fourth Aunt asked. "Daxin asked me to give it to you."

"Uh, I was just looking for a letter opener."

Fourth Aunt said, "He didn't learn of your father's death until the day before yesterday. Why don't you sit down and read the letter here while I go grocery shopping?"

"All right."

After Fourth Aunt left, Zhenguan found a pair of scissors and carefully opened the letter. How could two people's handwriting be so similar? As she unfolded the paper, she felt a tremor pass through her.

Zhenguan:

It has been so long since I last heard from all of you. My advisor has been ill (he is seventy, and all alone), so I moved into his dormitory to take care of him. I haven't been home often, and I only just heard about your father from Mother yesterday. I am so sorry for you. Please accept my condolences, I hope you will be strong. Give my sympathy to your mother as well.

Daxin

She read the letter twice, folded it, but couldn't resist opening it up to read again, and again. . . . Maybe this is how miracles in life are discovered?

II

Zhenguan's mother did recover slowly and gradually from the agonizing pain of losing her husband. Her strength and stamina, however, remained weak. So when her grandmother fell ill, Zhenguan was asked to move to her grandfather's to take care of Grandma on her mother's behalf. Her grandmother had spells of headaches that would last for two days, subside, and then return again. This went on for more than two weeks, giving everyone great cause for concern. Even First Aunt, who lived in Tainan, returned home to visit Grandma.

Of all the sisters, First Aunt and Zhenguan's mother looked the most alike. When they were still unmarried, First Aunt's husband-to-be wanted to take a peek at his bride-to-be. But in those days, decent girls about to be betrothed did not show their faces in public. So the matchmaker pointed to Zhenguan's mother, who was only twelve or thirteen at the time, and said, "That's her little sister; they look very much alike."

When Zhenguan's father passed away, First Aunt came to stay with her mother for ten whole days. Zhenguan remembered her first aunt telling her mother again and again, "Shuihong, the dead are dead, and the living must go on living!"

Back home, all the relatives had invited First Aunt to stay with them. But she insisted on staying with Zhenguan's mother, not only out of compassion for her grief-stricken sister, but also so that they might reminisce together about their childhood.

This particular evening, Grandma's room was packed with well-wishers. Zhenguan sat by her grandmother's bed, listening to the buzz of voices around her. She lifted her head when First Aunt walked in with her clothes packed up in her arms.

"First Aunt, aren't you going to stay for one more day?"

"No, I can't; the tickets have been purchased. Yincheng got them for me. But I'm going to sleep here tonight."

Third Aunt laughed. "I know, you've come to suckle at Mother's breast!"

Everyone laughed. First Aunt sat down on Grandma's bed and said, "Actually, I was the first to wean. You should laugh at son number five instead: he was breast-fed until he was seven or eight years old and already attending elementary school! Mother had to smear hot chili pepper on her nipples to make him wean. He would cry at first but, even then, would continue to suckle. Mother had no choice but to let him have his way."

"So how was he finally weaned?"

"Well, he would always have to suckle before going to school—"

"Standing?"

"Of course! He was seven going on eight already, and there was no way that Mother could carry him. One day, his classmates came to walk him to school, and . . . well, that did the trick!"

Even Grandma laughed. "Shuilian, how do you remember all of this?"

Of everyone in the room, Fifth Uncle's wife was the most embarrassed because they were talking about her husband. But it was indeed funny, and she couldn't help laughing along with the others.

"The youngest one in the family is usually spoiled rotten! How old was Mother at the time . . . at least forty, right? There probably wasn't even much milk left in her breasts!"

When night fell, the well-wishers departed, one after the other. Yinchan and her sisters proposed, "Since First Aunt is sleeping here, let's go to Yinyue's room."

"There's no need," both Grandma and First Aunt protested. "There's room enough for two more!"

Zhenguan changed into her pajamas and lay down next to First Aunt. She listened to the mother and daughter talk until there was no reply from Grandma, who had fallen asleep. Grandma was much better already, but still a little weak. She was, after all, advanced in years. It seemed as if her headache were a recurring ailment, but it was actually induced by grief over the death of Zhenguan's father. He had been orphaned at a very young age, and he treated his mother-in-law as if she were his own mother. No wonder he was Grandma's favorite son-in-law.

Zhenguan tugged at her blanket, and seeing that Yinchan and her sister were already asleep, turned to her first aunt and asked, "Did you know Second Aunt's husband?"

Her question caught First Aunt by surprise. She hesitated a moment before replying, "What's on your mind? Why do you ask?"

"I . . . guess I've always wanted to ask this question, having never known either First Uncle or Second Aunt's husband."

There was only the flicker of a night lamp in the room, and

in its halo, First Aunt's face seemed transformed into the face of Zhenguan's mother.

"Zhenguan, in your opinion, who is the fairest among us: your mother, Second Aunt, or me?"

After pondering for a bit, Zhenguan said, "Second Aunt has beautiful skin, whereas you and mother have pretty hands and feet, and brows and eyes. . . . Oh, I don't know how one can compare."

"You're a smooth talker," First Aunt laughed. "Actually, your second aunt, Shueiyun, is the prettiest among us. People called her Black Cat before she was married." In the native dialect, beautiful girls who knew how to pretty themselves up were referred to as black cats. Zhenguan tried to visualize what Second Aunt would look like if she were twenty years younger. If she hadn't been widowed so soon, if she hadn't had to bear twenty years of lonely widowhood, Second Aunt would truly be a very beautiful middle-aged woman. But now . . . During Chinese New Year, rice powder is packed into tightly bound sacks and placed under heavy rocks to squeeze out the moisture. That's what came to Zhenguan's mind when she thought of Second Aunt.

First Aunt continued, "Have you heard the expression, 'Black cats should marry drivers'? In those days, it was in vogue for pretty women to marry drivers."

"Why is that?" Zhenguan asked.

"Of course, it is an outdated saying now. But before Taiwan's retrocession, it was quite popular. Transportation in wartime was very inconvenient, and supplies were limited. Those who could drive were especially privileged!"

Zhenguan could imagine what that must have been like.

After all, in her grandfather's day, it took three days to walk to Tainan and one and a half days to walk to Jiayi. It must have been easy back then for drivers of vehicles to win young girls' hearts and to seek the favor of others.

So, Second Aunt's husband was a driver!

"And . . . ?"

"During the fiercest year of the war—you weren't born yet; such misfortune it was to be born at that time!—her husband sought refuge from the air raids at Grandpa's house. Shueiyun had a day off, so he caught some fish on the sly from our own fishponds and was walking home with his catch—"

Zhenguan interrupted, "But if he was catching fish at our fishponds, why did he have to be secretive about it?"

First Aunt laughed and said, "You have been blessed. You can eat whatever you fancy. During the Japanese occupation of Taiwan, however, the best produce was sent to the front lines for the soldiers at war. The Japanese military controlled all the supplies, and civilians were not allowed to keep anything in private. Once someone threw sugarcane scraps into your third great-uncle's backyard. The Japanese accused him of keeping supplies to himself, and they arrested and interrogated him for several days and nights. When he was finally released, he had black and blue bruises all over his body."

"But did Third Great-Uncle eat the sugarcane?"

"What sugarcane was there to eat? Even more ridiculous, the Japanese wanted to confiscate gold, so they tried to trick the womenfolk into revealing where they had hidden their treasures."

"Who would tell them?"

"No one, of course! So the perplexed Japanese said that they had a special tool to detect gold, and that anyone found hiding it would suffer the consequences."

Zhenguan had never known such hard times. "How were the supplies distributed?" she asked.

"There were different levels. The Japanese were level A, and they received the best clothing and food. Taiwanese civilians were level C."

"What about level B?"

"Level B supplies were distributed to those who were willing to give up their family names and take on Japanese names like Yamamoto."

"That is tantamount to claiming thieves as their fathers!" Zhenguan was indignant. "Our family names are passed on to us, how can we change them? How can anyone forsake his ancestral heritage?"

"Well, there are all kinds of people in this world."

Zhenguan was incredulous. "Did Second Aunt's husband encounter any Japanese soldiers while he was walking home?"

First Aunt shook her head slowly, awkwardly.

"Auntie, should we drop the subject?"

"No . . . I think you should know that your uncle was a man of principle. It was raining cats and dogs that day, and the land was flooded. The water in the streets was two or three feet high."

Zhenguan dared not ask any more questions. She lay quietly, motionless.

"Your uncle was wearing a farmer's raincoat and a hat woven with bamboo leaves. He dodged airplanes and Japanese soldiers along the way, and he almost made it home."

Zhenguan's heart was pounding wildly.

"At the entrance to the village, he fell into a fishpond that he had mistaken for solid ground. His body wasn't found until three days later."

Zhenguan closed her eyes, imagining her uncle's fate then, with planes and bombs in the sky, sentries and floods on the earth. The fishponds were an hour away, but he braved everything for the love of his wife and son. For men like her uncle, nothing was impossible.

"A hundred days after his death, matchmakers came to Shueiyun seeking out her hand in marriage." Zhenguan thought: Second Aunt could have basked in her husband's love for many lifetimes. Why would she want to remarry?

Aunt and niece looked at each other without saying a word. Suddenly Zhenguan sat up and looked at her watch. "Oh no!" she cried. "It's past ten o'clock already!"

"What's wrong?"

"Grandma wanted to listen to the Taiwanese opera, *Husband and Wife for Seven Lifetimes*. She asked me to wake her!" Zhenguan turned on the radio. First Aunt yawned. "You're only going to catch the tail end of it; why bother listening now? Tune in again tomorrow night. When are you going to visit me in Tainan?"

"I will," Zhenguan replied as a sorrowful tune arose from the radio. It was an old song, "The blossoms in springtime blossom only for spring." She didn't even hear the other lyrics; this line alone played in her mind, tearing her soul asunder.

"The blossoms in springtime blossom only for spring. . . ." The melody echoed, and she felt as if her very being were played out in the lyrics. Was Second Aunt the spring blossom? Or was it her uncle? It dawned on Zhenguan then how one's heart could die, truly die, with the loss of a lover. Her second aunt and uncle were both flower blossoms. They had bloomed for each other in the spring of their lives!

Everyone in the room had fallen asleep. Zhenguan lay down by the window. As she gazed into the night sky, the words "ask heaven about love" came to her mind.

eight

I

Zhenguan spent two years in Tainan.

At first, when she decided to leave home, her mother did not support her decision. So Zhenguan promised solemnly: "In two and a half years, when my brother graduates from school, I shall return." This made it easier for her mother to finally assent. Second Aunt also came to her defense, saying, "Shuilian is in Tainan, and she will take care of Zhenguan. You shouldn't worry about anything. In my opinion, Zhenguan is a good girl with a sensible head on her shoulders."

"I know I don't have to worry," her mother responded. "It's just that she's my only daughter, and I will miss not having her around!"

Zhenguan knew what her mother meant. She took her hand and said, "Ma, when I'm in Tainan I'll be able to work, make some money, and watch over Azhong. Boys don't really know how to take good care of themselves." Azhong, her younger brother, was starting his junior year in high school. Having foregone university herself, Zhenguan had high hopes for him.

"You're so young and inexperienced," her mother said. "How much money can you make?" Zhenguan did not reply. Actually, her first aunt had already gotten a job for her as a temporary clerk at the Office of Taxes and Revenues.

"You're my daughter, and I know you inside out," her mother continued. "You don't have to be in such a hurry to lighten the load on my shoulders. What's really on your mind?"

Zhenguan gulped and thought, She is widowed with children in her care. I am not capable of sharing her burden, but the least that I can do is to not make it any heavier than it already is.

"I have saved and scrimped what your father toiled to earn while he was alive," her mother said. "We also have the compensation fund that was awarded to us upon his death. I am a woman, so I cannot generate much revenue, but I can at least manage what we have. With our money, I have bought fishponds covering two hectares of land and entrusted them to your uncles and aunts. Even if our money loses its value over time, you and your brothers will still have some property to your names. If you want to continue your education, you should go to cram school or study on your own. Whatever you decide, you have my support. No matter what, this family will provide you with the money for books and for school."

Tears ran down her mother's face and pain tugged at Zhenguan's heart. Nevertheless, the decision was already made. "Ma, with my grades, what's the use of taking the exams? I'd be better off making some money like Yinyue and the others, and preparing my own dowry. . . ." She had meant to make her mother laugh, but as she heard her own words, she couldn't help but blush with embarrassment.

Mother and daughter shared the same bed and talked all night. The next day, they went shopping together and bought some flowery fabric to send to the dressmaker. On the day of her departure from home, Zhenguan was escorted to the station by her mother and two aunts. Her mother leaned on the window as the train was about to leave and reminded Zhenguan again, "Be understanding, be civilized, and associate only with good people. At the same time, learn how to deal with those who are nasty without intentionally crossing their path. Remember: bad people ride bad horses, and the malicious will bear the consequences of their own misdeeds."

As the train moved away from the platform, Zhenguan pressed her handkerchief against her eyes to hold back the tears.

From Tainan, Zhenguan would return home for all the festivals: Lantern Festival in January, Tomb-Sweeping Day in March, Dragonboat Festival in May, Hungry Ghosts Festival in July, Moon Festival in August, and the Lunar New Year in December. And thus, two years passed by quickly. Azhong was already in his senior year, his university exam only three months away!

Home was still home, attracting Zhenguan like a magnet. But . . . something was holding Zhenguan back now. She had come to know Tainan.

Every morning she would walk thirty minutes to work, and at sunset, she would stop by First Aunt's. It wasn't a long walk, but Zhenguan took her time, slowly, like an old woman with bound feet. She had not realized at first how beautiful the city of Tainan was, its avenues lined with flame trees and ablaze with fiery flowers that leaped into her eyes when she looked out the window, walked on the streets, or gazed up at the sky.

Zhenguan felt immensely thankful that her forefathers, who had come to Taiwan as pioneers of the wilderness, had had the vision to build a city with such beautiful trees. Every time Zhenguan passed one, she would look up into the flowery sky and her heart would fill up with admiration and gratitude.

Her first aunt and uncle often teased her, "You're such a strange girl, preferring to walk rather than to take the bus!"

And she would respond, "I did take the bus at first, but it was difficult to stay seated. Whenever the flame flowers came into view, I had to get on my feet and start walking!"

All flowers bloom in the eye of the beholder. To Zhenguan, the flowers of the flame tree represented a spirit that wasn't meant to be taken lightly. The others could not fully understand her sentiments. Yinchan wrote in her letter to Zhenguan, "If you love the flowers so much, why not marry a native of Tainan so that you can stay there forever!" Zhenguan missed Yinchan the most. Of all the cousins, they were the closest. Yinchan sometimes teased her and joked around with her, but it was only because they were the best of friends.

Yinchan's words were merely words. Both girls knew that no matter how times changed, home would always remain foremost in their minds; their hearts were anchored to the sea water and the night skies of their hometown.

II

Returning from work one day, Zhenguan found her brother reading a letter. The envelope was lying on the table, and the handwriting again gave Zhenguan a jolt: it was so much like her own. So what? she told herself. Quite a lot of people in this world have similar handwriting, after all!

She asked, "Azhong, who is the letter from?"

"Oh, it's from our cousin, Daxin," he answered, pulling another letter out of the drawer. "Here's one for you."

Of course, it had to be him!

"When did you two starting writing to each other?"

Her brother laughed. "Didn't you know that Daxin has been tutoring me by mail for a semester already? The summer before my senior year in high school, Fourth Aunt asked him to write to me. Now if I don't score at least 90 out of 100 on my physics and chemistry exams in July, I will be too ashamed to face my own relatives!"

Zhenguan thought for a moment. "He must be in his senior year in university by now, right?"

"Yeah, he's preparing for the military exam and for his graduation exams . . . that's a lot of preparing, but I wouldn't worry because he is such a good student," said Zhenguan's brother, his rosy-cheeked smile showing off two rows of sparkling white teeth.

"Speaking of which, dear brother, you'd better study hard!" Zhenguan said as she opened her letter. She had never replied to that letter Daxin had written her two years ago.

Dear Zhenguan:
I haven't heard from you for a very long time. It was only recently that I learned of your whereabouts from Azhong.

I was a guest at your house the summer before eighth grade, and a bone got stuck in my throat as I was eating fish. You might not recall the incident, but I remember clearly that it was you who came to my rescue with the malt sugar! Since it seemed as if you didn't want anyone to know, I decided to keep silent.

It's been so long since then, but I have thought about the incident often. It's about time that I express my gratitude: thank you very much.

Sincerely yours,
Daxin

Zhenguan folded the letter carefully after she finished reading it. The next day, she wrote a courteous response, thanking him for tutoring her brother. Several days later, another letter arrived.

Dear Zhenguan:
I saw your letter lying on my desk when I came home today. I was at first surprised, and then very happy, for I wasn't expecting you to write back! Please don't call me Mr. Liu, though. Doesn't that sound too formal? Just call me by my name, okay?

I've heard that you like flame flowers, and you walk in reverence when you see them. If the flowers knew, they would bloom all year round in your honor. Flame flowers are to Tainan what azaleas are to Taipei. They are what they are because of Tainan, just as azaleas wouldn't be azaleas outside of Taipei. If the two were switched around, they surely would not bloom. Don't you agree?

As I look out the window of my laboratory, I see a sea of azaleas. In the month of March they bloom in a dizzying array of pink, white, red, and purple. Please find enclosed an azalea blossom that I have just picked . . . although by the time it reaches you, it will probably be crushed!

Best wishes,
Daxin

Zhenguan held the soul of the flower in her hand. The brownish red blossom was indeed withered as Daxin had predicted. What an interesting person! But how was she to answer his letter, not knowing what to call him? She didn't even address Yincheng and her other male cousins directly by their names!

A few days later, she finally wrote him a short note:

Dear Brother:

In our grandfathers' and great-grandfathers' day, there were few literate and well-learned men. But as children, we heard them chant, "Men from the four seas are all brothers." Shouldn't we share their sentiments?

I have received the flower you sent. You might laugh, but that was my first encounter with an azalea blossom! As you said, there are none in Tainan, nor are there any flame flowers in Taipei. I guess everything has its own place in this world!

All the best,
Zhenguan

Three days later, another reply. Zhenguan thought: What's wrong with this person? Doesn't he have to prepare for examinations? or maybe he is so well prepared already that . . .

Dear Zhenguan:

Here's a question: I have no way of knowing; what do you look like now? The last time I saw you, about nine years ago, you were only twelve or thirteen, having just graduated from elementary school!

What is so wonderful about the flame flowers? Why are you so taken with them? Can you send me a blossom and educate this Taipei bumpkin?

Do you know what I'm like? I am the oldest child in my family. I am stubborn, sensitive, and headstrong. I am used to walking alone at night, and I like to gaze at the moon quietly from high places. The moon is like a crescent, and my mind is like a pool, still as the water in a well. Underneath the calm surface the currents are gushing and turbulent; and yet, the well is an infinite source of trust, hope, and love.

I enclose a recent photograph of myself. Do you still recognize me after all these years?

Yours,
Daxin

It was a graduation picture. Zhenguan couldn't imagine how the little boy who read kung fu novels and burned holes in the mosquito netting had grown into such a handsome gentleman. It is believed that one's fame and fortune can be predicted from the appearance of his hands and feet; his intelligence, from the eyes and ears. Daxin's eyes were clear and bright, but reserved and modest. He had the classic look of a scholar, with those handsome brows. But it was his facial expression that was most striking, like that of the Nobel Prize-winning Japanese physicist Yukawa Hideki.

Zhenguan did not reply to Daxin's letter for more than ten days. In that time, she had rushed home to serve as bridesmaid at Yinyue's wedding. All the female cousins rejoiced at their reunion and stuck together day in and day out, like glue. On the eve of the wedding, the five of them stayed up all night chatting. Actually, there were six girls in all, counting Yinxing, but since she was only fourteen going on fifteen, she had little to say and fell asleep amid the chattering cousins. Nonetheless, she needed to be in the room because even numbers were considered auspicious.

On Yinyue's wedding day, Zhenguan and her cousins escorted the bride all the way to Saltwater Town, where the bridegroom lived. His family had planned a huge banquet, and they feasted and reveled until late afternoon. But that morning, when cars were arriving at the front gate to pick up the guests, Yinyue had been in her bridal chamber, holding on to Zhenguan's hand, refusing to let go.

Seeing her cousin weep with her head bent, Zhenguan too was overwhelmed with emotion. As she wiped away the bride's tears and powdered her face, she said, "Come now, whoever cries will break the bucket." Her words brought a smile to Yinyue's face.

That night, on the way home, Zhenguan sat beside her Fourth Aunt, who asked her, "Has Daxin written to your brother?"

"Yes, he has been tutoring Azhong. If Azhong gets into his first-choice school, he will certainly have his teacher to thank!"

"Ah," her aunt sighed. "Actually, Daxin has been having a rough time lately. . . ."

Zhenguan sensed something strange in her aunt's tone. She didn't feel she was in any position to pry further, but her aunt continued, "There's a girl in his class, and they have been a couple since their freshman year. But last semester, without any warning, she married a visiting professor and left for the United States. . . . Actually, it's just as well that she changed her mind, heartless person that she was. But Daxin, ever stubborn, has taken it quite badly."

Zhenguan listened quietly, sympathetically. After all, her feelings toward Daxin were not romantic in nature; rather, she had always regarded him as a kindred spirit. Poor forsaken brother!

Another day passed, and Yinyue went back to her maiden home to attend the wedding banquet prepared by her own family. The celebrations continued until the sun's rays disappeared in the west. The chauffeur knocked on the door several times for the bride, who finally bade farewell to her parents in a gush of tears.

In the meantime, Zhenguan had packed her bags and was ready to return to Tainan with First Aunt. She said good-bye to everyone but couldn't find Yinchan. She tracked her down at last in the kitchen, where she was helping the cook clear the tables.

The leftover soups and banquet dishes were all mixed together. Any three-year-old child with teeth knew that the "tail of the feast" was delicious. Since childhood, Zhenguan had relished this treat after wedding banquets and festivals at home, when they would enjoy the leftovers for five or six days in a row, heating them up for meal after meal. When the pot finally emptied, they would start dreaming of the next wedding or happy occasion. Was it the festive atmosphere of celebration that they were so reluctant to leave behind . . . or was it the taste of the leftover "tail of the feast"? So many fond memories. . . .

"Yinchan, I'm leaving!"

Seeing that it was Zhenguan, Yinchan filled a big bowl and brought it to her, saying, "Finish this up before you go!"

"Give me a break, dear, I'm too full!"

Yinchan, not about to take no for an answer, stuck a spoon into her hand and said, "You're going to get hungry on your way back, and you won't have any of this down in Tainan!"

"But—"

Yinchan laughed. "But what? Even three-year-olds know that this is delicious!"

They finally settled by finishing the bowl of leftovers

together. Zhenguan said jokingly, "When you get married, we won't even have to share the leftovers with neighbors. All seven or eight pots of leftovers will be for the bride herself!"

"Yeah, that ought to last for about ten days!"

The two girls laughed, and finally Yinchan helped Zhenguan with her bags and saw her off at the train station. By the time Zhenguan arrived in Tainan, it was already nine o'clock in the evening. First Aunt, tired from the journey, went straight to bed after washing up. Zhenguan went upstairs to find her brother still awake, so she gave him ginseng sent from home and relayed her mother's messages. When she returned to her own room, the first thing that she saw on her desk under the lamp was an envelope with familiar handwriting. Her brother had placed it there for her.

She sat down to steady herself, but her heart was thumping wildly. She couldn't find her letter opener, and she didn't want to make a lot of noise hunting around for it, so she tore the envelope open by hand. She wasn't neat about it and ended up with a jagged tear. What could Daxin have written? After a moment of hesitation, she finally unfolded the letter. Under the light of the lamp, the words leaped up from the page.

Dear Zhenguan:

I just bought a biography on the Tang Dynasty poet Li Ho. It is very good! I have also read Tang Dynasty legends, Ming Dynasty novels, *The Peony Pavilion, The Everlasting Temple,* and other works of literature recently. Reading an essay or a novel is no easy task. The reader is tempted, forced to depart from reality and his present state of stability (or is it complacency?), to pitch himself into the past, or an expectation, or a melancholy state. It is inevitably turbulent.

When reading, one is caught between reality and illusion, floating here and there, sometimes caught in tempest and excitement, sometimes losing oneself in the sublime, sometimes floating beyond the dusty world, sometimes falling back into the solemnity and constraints of life. . . . Moving between the two states is a kind of pushing and pulling, a kind of ripping apart. If only one could achieve harmony!

A chemist's footnote: sublimation is when a solid substance, bypassing the liquid phase, is transformed directly into a gas. This is an abrupt but astonishing process, much like the sudden transformation of a hardened criminal into a righteous soul.

Best wishes,
Daxin

Zhenguan folded the letter and shut her eyes. Why had she opened this letter in the first place? She shouldn't have read it, for it marked the beginning of her fondness for Daxin! ". . . sometimes floating beyond the dusty world, sometimes falling back into the solemnity and constraints of life. . ." How similar they were! The same books! So many coincidences! How could she not take him seriously?

III

Dear Chemist:

Enclosed please find the petals of two flame flowers. I think they are deeply enchanting.

I also enclose a group picture taken with my colleagues at the office. Since you asked, see if you can guess which one is me!

Zhenguan

Three days later, a letter came from Taipei by express mail.

Dear Zhenguan:
The flame flowers are wonderful indeed. I can feel it: I must have known them in a previous lifetime, and now am reunited with them again in this one. Perhaps I should move to Tainan, no? My professor once said that the purpose of studying is to encounter good affairs, good sentiments, good people, and good things in life.

I have received the photograph. The only thing that I can be sure of is that you are not one of those men wearing ties! A good guess? I'd better stop while I'm ahead! (Actually, I do know which one is you! Ha!)

Daxin

If she hadn't returned home to attend Yinyue's wedding, if she hadn't sat beside Fourth Aunt and heard her story about Daxin, Zhenguan would have responded to the letter promptly. But now . . . she knew that he had gone through an ordeal, but she was starting to take him more and more seriously. It would not be easy for her to sustain their casual and lighthearted acquaintance.

After several days of torment, she received another letter.

Dear Zhenguan:
Let me tell you a story about what happened on a campus filled with azaleas. It is the love story of a friend. . . .

In his freshman year, he was wild and bold, and she was a lily of the valley. The harsh winter had passed, and when spring arrived, they took off their vestments of shyness and reserve and fell madly in love. They could be seen all over the campus, their footsteps heard on the tree-lined boulevard, by the greenhouse, in the old school president's graveyard, and especially at the pavilion by Building Number Six . . . the pavilion was their special place. All their vows and promises were made there.

Wherever they went, they would carry a book with them. It put them at ease and served as a pillow as they lay on the grass looking at passersby, although she preferred to lean on his shoulders. Sometimes they hid from the crowds for privacy, to avoid prying eyes (some people have sick minds!).

However, within a month, while he was busy finishing up his studies, she had married someone else and left the country. But they had exchanged vows, planned to study abroad together! How could she? Alas, perhaps it is for the best. They won't have to see each other's hair turning white with age.

My friend passed this sad story on to me. But people living in times like these shouldn't drown themselves in such common tragedies—

The letter was not signed and seemed unfinished. Zhenguan could sense the struggles in his mind! He didn't want to keep this from her, and yet he couldn't give expression to it, so he opted for this clumsy description. No one but those involved can fully grasp the vows exchanged between two lovers. Zhenguan felt pained, for she hadn't expected such a past from him. She had only respect and tender feelings for Daxin, such a bright person, full of life and lucidity. Nevertheless, she couldn't resist the temptation to tease him just a little.

Dear Protagonist:

How touching! Great love stories live forever!

In the novel *Water Margin,* the bandits who rallied together on Mount Liang to rebel against the Kingdom of Liang pledged lifelong loyalty to their cause. I am sure you can understand such devotion.

But love is never mistaken! If you did love that person, then it will last a lifetime! True love doesn't look back, it doesn't regret. If she won your heart, and if you love her, then that alone should suffice. You needn't claim that person as your own. The Chinese philosopher Chuangtze said: "Gold is hidden deep in the mountains and pearls deep in the ocean." . . . As long as she is part of the scenery of this world, as long as she is alive and well, life is beautiful!

Be strong!

Zhenguan

When she mailed the letter, she had not thought it inappropriate. But a week passed by with no reply with Daxin, and she started to suspect that maybe she had done wrong. He obviously hadn't wanted to lay everything out in clear daylight. Why did she have to call his game? Life is filled with realities and illusions. So what if she got to the bottom of things? She was a silly girl, it seemed, an idiot in this dazzling game of life. One doesn't have to take everything so seriously!

On the tenth day, his letter finally came:

Dear Zhenguan:
I have received your letter. I was angry, a little bit; why did you have to drive me into a corner? Okay, I admit that I am the person in the story! I also admit that I have been guilt-ridden these days. Love, love, love. Is it an easy concept for you? Do you know how many times a person has to stumble before he reaches the truth?

Actually, I'm not really mad. I should thank you for saying what you did; for if you hadn't, I would probably be even more miserable than I already am.

I will be graduating in ten days. I have attended banquet after banquet, stuffing myself. My brain is sinking into a stupor and my stomach beginning to sag!

How are you finding Tainan?

Daxin

Zhenguan counted the days. Her brother's graduation was just around the corner, and she had been in Tainan for two years and four months already. How unpredictable is life! When she made that promise to her mother, she had not suspected how attached she would become to Tainan's geography and landscape. She hadn't predicted that she would come to know Daxin while living in this city.

Nonetheless, it was time to bid farewell. There would always be a place for Tainan in her heart. She realized now that a person didn't have to spend all of her days in one good place. Knowing the mountains and the rivers, the sun and the moon, the people and the customs of Tainan . . . that was enough. So as Zhenguan packed her things, she felt ready to leave.

She left Tainan to fulfill her promise to her mother. But that wasn't the only reason: she knew somehow that Daxin would come looking for her. She had to put a stop to it first! Daxin was like a mountain of treasures: the deeper she dug the more she found to like. But out of pride and indignation, she said to herself: No more! Maybe she was angry with him. Maybe she was angry with herself. Fires burn to ashes, and he had burned already. Why had they not met first? Alas, let the two of them pay the price for that!

The next day, Zhenguan handed in her resignation at the office. As she left, it suddenly hit her: tomorrow she would be here no longer. In an effort to cast her shadow over the now-familiar pavement of Tainan before leaving, she decided to walk the streets. That afternoon, she walked all over the city.

It was only at dinner that night that she finally informed her aunt and uncle of her decision. Both were surprised. "But you're doing so well here, why leave?"

Zhenguan gave them a pained smile. "I don't want to go, but I promised Mother. . . ."

First Aunt laughed. "If that's the problem, don't worry; I'll talk to her."

"But no—" Zhenguan said hurriedly. "The last time I went back home, for Yinyue's wedding, Grandma and Grandpa made me promise to return soon too!"

Knowing the filial daughter that she was, First Aunt did not insist on keeping Zhenguan with them further. "In that case, then, just stay a few more days!" she said. "I can't stand to see you go!"

Zhenguan felt torn.

When she had first started working, before she'd received her first paycheck, her aunt had been worried about her not having enough to spend. So at night, after Zhenguan had fallen asleep, she would quietly go into her room and stuff money into her pockets. In the early morning, Zhenguan would find the money when she was dressing. At first she didn't know where it had come from; but one night, she was still awake when First Aunt came into her room, and through the mosquito netting, she saw First Aunt slip the bills into her little purse. Zhenguan waited for her aunt to leave the room before sitting up. Her eyes filled with tears.

And this went on for a whole month, until Zhenguan got her paycheck.

Beneficiary of such benevolence, Zhenguan vowed to herself: I will allow the tree of my life to grow tall and to flourish so that one day, I will be able to repay my loved ones.

Zhenguan ended up staying in Tainan for a few more days, and she mailed this letter before boarding the train:

Dear Daxin:

Congratulations on your graduation from university!

I have left Tainan already. Even though I love the flame flowers and I will miss the place, I shall be content with the thought of having lived here once. In the future I can visit Tainan as often as I want in my dreams.

Zhenguan

nine

I

A month after Zhenguan's return home, two very important things happened. First, her brother scored very well on the university entrance exams and got into the school of his first choice. Second, the family heard from First Uncle, who had been missing for thirty years.

First Uncle had lost contact with the family after he was conscripted by the Japanese army during World War II to fight in southeast Asia. After the war, some of his fellow soldiers returned to Taiwan, but no one knew First Uncle's whereabouts; no one even knew whether he was dead or alive. For thirty long years, Suyun, his wife, waited for him to return, raising their two sons on her own. And now, all of a sudden, there was a letter from him, sent from Tokyo. It created an uproar in the family.

Most respected Father and Mother:

Your unfilial son Guofeng was conscripted to fight in southeast Asia. I escaped death many times and survived the ravages of war, thanks to the merit of our ancestors. Finding myself in a strange land with only the shirt on my back and not a penny to my name, I swore that I would make something of myself before returning home. I now run a quite successful establishment of my own.

Though I have succeeded in my ambition, the thought of you has always been in my mind. Tokyo is a fine city worthy of its fame, but it is not my homeland. Thirty years, and not a day has gone by when I have not thought of home, the home of my spirit and soul. Before my homecoming I am writing this letter to inquire about my brothers and sisters.

How is Suyun? My greatest guilt is that I have started another family here with wife and children, leaving Suyun on her own for thirty years. My Japanese wife dares not return with me to Taiwan. She is Japanese, but she is familiar with Chinese customs and etiquette. Although she has seen me through difficult times, our union has not been approved, and shadows of doubt have been cast over its legitimacy. I solemnly seek your advice on this very delicate matter and shall abide by your counsel.

Your most unfilial son,
Guofeng

The letter was passed around all day, then folded neatly and placed on the family altar. Almost everyone had read it except for the person whose life and interests were most intimately affected by its contents. Not a sound or query came from her at all. Zhenguan knew that her aunt, Suyun, did not read much.

But from what the others had been saying, she must have pieced things together. Zhenguan thought, if there were a reason at all for her silence, it had to be fear at the thought of such a homecoming! The news, after all, came out of nowhere; anyone would have been taken by surprise, dazed, unable to distinguish dream from reality.

Such a development, of course, called for a family conference, and everyone gathered around the table to talk. Zhenguan heard her grandmother ask her grandfather, "Old one, what do you think?"

Grandpa looked at her aunt and said, "We should ask Suyun. All these years I have known my daughter-in-law and not my son; she has taken his place and done all for him that he should have done himself. . . . Why ask me?"

So everyone turned to Suyun. Zhenguan saw that her eyes were red, and she was unable to speak.

"Suyun. . . ."

"Mother. . . ."

Mother-in-law and daughter-in-law called out to each other but their voices hung in the air. There was so much to be said; where should they begin?

"I know of all your pain and suffering, and there is no reason for you to swallow any more bitterness. Guofeng—"

"Mother . . ." the words finally came haltingly from Suyun's mouth, as two lines of tears streamed down her cheeks. "I am forty, going on fifty, and I am a grandmother already. My thoughts no longer run shallow or narrow in mind or spirit. I think: the more in the family, the merrier." She wiped her tears with the corner of her handkerchief and couldn't speak anymore. Grandma took her hand and said, "Let me stand where you stand. I will give you my firm support!"

Zhenguan realized that her aunt's tears were tears of happiness and gratitude. First Uncle had been gone for thirty years, and she must never have imagined that he would still be alive to share months and years of living in this world. This thought alone was enough to make her cry.

"Mother, men are—"

"Yes?"

"Whatever he decides will do! I'm just so happy that you have found your son again! And Yinshan and his brother will see their father alive. . . . My tears are of happiness, not sorrow."

Silence fell on the front hall as everyone became lost in their own thoughts, and for a while no words were spoken.

Finally, Grandma said, "You are a mature and understanding person. As your elders, we feel a genuine fondness for you, and the younger members of this family all hold you in the highest regard. Should the Japanese woman return with him? Your father-in-law wants to leave the decision up to you."

Aunt's head was bowed, but at this she sat up straight and said, "Father and Mother, you two are the elders, and the decisions of this family, large or small, should be yours to make! But as for my own opinion: she has taken care of Guofeng all these years, making sure that he was warm and well fed . . . such merits should compensate for any misdeed. Furthermore, when Guofeng left home, Yinshan was only three years old, and Yinchuan was still a baby in swaddling clothes. I have been at Guofeng's side for only five years, whereas she has been with him for thirty! If he were to reject her now, Guofeng would not be a man of honor. Our family has been of good moral standing for many generations, and we should not have anyone tarnish our name!"

That night, Zhenguan was still thinking of what her aunt had said. Sleepless, she tossed and turned for a long time.

"Grandma, what do you think about this affair with First Uncle?"

"What do I think?" the old woman repeated, as if asking herself. "It's all like a dream!"

II

It was the seventh day of the seventh lunar month. The sun had just set in the west when suddenly a gust of wind and a whirl of clouds brought forth a scattering of rain from the sky. It always rained this time of year, so people were expecting it. In fact, it would have been strange if it hadn't rained.

Zhenguan, Yinchan, and the sisters were making rice balls in the kitchen, remembering to put a dent in the rice balls to hold the tears of the spinner-girl. As she kneaded the dough, Zhenguan suddenly felt an urge to walk into the front hall. Her feet were moving involuntarily, while her fingers were still busy rolling the rice balls. Just as she was about to make a dent, she came to a standstill.

The people in town seldom kept their front gates closed. Zhenguan stood in the courtyard and saw a man at their gate. It seemed as if he were having difficulty making up his mind whether to come in or not, though there was nothing suspicious about him. As Zhenguan moved toward the visitor, she thought: Two thirds of the men in the household have left for Taipei to pick up First Uncle at the airport. If this man had come to see Yinchuan or Yinan, he had made his trip in vain. "Whom are you looking for?" she called.

The weather was sweltering hot, and though the man had not rolled up the long sleeves of his white shirt, he looked quite comfortable. "I—"

He looked into Zhenguan's eyes then. She gave no signs of joy or even recognition and seemed rather to give him the cold shoulder. He smiled. "Zhenguan, I am Daxin."

Such a person, popping in on her like this and catching her by total surprise! Visitors were visitors, but this was no ordinary visitor! Here was the person who had helped her brother with his studies, to whom they were all indebted and grateful. And of course, he was Fourth Aunt's nephew. . . . "Oh, it's you!" Zhenguan said. "Please come in, let me go find Fourth Aunt!"

She helped him with his bags, led him to the front hall, and summoned Grandma, Grandpa, and the others. Thinking that they would keep him busy for some time, she snuck back into the kitchen.

So he had come just like that. She was a bit angry with him, but how strange it was! There was something almost telepathic about it. Why else would she have left the kitchen so suddenly to find him standing at the door? In the commotion she didn't even get a good look at his face. Could that brief encounter even be considered a meeting between the two of them? Picking Chinese Lovers' Day to make his entrance: was that merely a coincidence?

Making rice balls was a mechanical process that could be done almost unconsciously, but as she rolled and pinched the rice balls, Yinchan cried out, "Your palms are sweating! And I was wondering why the dough was wet!"

Zhenguan saw that the newly made rice balls did contain tears in their tiny dents, glistening wet. She smiled. "We're almost done, let me go home and summon Azhong!"

"Why?"

"We have a visitor from Taipei: Fourth Aunt's nephew. Azhong must come and meet his tutor!"

When Zhenguan got home, her brother had just left with one of the boys. She had taken the shortcut and missed them on the way. Her mother, preparing food for the evening rites, said to Zhenguan, "Azhong left in such a hurry that I didn't have time to remind him to invite Daxin over for dinner. Will you make another trip to Grandpa's?"

Zhenguan helped her mother with the bowls of sticky rice and said, "Why worry? He's going to be well taken care of there. It's his first night here, and Fourth Aunt is not going to let her nephew go anywhere else for dinner. Not to mention Grandma! Why fight over him?"

Second Aunt joined in. "Yes, and you want Zhenguan to go over there? Nobody who does will return tonight! Besides, who's going to help you with the big pot of sticky rice that you just cooked?"

"What do you mean?" her mother asked.

Second Aunt laughed. "They have a visitor there, and the atmosphere is festive! Since they're going to prepare a feast anyway, it doesn't matter whether it's for one guest or ten. Anyone who visits will certainly be detained as a guest. Azhong's not going to be able to make it back for dinner, and certainly not Daxin!"

Sure enough, they waited until after seven, and Azhong did not return for dinner, so they started without him. Afterward, his mother glanced at the pot and said, "All these leftovers! We're only missing Azhong for dinner, and look at how much we have left. If Zhenguan had gone too, I wouldn't have had to cook tomorrow!"

Zhenguan laughed, saying, "Boys have big appetites; I can't compete with them. With Azhong and a guest, we wouldn't have had enough!"

They chatted until it was time to listen to Taiwanese opera on the radio. Zhenguan's mother and aunt retired to their room, and her little brother went to his to do his homework. Zhenguan was alone, so she went back to her own room to sit quietly, though her heart was still in a state of turmoil. She had planned to sew with Yinchan tonight, but the unexpected visitor had thrown her off balance, and now she didn't know what to do with herself.

There was a transmitter radio on the desk that Azhong had assembled in one of his experiments. She switched it on and was greeted by the song "Peach Blossom Crossing the River." In the song, an old man on a ferryboat teases a young woman by the name of Peach Blossom who wants to cross the river: "I'll take you across the river, but you must marry me first!" Peach Blossom replies, "Let us have a singing contest. If you win, I'll be yours; but if you lose, you'll take me across the river." And Zhenguan listened to the playful duet:

> In the first lunar month, as others welcome their husbands, a single woman stays in her boudoir. Eating betel nuts and powdering her face, coral in hand, she waits for a husband.
>
> In the second lunar month, with spring just around the corner, a good-for-nothing pushes the ferryboat, eating on deck and sleeping in the cabin. If you drown, the water ghosts will capture your soul.
>
> In the third lunar month, as rain starts to drizzle, the flirtatious girl feigns modesty. I am Yang Zongbao, the general, and you, Peach Blossom, are Mu Gueiying, the female warrior, forcing me to marry you.

In the fourth lunar month, as spring sets in, the good-for-nothing sits by his ferryboat, having no rice to cook three meals. How dare you dally with me!

In the fifth lunar month, it's Dragonboat Festival. Peach Blossom, with her good looks and flirtatious nature, runs after people with her umbrella, falling in love with a handsome but dull fellow.

In the sixth lunar month, temperatures rise, and the good-for-nothing takes passengers on his ferryboat. There's no one to mend his clothes when they are torn, and bugs start biting when the clothes are drenched with sweat.

In the seventh lunar month, leaves start falling from trees. Having married Peach Blossom, I strut with pride, but neighbors laugh and say that I have hit rocks with my spade.

In the eighth lunar month, white dew forms, and the good-for-nothing pushes his ferryboat. He wants to eat but he won't work; if he loses his oar, he'll be in for hard times.

In the ninth lunar month, the persimmons ripen, and Peach Blossom's beauty is potent. An old man like me can take the sting, but sting the young and they will wilt.

In the tenth lunar month, it's time to replenish oneself in preparation for winter. Quit daydreaming about me, you old man; there's no one to wake you when you sleep late and no one to sleep by your side on your old straw mat.

In the eleventh lunar month, when winter is just around the corner, I discover that you have camouflaged your big feet as dainty little ones. Your feet are actually bigger than my oars.

In the twelfth lunar month, special cakes are offered to honor ancestors. Those with spouses have an easy time, but you, old man, can only fan the cold wind at the side.

Zhenguan laughed as she listened. The woman was a tart, and the old man was so cocksure, but both were gutsy and admirable. They meant no harm; they were simply two people with high self-esteem.

Just then there were two thumps on the door, and Zhenguan called out, "Who's there?"

"Zhenguan, Daxin is here; don't you want to come out for a while?"

That person . . . what did he want from her? He had many reasons to be there: to visit relatives, to sightsee. . . . It's not that she wasn't welcoming, she just didn't know what to say to him. If they hadn't been writing to each other, he would just be another visitor, and she could treat him politely. But now they were on familiar terms, and the situation had become more complicated. She just didn't know how to face him! If she were truly angry at him, then she could put a resolute end to her confusion. But of course it wasn't that simple. First Aunt had taught her that one cannot always make a big fuss, that one must let go of certain things. So she wavered from one stance to the other as if she had two feet planted on two different boats.

Zhenguan put on a grass-green dress with yellow and white dots. The visitor sat facing her mother. When he saw her walk in, he stood up, then sat down again. Zhenguan poured him a glass of ice water, only to find that he already had a glass in his hand. Everyone else had a glass of water too, so she started drinking the water herself. As they talked, Zhenguan continued drinking. She was on her third glass when her mother said, "At dinner I asked if you wanted seconds, and you said you were too full to eat any more. How can you drink so much water now?"

Zhenguan didn't say anything, but Daxin answered for her. "The stomach for eating ice differs from the stomach for eating rice! That's what my sisters always say."

Her mother, aunt, and brother all started laughing; Zhenguan kept a giggle to herself.

Later, Daxin said he wanted to walk to the beach to look at the ocean. Mother and Second Aunt both urged Zhenguan and her brother to accompany him. Zhenguan consented and led the way, walking ahead of the two boys. They soon caught up with her, and the three of them walked side by side. Then, somehow, Zhenguan's brother pulled ahead while the other two followed behind.

This was the moment that Zhenguan had feared most. She walked slowly, staring at the tips of her shoes. Her emotions were all mixed up, and yet she somehow felt trusting and at ease. She glanced at Daxin's old-fashioned shoes and had to suppress her laughter. It was the seventh day of the seventh lunar month, a day for lovers, and walking by her side was a very attractive man wearing the ugliest pair of shoes she had ever seen.

Daxin finally spoke. "Hey, have you noticed that July seventh according to the Western calendar and the seventh day of the seventh lunar month according to the Chinese calendar both have something to do with bridges?"

Zhenguan smiled, "Hmm . . . now that you mention it . . ."

Daxin continued, "I was also listening to 'Peach Blossom' just now. It's really something! I wonder why it escaped my attention before. We heard it on the radio all the time when I was in elementary school. The lyrics and the melody are both very nice. . . . Can you sing it?"

Zhenguan thought, Even if I knew how, I wouldn't sing it for you! But she couldn't voice her feelings, so she just smiled mysteriously.

The rows of street lamps resembled strands of pearls sewn onto the dark velvet of the night.

Daxin said, "I don't know about you, but I think that she and the ferryman will make quite a couple!"

"Who?"

"Peach Blossom!"

"Oh."

"Women like Peach Blossom win the hearts of all men, don't you think?"

"How would I know how men's hearts are won? After all, I am a woman!"

Daxin laughed. "Exactly, so how could you not know? Isn't there a saying in Buddhist texts: 'Holding a flower with a smile'? A smile alone is enough, no words are necessary!"

Zhenguan was quiet.

"Hearing the song is almost like meeting her in person," Daxin continued. "Peach Blossom is ageless; she lives in China's history, like a grandmother, and like a little sister. . . . You might say that she has been singing her playful banter since the dawn of time and the beginning of civilization!"

Zhenguan laughed, suddenly happy, thinking about Peach Blossom and the person beside her.

Daxin said with a chuckle, "Hey, what are you laughing at?"

"With a bosom friend like you, Peach Blossom is indeed a thousand years old," Zhenguan replied. "She can live forever with no need for reincarnation!"

"And . . . ?"

"Well, I admire her tenacity, seeking new hope in the face of desperation. She lived fully, as if nothing in the world could thwart her. I'm sure that, even thrown over the steepest cliff, she would cling on to life and—"

"—and return, singing a song of triumph, right?" he finished her train of thought seamlessly. Could two minds really be so much alike? Zhenguan was more bewildered than ever.

The three of them arrived at the dock. They looked at the fishing boats and the sea lit with fishing lanterns and then walked toward the back of the bay, hugging the coastline. Daxin kept talking all along the way. Zhenguan thought: This man didn't come for a view of the sea, he came to talk!

By the time they returned to their starting point, it was already half past nine. Zhenguan's brother had met an elementary school chum on the way back and had gone to his house to visit. The remaining two walked very slowly, their footsteps heavy as cows. . . .

Zhenguan stopped at the front door of her house and looked up at Daxin, saying, "It's late, so I'm not going to ask you to come in. Can you make your way back to Grandpa's?"

Daxin smiled, "If I were to say no, would you escort me back?"

"This—" Zhenguan was flustered. "—that is, we'd have to wait for Azhong to come back. . . ."

Daxin laughed. "Don't worry! I counted the number of street lamps on the way! I know them better than the Taiwan Electric Company workers!"

Zhenguan laughed now too. "I knew you were just pretending that you'd get lost."

The two looked at each other and then smiled, saying goodbye. As Daxin turned to walk away, Zhenguan said from where she was standing, "Walk safely, and happy birthday!"

Daxin was caught by surprise. He turned back to face her—like a rubber band stretched in the wrong direction, Zhenguan thought.

"Oh! How did you know?"

Zhenguan was expecting the question. "Why wouldn't I know?" she answered. "Who doesn't know that you were born on the same day as Emperor Wu of the Han dynasty?"

Daxin was even more surprised. "No, really. Don't keep me in suspense, let it out!"

"It's a secret."

"Come on, I am bursting with curiosity!" Daxin prodded.

"Okay, I'll tell you," Zhenguan conceded. "I found out about your birthday nine years ago. It was the seventh day of the seventh lunar month; you had just returned with the others from the seaside. The adults all retired to bed, but Fourth Aunt went to the kitchen to cook a chicken egg and a duck egg for you."

"Oh . . . so that's how you knew!"

"Yes, that's the custom here in the south."

"In Taipei, we eat noodles cooked with pig's knuckles on our birthdays."

"Yes, but here that's for people over twenty years old. Before that, children are given a chicken egg to represent a chicken, and a duck egg to represent a duck. So it's like eating a whole chicken and a whole duck!"

Daxin laughed. "Chinese culture is so rich and deep. Foreigners would probably have a hard time understanding how an egg could represent a chicken!"

"Well, it certainly isn't a science!"

"Such is the nature of our culture: no matter what, there will always be room for contemplation. . . . Oh, Azhong's back!"

Azhong ended up walking Daxin back to Grandpa's. After they left, Zhenguan bathed and got ready for bed, but she did not feel at all like sleeping. There were so many things on her mind!

She thought about First Uncle's imminent homecoming, First Aunt's love for her husband, her own father, Second Aunt's husband. . . . Life and death were a world apart! Departure in death meant separation forever. But departure in life meant that as long as one was alive and breathing, he could make it back home. It didn't matter how long it might take or how difficult the journey might be. . . . Yinshan could still see his father's face, but Mother and Second Aunt were to remain heartbroken all their lives.

And her thoughts turned to Azhong. He was moving to Taipei to register for university: Taipei, the city that nurtured Daxin, a man so unique and full of spirit. . . .

Zhenguan reached out to shut the window, feeling peaceful and luminous inside.

III

It was two or three in the afternoon, and everyone was taking a nap. Zhenguan lay in her own room, drifting in and out of sleep. The sewing machine creaked in the next room: her second aunt was altering an old dress that was no longer in fashion.

The same sweet dreams visit me every day
And I awake to be greeted by emptiness
So I waste away
All is in vain
Memories bring only pain

And the dreams bring more memories
The same sweet dreams visit me every day
And the moonlight shines through my windowpane
Illuminating my room full of loneliness. . . .

Zhenguan realized that it was Second Aunt's voice. The love-smitten souls of the world! Twenty, thirty years had passed already. In that time young saplings can grow into towering trees, and ambitions can be realized through perseverance. But her second aunt was still locked in her chaste and closed world, bitterly reminiscing about her beloved husband.

Love knows no end
Until the end of time
My grief runs deep as a well
As I search this life and the afterlife
For my beloved.

The thought of love kept apart by life and death struck a heavy chord in Zhenguan's heart, and she felt a tightening in her throat.

At that moment, laughter and merry conversation drifted into the room; Zhenguan recognized the voices of Azhong and Daxin. The two of them had left the house early in the morning with their fishing gear, and they had asked her to join them on a fishing trip. Why had she turned them down? she wondered now. Was it timidity? Before the eve of July seventh, she had thought of Daxin from time to time, but she'd also had other things to think about. Since the seventh of July, however, thoughts of Daxin had taken over, leaving no room for anything else.

But she didn't want things to happen so fast, she didn't want to see him every day. The faintest thought of him now was enough to send her head spinning; how could she endure the intensity of the feelings that would overwhelm her if they were to face each other?

Zhenguan pulled out a box and was about to go through all the letters that Daxin had written to her when she was interrupted by her little niece, Aman, the five-year-old daughter of Yinshan. She knocked on Zhenguan's door, saying, "Auntie, Auntie!"

Zhenguan put the letters away and opened the door to greet her niece. "Little Aman!" she said, picking her up and pecking her chubby cheeks. "Where are Mama and Grandma? Who brought you here?"

The little girl looked up at her with her jet-black eyes, puckered her little pink lips, and replied firmly, "I came by myself! I wanted to see you and Great-Aunt!"

"What for?" Zhenguan asked with a smile.

"I wanted to ask Great-Aunt for some rice so that you can sew little rice bags for me!"

Such a logical and straightforward answer! Zhenguan felt a surge of warm feelings for her little niece and wanted to pamper her. "So, you've already mastered the game of picking up little sacks of rice?" she asked.

"Not yet, but I want you to sew the little rice sacks for me now, so I'll have them to play with when I'm old enough."

"Picking up little rice bags" is a game often enjoyed by young women in their boudoirs. Five pieces of cloth in various colors are sewn into triangular sacks the size of coins, then filled with sand or rice or beans. There are different ways of playing with the little sacks. In the first round, the player throws a little sack up and, while it is still in midair, picks up one of the four remaining sacks and moves it to the side, repeating until all five sacks are in the same heap.

In the second round, two sacks are picked up at once. In the third, only three of the five sacks are used: the player picks them up one by one and transfers them quickly from the left to the right hand so that the two sacks in the right hand, when thrown up into the air, land skillfully on either side of the right wrist. Then the sack in the palm of the left hand is tossed upward and the two sacks must be picked up again, quickly, before the sack lands. The last round is the most difficult. The sack tossed upward must land on the back of the hand while the thumb and index finger pick up one of the four sacks from the tabletop and fling it over the back of the hand without dropping the sack that is already there. Zhenguan had been playing this game since she was seven, and she still couldn't master this last move.

She asked the little girl, "Isn't there a pail of rice in the pantry? What did your mother say?"

The little girl pouted. "Mommy wouldn't give me any rice. She said that rice is not to be played with."

Zhenguan pinched her cheek and said, "She's right! Rice is a grain that has been planted as food for you and me, and we must not waste it." The little girl listened raptly as Zhenguan continued, "Some people don't sew the sacks well, and the rice spills out when they play with them. This upsets the deities above—"

"Uncle—" the little girl called out suddenly.

She turned to see Daxin. He must have been standing behind them for some time already. "So, the fisherman has returned," she said softly.

Daxin's nose was red from the sun. He grinned. "Yeah, I came back just in time to sit in on your class!"

Zhenguan put her niece down and the two walked toward the front hall. "Do you want to see what we caught?" Daxin asked.

"Didn't you leave your catch of the day with Fourth Aunt?"

"Don't worry, there's enough to go around. We can all have fish for dinner."

Azhong had already emptied the fish into a large pan, and Zhenguan took a peek. "Wow, this must have been a good day for fishing!" she exclaimed. "You seem to have caught all the fish in the sea!"

Zhenguan's little niece grabbed the largest fish and said, "Auntie, I want this for dinner!"

Zhenguan laughed. "You'd better ask your uncle whether he wants to give it away."

"Of course." Daxin chuckled. "Tell your aunt here to cook it for you!"

Zhenguan put the fish back and went to wash the smell off the little girl's hands. When they returned, Azhong was nowhere to be seen. Daxin was reading a newspaper. The little girl sat down and tugged at Zhenguan's hand, saying, "Auntie, let's play a game."

Zhenguan held out her hands, positioning her left index finger in the middle of her right palm, stretching her fingers out like an umbrella. Zhenguan's niece touched her palm with her little fingers. They chanted a nursery rhyme in unison, and the little girl was to extract her fingers as soon as they reached the end of the rhyme. If she wasn't fast enough, her hand would be trapped by Zhenguan's fingers. This time, Zhenguan won the game.

Aman giggled. "Now it's my turn to catch you in my umbrella."

The two of them had a grand time. Watching them, Daxin said, "I cannot help but envy her. Let me tell you something, have you heard it before?"

"I won't know until you tell it to me!"

Daxin chuckled. "Okay, here it is: We are true to ourselves between the ages of one and ten. But once we turn eleven, we are no longer pure."

Zhenguan had indeed heard this theory before! It was said that all living things are destined to live a certain number of years, and that mankind was allotted only ten. When man learned of this fate, he cried with sorrow. The other creatures—such as the monkey, the dog, the ox—all pitied him, and each donated ten years to the life of mankind. From then on, it was thought that one who reached eleven was no longer truly himself. Only certain people of remarkable character might have control of their own destiny. Sages and saints have been known to extend their meaningful existence far beyond ten years through hard work and discipline.

As they talked, Daxin joined in their little game. When his hand was caught by Aman's for the third time in a row, Zhenguan could have sworn that the man before her was but a ten-year-old boy!

ten

1

The two people most affected by First Uncle's homecoming were Zhenguan's mother and Second Aunt. Her first aunt also came home from Tainan. The reunion of father and son, husband and wife, sister and brother, uncle and niece . . . what a joyous occasion! It seemed as if they had been separated forever. Tears were inevitable at a time of such great happiness. They even ran down the powdered cheeks of Zhenguan's newly acquired Japanese aunt, clad in a kimono.

First Aunt was the perfect hostess, overlooking not a single detail. But though she had comforting words for everyone, her own eyes were red all the time. Facing his wife, First Uncle seemed to be filled with shame. Zhenguan noticed that he tried to speak to her several times but always held back at the last moment. First Aunt's magnanimity garnered everyone's respect and admiration. All witnessed how she extended her hospitality to First Uncle's Japanese wife, fetching her water to freshen up, passing her food and soup, treating her like a guest of honor.

They were always taught to treat each other with courtesy, but Zhenguan only came to understand what this truly meant when she observed the demeanor of her first aunt. Her relationship with First Uncle had transcended that of husband and wife. Zhenguan could sense that they were like brother and sister as well. First Uncle was First Aunt, and she, him. No words were necessary when two people reached such a stage; all could be left unsaid.

As the tearful reunion took place in the front hall, Zhenguan's mother and second aunt stole away to cry their own tears. After greeting their long-lost brother, each retreated to her own room without disturbing anyone. Life and death were two worlds apart. At this moment, they would rather that their husbands had wed someone else than been separated from them by death! Nevertheless, life stretches on with no end, and those sharing this lifetime enjoy the same moonlight bathing thousands of mountains, and the same water glistening on a thousand rivers.

Her second aunt entered Fourth Aunt's room. Zhenguan waited at the door for a short time and then went to seek out her own mother in Grandma's room. Her mother was standing by the bed with her back to the door, sobbing, her face buried in her hands. Zhenguan approached quietly and passed her a handkerchief. She did not know what to say; all she could do was weep along with her.

Why do people yearn for romantic attachment? It is the source of such heartache and pain, and the torment outlasts death! She remembered the poet Su Dongpuo's words: "If alive, I shall return to you, if death is the cause of our separation, you shall live in my mind forever." This is the story of all our lives. First Uncle was living, so he had found his way back home! Zhenguan's father and second uncle had passed away, but they would be remembered by their loved ones for generations to come.

After dinner, Grandma asked Zhenguan's mother and aunt to stay overnight. Her five sons and three daughters were finally reunited under one roof. Zhenguan could imagine how overwhelmed with joy her grandmother must be.

With one foot outside her grandparents' door, Zhenguan ran into Daxin. He knew her well enough to understand why she would choose to leave under such circumstances. Zhenguan looked at him, then continued to walk on; he stayed by her side. Feelings, true feelings, are spawned at moments like this. They walked next to each other for quite some distance, their shadows changing from tall to short and short to tall as they passed under the street lamps.

Finally Daxin broke the silence. "Are you feeling better now? I saw you crying at noon, and I didn't know what to say."

Zhenguan did not reply. She wondered how he had managed to catch her crying.

Daxin continued, "I can understand your feelings, but seeing you cry, I felt . . . strange!"

Zhenguan tilted her chin up. "I'm not crying anymore! I'm all right now."

"Okay, let's not talk about it anymore." Daxin smiled. "I know you're happy that First Uncle is back home!"

"Yes, I haven't seen him since I was born. But today, when I stepped into the front hall and saw him sitting there,

I recognized him immediately. I felt as if I knew him already."

Daxin was incredulous. "So, when you ran into me on the seventh day of the seventh month at the door, did you say to yourself: Yes, this must be Daxin!"

Zhenguan smiled. "I refuse to answer that question!"

As they talked, Zhenguan's house came into view. Zhenguan knew that her mother and brother were still over at Grandma's, and with no one at home, it wasn't appropriate for her to invite Daxin inside. She looked up at him and was about to say something when he suddenly suggested, "Are you going to call it a night already? If not, why don't we go to the beach to enjoy the moonlight?"

Zhenguan didn't say no, nor did she say yes. She looked down at her feet . . . and they continued to walk, almost as if of their own volition. "As a man, I can understand First Uncle's feelings," Daxin said. "Ethics, family, and nostalgia for his homeland have brought him back. But there must be another force that has drawn him home, despite the difficulties that have stood in the way of his homecoming."

"What do you mean?"

"I don't really know how to put it clearly; but you, you are a part of the force, so you must understand!"

"I think I do. This force runs through my veins as well, just as it does for First Uncle, for Grandpa and Grandma, for Yincheng's twenty-day-old baby. This family is one; it is a circle, strong and resilient, and it cannot be broken. . . . Even my deceased father and Second Uncle are still part of it, inseparable. First Uncle was torn away forcibly, transplanted to foreign soil; he would never have been whole again if he hadn't returned. . . ."

Daxin finished her thought, ". . . that is, he'd be alive but not truly living! He could never have been happy again, or even capable of happiness."

Daxin was always able to read her mind. Zhenguan did not know what to say. Noticing her silence, Daxin asked, "Why aren't you speaking?"

His solemn expression made Zhenguan laugh. "What else is there to say? You just said it all!"

And the two broke into laughter together. Daxin continued, "Zhenguan, I know how you must be feeling. But I couldn't have expressed it as you have."

This was the first time he had addressed her directly by name, and Zhenguan did not feel fully at ease. She paused before saying, "That's because you're not in the circle."

Daxin retorted, "Who says? I am also family! Think about it: my third aunt is your fourth aunt!"

Zhenguan knew she would not convince him, so she said no more.

"You just used the circle as a metaphor: how apt that is," Daxin commented. "I think that the Chinese are truly a cohesive people—not at all like a dish of scattered sand, as some might say."

Zhenguan added, "Those who would say such things do not understand our people. And they certainly do not speak for us!" Daxin applauded her comment as she continued, "But perhaps there are the likes of them among Chinese people too. Well, we're here. . . ."

The two shared a moment of silence as they arrived at the old harbor. They saw fishing vessels equipped with their own power generators lined up one after another at the dock. Daxin bent down to touch one of the fishing boats and said, "I really love this place. In Taipei, we live in apartment houses, and one spends his entire life not understanding what it means to know all of his neighbors! From Third Uncle and the others, I have learned what the *Book of Rites* really means: one must first be a son before one can be a father!"

The moon finally surfaced. Under its light, caressed by the gentle sea breezes, Zhenguan felt a song at the tip of her tongue:

The spring flowers on the hilltop
Blossom in red and white
In love with springtime
Completely at ease, they blossom. . . .

Looking at Daxin beside her, Zhenguan felt completely at ease too. He was wearing a white shirt and white dress trousers with stripes; he even claimed that his trousers were the best that one could buy. How did he come to be so confident in himself? Indeed, men ought to be proud and resourceful. And yet, he was also humble and modest at the same time! Such traits and characteristics are supposed to be conflicting, but in him they somehow managed to strike a balance, two extremes coexisting in perfect harmony!

It was certainly a good thing that the two of them were so much alike. But it suddenly occurred to Zhenguan: what if they were to clash one day? What kind of damage would that cause? Take his stubbornness, for example. He had been trying these past few days to convince her that he cared for her. The girl from once upon a time was but an unhappy memory, though a crucial element marking his transition from boyhood to manhood. He had not said he'd forgotten her, but to Zhenguan, it was a sign of his generous nature that he never spoke ill of her. He was always true to himself.

To say that he wasn't still thinking about her would be a lie. But Liao Qinger had become just another name in the school yearbook. Once he was showing Zhenguan a calendar from his university days because it was filled with caricatures that he had sketched. When she flipped to the last two pages, she saw the red stamp of a name chop and exclaimed, "Liao—qing—er—what a pretty name. . . ."

"That was her name." He said it very calmly. Zhenguan smiled at him and continued flipping through the pages. What he meant was that all had become past tense. He didn't say it aloud, because he was thinking: You should know! Sometimes Zhenguan wished that he would voice his thoughts so she would feel reassured. Actually, not so much for reassurance, because she wasn't jealous, but she didn't want to dwell on bygones. In fact, she felt the pain that he had gone through. She sympathized with his suffering. Now that she knew him so well, she was at a loss about what to do with her fluttering heart. Grandma once said, "Given a choice, choose the one who was wronged, not the one who wronged someone else. All the debts of this world, be it a debt of love or a debt of money, have to be repaid someday—if not in this lifetime, then in another."

And it suddenly hit Zhenguan: Daxin was perfect! His entire being was complete and whole!

"What's on your mind?"

Zhenguan didn't say anything, she just smiled mysteriously.

Daxin asked, "Do you know what I'm thinking about?" Zhenguan shook her head, and he continued, "Have you ever heard the saying: 'To find eternity in a moment's thought'?"

"Is that from the Buddhist texts?"

"Yes, exactly."

Daxin inhaled deeply and uttered slowly, "To see the universe, to capture eternity, in a moment of lucidity. . . . The Ming Dynasty scholars had a similar idea."

The two talked and walked until they reached the far end of the harbor. Zhenguan looked up at the moon along the way, her heart brimming with a song:

The moonlight shines over us
To have a bosom friend
Is life's greatest happiness
Sure and steadfast
The sky is radiant
And the road is wide.

II

The fifteenth day of the seventh month was Ghost Festival.

At dusk, every household would lay out feasts and burn paper money to placate the wandering ghosts. Smoke and incense filled the air of the little town by the sea. It was a smell that lingered in one's mind forever! The scent followed Zhenguan everywhere. To her, it seemed like a bridge to the netherworld.

Her mother had cooked up a few extra dishes. For one thing, they were to be placed on the altar, and for another, she was going to invite Daxin over for dinner. Once the delicious food was laid out on the altar as an offering to their ancestors, Zhenguan's mother summoned her to fetch the guests. When Zhenguan arrived at Grandpa's house, she sought out Fourth Aunt, who laughed. "So you're inviting him for dinner! Good, you must have cooked up a scrumptious feast!"

"Yes, it is quite a feast indeed."

"So am I invited?"

"Of course!" Zhenguan tugged at her aunt's arm and added, "Uncle too! Let me go tell Grandma—"

"No, don't!" Then her Fourth Aunt chuckled. "Just kidding. Look, you're tearing off my sleeves!"

Zhenguan laughed as she let go of her aunt. "I really do mean it! Won't you join us for dinner?"

"Next time, I'm actually too busy today to join you. Why don't you fetch Daxin? He's back there in the study."

The door to the study was usually wide open, but Zhenguan found it shut. "Hello, who's in there?" she called out. Daxin was standing in front of her all of a sudden. He raised his eyebrows and grinned from ear to ear, looking like a mischievous eight-year-old boy playing hide-and-seek with his sister.

"Ah, the mademoiselle has come! I didn't think you would dare!"

"And why not?"

"Since the day I arrived, you have been in every single room of the house except for this study. I thought you'd taken an oath not to venture here!"

"What nonsense! I have my mother's orders to invite you for dinner!"

"So you're here to extend an invitation!"

"Yes. Can we dispense with all the pomp and ceremony?"

"All right, but do come in and sit down for a while."

"But . . ."

Seeing that she was hesitant, Daxin did not push her. "Well, at least allow me to put these away first!" He was holding a piece of rubber and a small carving knife in his hand.

"What's that for?"

"Engraving name chops."

"Can I see how you do it?" Zhenguan asked with genuine interest.

"You'll have to come in if you want to see my work. Or do you want me to move all my stuff out here?"

Zhenguan smiled and followed him into the study.

The desk was messy, covered with tools of every sort. Daxin turned around to get ink for the stamp, applied it to the name chop, and prepared the paper. Zhenguan didn't allow herself to sit idly. She reached out to help Daxin arrange the paper on the desk. Their fingers touched for a brief moment before Zhenguan quickly retracted her hand.

Daxin finally made an imprint with the chop, and Zhenguan almost let out a gasp when she saw it: it was her name, red ink on white paper, in a beautiful and stately ancient Chinese script.

"It's amazing! How did you do this?"

"I don't know. It seems like I just learned how to engrave name chops overnight. Do you want me to teach you?" Daxin asked with a smile.

"First tell me how you taught yourself!"

"It's no big deal, really. When I was in tenth grade, I lost my father's name chop and engraved another one to replace it. So, in a way, I had to take up name chop engraving out of necessity!"

People like Daxin had the uncanny ability to make others go out of the way to do things for them.

Daxin continued, "You know, rubber is light, but look at the imprint of this name chop: why do you think it appears to be so solid and full of strength?"

"I have no idea, tell me!"

"There's a secret here. I rubbed the name chop on the ground to smooth the sharp edges after the engraving was done. It's a little trick that I thought up on my own!"

Zhenguan was impressed by his ingenuity. Daxin placed the name chop in her hands and asked, "Well, aren't you going to put it away?"

"I . . ."

"I want it to be a present."

Zhenguan held the name chop in both hands, and when she looked up at Daxin again, she knew she was lost. She had ventured on a path of no return.

As he was putting on his shoes, Daxin said, "Speaking of name chops, there's a story that always comes to mind, and it still makes me laugh. When I was a sophomore in university, my classmates found out that I had this talent, and they all came to me. Before long, I was engraving name chops for all of their boyfriends and girlfriends!"

"So you were doing good business!"

"Actually, I didn't charge them anything. At the time, there was a bookstore called The Ph.D. near the main entrance to the school. I went there once every couple of days to buy rubber, and as time went on—"

"You ran up a huge debt!"

"No, as time went on, the saleslady at the bookstore thought I had ulterior motives!" Daxin laughed as he spoke.

Zhenguan laughed as well, saying, "I bet she turned you down the next time you were in the store!"

"Guess again! I didn't have the guts to go back there. I had to cross the street to buy my supplies at another store!"

The two laughed and said good-bye to the elders before heading toward Zhenguan's home. Zhenguan was struck by a strong smell in the air as soon as they stepped out onto the main street, while Daxin was mesmerized by the scene before him: an old lady with bound feet was burning paper money in front of her house. As it burst into flames, she sprinkled wine in a circle around the golden urn that contained the burning paper money. She was chanting something. "Do you know what she's saying?" Daxin asked.

"Of course." Zhenguan winked. "My mother and grandmother chant the same thing: follow the circle, make a fortune!"

"Even the smallest act bears the most abundant meaning," Daxin exclaimed. "Follow the circle and make a fortune. Making money is but a commonplace and ordinary wish—"

"But the wish comes to life with her chants!"

"Yes, how true! She utters the wish over and over, but with such solemnity. In this whole wide world, only we are blessed with such perfection! What's wrong?"

"You have put it beautifully!"

"What I meant was, why have you stopped talking?"

"Because nothing more needed to be said."

Daxin smiled. "In Taipei, I rarely noticed the subtle beauty of our culture. I have to thank you for opening my eyes!"

"No, please, I don't deserve your thanks! I was thinking, though, if you continue to be so perceptive. . . ."

" . . . one day . . ."

"One day you might become an expert in folk culture!"

Daxin laughed. "Our folk customs and way of life contain a wealth of beauty and wisdom. The more you understand, the more you appreciate."

Before they knew it, they had arrived at Zhenguan's door. Her second aunt was waiting for them, and Zhenguan's mother was setting the table. "Good, you came," she greeted Daxin with a smile. "I thought you were putting up a fight, given how long it took for Zhenguan to get you here!"

Daxin fixed a gentle gaze on her and said, "That certainly wasn't the case. As a matter of fact, I had been preparing for this invitation since noon!"

"How so?"

"Today, during lunch, I accidentally dropped a chopstick. Grandma told me it was a sign that someone was going to invite me to dinner tonight. And sure enough . . . !"

Everyone broke into laughter.

Since Azhong was away from home for military training before his enrollment in university, Zhenguan's mother piled all the good food into Daxin's bowl. Seeing his embarrassed gratitude, Zhenguan hid a smile.

After dinner, Zhenguan continued to take care of their guest. They walked here and there, finding themselves again at the beach.

Daxin asked, "Do you know what day it is today?"

"What? Don't tell me it's your birthday!"

Daxin made a funny face and said, "No, it's Ghost Festival! What a poetic day it is! Just think: all around, in every corner, ghosts are looking at each other with tears in their eyes, ghost friends who haven't seen each other for so long are making up for lost time."

Zhenguan covered her ears and ran from Daxin. Surprised, he ran after her and asked, "Are you afraid?"

"I have been reading ghost stories in *Tales from a Leisurely Studio*," Zhenguan said. "Do you want to scare me even more?"

Hearing her, Daxin cleared his throat and said dramatically, "I officially retract my words!"

A boat was perched next to them, close to shore. Daxin turned and leaped onto the deck. Zhenguan was going to do the same, but when she looked down into the shiny black water, her feet froze.

"Ha, you're as cowardly as a mouse!" Daxin laughed, extending a hand to her.

The moon was reflected on the surface of the water, and heaven and earth were bright and vast. Daxin sat on the deck, singing one song after another. Zhenguan listened but heard not a word. She was thinking about how Daxin had touched her shoulder just now.

"I thought you grew up on boats!" Daxin said. "How can you be so timid?"

Zhenguan replied, "Hear me out first. When I first started going out to sea on boats, you weren't even around! Every year, on the night of the Mid-Autumn Festival, the folks in town would gather here and pile into the fishing boats. The boats would sail out, all fifty, sixty of them, to the white sand beaches across the sea, where people would disembark to enjoy the view of the full moon. I've been coming out here with the elders every year since I was a three-year-old toddler! What do you think of that?"

Daxin exclaimed, "Wow, you do know how to enjoy life here! The view of the moon in the sky and on the surface of the water must be breathtaking, most certainly a sight not to be missed! It's a pity. . . ."

"Why, what do you mean?"

"You shouldn't have told me about it. I am about to start compulsory military service, and I won't have the opportunity to enjoy the moon this year at the Mid-Autumn Festival."

"But you can see the moon anywhere. The moon is the same whether it is in the south or in the north, no?"

"I know it is the same moon, but hearing it from you is reassuring."

"Reassuring?"

"Well, realistic, anyway."

The two exchanged a smile. Although their bodies were two or three feet apart, there was no distance between them.

Daxin continued, "Come on, reassure me some more!"

Zhenguan thought for a moment and then said, "There is a Buddhist sutra. Let me recite it: 'All the mountain peaks share a moon, and spring descends on all households alike; a thousand rivers reflect a thousand moons, the sky stretches on forever when there isn't a speck of cloud.' "

"Beautiful! Where did you find these words?"

Deciding to tease him a bit, Zhenguan said, "Buddhist texts, silly!"

"Which one?"

"*Record of the Buddha's Earthly Life*!"

Flustered, Daxin edged closer to her. "Why haven't I heard of this book before? Can you lend it to me?"

"Sorry, but it's not for loan!"

"Oh, what I am to do then?" Daxin seemed distraught.

Seeing his reaction, Zhenguan realized how serious he was. She broke into a smile and said, "I fooled you, didn't I? You can have the book if you want. Buddhist texts are meant to be shared by all!"

Daxin also laughed. "I fooled you too! I knew that you would lend me the book. But since I won't be able to read it until we get back, why don't you explain the words to me now?"

So he subtly outwitted her again, Zhenguan thought as she said slowly, "The Indian King Asoka invited all the monks in the realm to a vegetarian feast. Everyone came but the Arhat, Pingfulu, who did not arrive until the sun had set in the sky. The king asked him, 'Why are you so late?' and the Arhat replied, 'Because I have attended all the banquets in the world.' 'How is that possible?' King Asoka demanded. The Wise One said, 'Let me tell you . . . ,' and he recited the poem that I have just shared with you."

For a moment, both were silent. When Zhenguan looked up, she saw that Daxin was gazing at her intently. His eyes were clear and vibrant, shining like morning stars in the darkness. "Do you know what I'm thinking?" he asked.

"Tell me." Zhenguan gazed out at the flickering lights of the fishing vessels at sea, the sights of her hometown, the water, the night scene; and there was Daxin right before her, indeed a gentleman as in the classics, with a simple and provincial quality, yet sophisticated, smart, sincere. . . .

Daxin said, " 'A thousand rivers reflect a thousand moons.' The line is from a Buddhist sutra, composed by a Buddhist monk. But I think it also applies to the unwavering devotion of someone totally committed to love. What do you think?"

Zhenguan didn't say anything, although she knew exactly what he meant.

"Shall I cite examples?"

"Yes, I'm a good listener!"

Daxin's expression became serious. "Does it not remind you of the verse, 'This love lives as long as I shall live?' "

As if a torch had been lit up in her heart, Zhenguan felt an inner radiance. It was as if she and Daxin had been born on the same day, the same month, the same year. How else could they be so much alike? They must have sworn while they were still in their mothers' bellies that if they were born the same sex, they would be as close as siblings, and that if they were born as opposite sexes, they would be lovers, husband and wife.

"Do you agree?"

"I'm still thinking. Should I say yes or no?"

Daxin couldn't resist laughing. "I know what you're thinking: that the first verse is grander in scope, encompassing heaven and earth, whereas the second deals with love and is smaller in scale—right?"

Zhenguan laughed. "Actually, since the beginning of history, love has always been writ large. How can we belittle it? Don't you know that love holds heaven and earth together? I'll give you credit for what you said though!"

They took a shortcut on their way back. Open-air performances were being held in the empty lot in front of the temple. On the east side of the lot, a performance honoring the deity of the temple was being staged; on the west side, a love story. A man and a woman were standing on the stage. They had declared their love for each other, but there were still words to be said. The man proclaimed, "Don't worry, I won't be distracted; I'm a man with a good head on my shoulders!" And the woman sang, "My love, fame and fortune I love not!" Then he asked her, "What do you want?" "I love you, my hero," she replied.

Zhenguan stood by Daxin, watching the performance, her heart fluttering with the lyrics of the song. This was the first time that she had been with him in front of so many people. In the crowd, with everyone's shoulders touching, this man was the closest to her. Seeing his face, attentive, she thought of the lyrics and suddenly felt overwhelming gratitude for heaven and earth, and for her destiny.

eleven

I

Yincheng's son was one month old.

One day, Zhenguan was getting ready to wash and cook the rice when her second aunt came in. "Auntie, what brings you here so early in the morning?" she asked.

"Put the rice away, everybody is waiting for you," her aunt said with a smile, setting Zhenguan's rice pot aside.

"But I thought that the sticky rice they were cooking to celebrate the baby's first month wasn't going to be ready until noon!"

"How is it going to be ready if you don't go and help?" Second Aunt broke into laughter. "Oh, I see: so you were planning on arriving at noon to enjoy a feast of sticky rice without pitching in first! That won't do! I'm waiting for you to go over and help with the preparations!"

"Yes, I should help, but what can I do? There are so many master chefs there already! There isn't even room enough for me to stand in the kitchen, so I figured I could help best by eating the sticky rice later!"

"You can't be serious! Hurry now, go change."

Zhenguan's aunt pushed her out of the kitchen and walked toward her mother's room, saying, "Your brother came back with more than ten *jin* of fish and oysters and said that they were to be cooked for breakfast. You'd better hurry to the table before it all gets cold."

Zhenguan's mother came out of her room, laughing. "We'll see the bottom of the pots before it gets cold!"

It only took Zhenguan ten minutes to change and walk over to Grandpa's. The dining room was already full by the time she arrived. At the men's table, two people stood out: her first uncle and Daxin. Her first uncle caught her attention because she hardly knew him as a child, and Daxin—well, he already occupied her heart. As she took her seat, she looked up to meet Daxin's gaze. Zhenguan smiled to herself, thinking: How much one's eyes can say! He was certainly dreaming up something to tease her about later!

After breakfast, Zhenguan helped her cousins with the dishes; then they washed a big basketful of cilantro, which took up most of the morning. Seeing nothing else that she could put her hands on in the kitchen, Zhenguan was about to leave when Third Aunt handed her a kitchen knife and said, "Grandma told us to fix a refreshing soup for lunch. The sticky rice is going to be quite greasy. We need something to wash it down, or no one's going to want a second serving. Why don't you go and cut us some snake melons from the back garden? Here's a sack!"

Zhenguan took the tools from her aunt. "Such a big sack!" she exclaimed. "Do you want me to fill it?"

"It's up to you," Third Aunt answered as she turned to stir-fry the sticky rice, beads of perspiration forming on her forehead and nose. "Cut the ones that are big and ripe enough. Your first uncle said he hasn't tasted snake melon in thirty years!"

As Zhenguan stepped out of the kitchen with knife and sack in hand, she ran into Daxin, who said to her, "You seem very busy; but can I ask you a question?"

"Yes, go ahead!"

"Early in the morning, on my second day here, I heard the mesmerizing sound of a bamboo flute. And I have heard it almost every morning ever since. Can you tell me what it is?"

Zhenguan consciously avoided his question. "So, you're an early bird!"

Daxin laughed. "I've been meaning to ask you about this for some time, but every time we meet we get so caught up talking about everything else that I haven't gotten around to it. This morning I woke up at the crack of dawn, so I decide to track down the flute. . . ."

Zhenguan had done the same thing before, so she decided to stop beating around the bush. But first she asked him what he had found.

"When I got to the main street, the flute player had already darted into the winding alleys. But the sound of the flute still lingered in the crisp air. I felt a sense of loss, as if I were unable to find something elusive. . . . Are you still going to keep it a secret?"

"All right, I'll tell you: it's the butcher who castrates pigs!"

"I know you would never lie to me, but . . ." Daxin seemed doubtful. That was certainly not what he had expected to hear!

"But what?"

"I'm not suspicious of your answer." Daxin smiled. "I'm just surprised something like that would sound so musical!"

"The first time I heard it—I forget when exactly, but I was very young . . . when the adults told me it was a butcher castrating pigs, I remember thinking: when I grow up, I'm going to castrate pigs too—"

Daxin was laughing loudly before she had even finished. Zhenguan started to laugh too. "Do you know why I majored in chemistry?" Daxin asked.

Zhenguan squinted, eyeing him up and down as if it would help her guess. "Because . . . because . . ."

Daxin chuckled. "I almost flunked high school chemistry, so when I got into university, I made up my mind to really find out what it was all about—simple, huh?" He turned to look at Zhenguan, and the two exchanged a knowing smile.

In the back garden, three little children could be seen laughing and chasing one another outside the bamboo fence. Zhenguan watched them frolic for a while and then started to hunt for snake melons hanging from the trellis. The vine twisted and turned, tangling all the melons, branches, and leaves together. Zhenguan found a big fat melon and was about to cut it off at the stem when Daxin called out from behind her, "Can you guess what I'm thinking?"

Without turning her head, Zhenguan answered, "It must be about the pastoral poet Tao Yuanming!"

"Wrong! I was wondering what you were like as a child."

Zhenguan acknowledged him with a "hmm" and went back to cutting the melon. Daxin continued, "Actually, you're right.

I could well have been thinking of Tao Yuanming: 'My fields will be running wild, what holds me back?' "

Hearing his words, Zhenguan dropped the melon and turned to him excitedly. "Which lines in particular appeal to you?"

" 'Wet are my clothes with evening dew, little does the cold dew bother me, as long as I have my will.' What about you?"

"The same!"

All of a sudden, Daxin exclaimed, "Hurry, look here!"

He seemed so excited that Zhenguan figured he must have discovered something truly rare and unusual. She put down her knife and got up close to Daxin, curious to examine what he had to show her. It was a tiny snake melon in the process of transforming from a flower; its upper body was already the size of a little cucumber, while its lower body was still a yellow bud. So this man from Taipei City had never seen a flower turn into a melon! Zhenguan tried to stifle a chuckle.

"Why are you laughing?"

She covered her mouth quickly. "Oh, nothing, nothing!"

"The face of a melon and the body of a flower. . . . Life is full of wonders!"

Zhenguan was thinking about the verse: "This love lives as long as I shall live; no, it lives even when I no longer live . . . though the flower has disappeared, the tender melon perpetuates the love—"

"I know what's on your mind!" Daxin said with a smile.

Zhenguan turned to resume her work. She picked up the kitchen knife and tapped it twice, saying, "Good, then I don't have to tell you!"

On their way back, Daxin helped Zhenguan carry the sack. When they were a few yards away from the kitchen, Daxin handed it to Zhenguan and said, "I'm going back to the cottage."

She thanked him and walked toward the kitchen with the sack of snake melons. But when she turned her head, she found that Daxin was still standing there, watching her. She winked at him teasingly before stepping into the kitchen.

There, they were just moving the sticky rice from the stove to the table. Having fulfilled her mission successfully, Zhenguan was going to sit down on a stool when her third aunt handed her a little pot of sticky rice. "Where is Fourth Aunt's nephew?" she asked.

"I think he's in the cottage."

"My hands are greasy. Can you bring this pot of sticky rice to our guest?"

Pot in hand, Zhenguan asked, "Aren't we supposed to give this out to all our neighbors?"

"Yes, but we have to take care of them one at a time. Many of your cousins are off at work, and we have visitors in the main hall. Your sister-in-law's family has just come with presents. Why don't you take this to the cottage first?"

Zhenguan stood up to fetch a bowl and chopsticks, saying, "I'll deliver the rest of the sticky rice when I get back!" Leaving the kitchen, she headed toward the cottage. Daxin emerged before she had even arrived at the door.

"My, you have a keen sense of smell!"

"Yes, I do indeed. I can't resist the aroma of sticky rice!"

Zhenguan politely put the pot on the table, then set down the bowl and chopsticks. She turned to leave, saying, "I'll be on my way now. Enjoy your meal!"

"Wait a minute, wait a minute! This won't do! How am I supposed to finish all this food on my own? You'll have to help me out!"

"I'm sorry, but I can't right now. I have to deliver more sticky rice to our neighbors."

"Can I come along?" Daxin wanted to tag along just to keep her company. Seeing Zhenguan's expression, however, he suddenly realized: the only reason she had been able to walk with him to the beach and all over town was that he was a guest. In this conservative little village, guests were held supreme. But becoming her helper would be tantamount to a declaration of friendship. Maybe they would have such a day, but it wasn't time yet, a fact that was painfully clear to both of them. Before Zhenguan had a chance to speak, Daxin quickly amended, "Actually, why don't you go and make the deliveries? I'll just stand here at the door, where I can see you."

Zhenguan was deeply touched. She lowered her head slightly, nodded, and walked out the door, not daring to look back at Daxin. She knew that if she had looked at him at that moment, her love for him would have gushed over like a waterfall, like a river of no return.

In the kitchen, all the sticky rice was laid out on the table, awaiting delivery. Zhenguan took platter after platter to the neighbors. Daxin noticed that she would always return from each trip with half a platter of white rice. "Where are you getting all that rice?" he asked.

"Take a guess!"

"Hmm, let's see . . . it must be a token of appreciation from the recipients of the sticky rice."

Zhenguan laughed. "You're right! This a gift in return. We Chinese always give something in exchange when we receive presents. None of our neighbors would allow me to come back with an empty platter. Just now, on my last delivery, there were children playing in the front courtyard. They were not aware of this custom, so they took the sticky rice and said thank you. I was almost gone when their mother, who was in the backyard hanging out clothes, came running after with me with a bowl of rice to pour into the empty platter."

Daxin clasped his hands together. "Ah, the courtesy that is integral to the entire Chinese way of life is evident in even the smallest act."

Touched by his words, Zhenguan said, "It reminds me of when I delivered sticky rice along the main street with Yinchan."

"Did you make any wrong deliveries?"

"Not a chance!"

"Then . . ." A big smile was already forming, revealing itself slowly in the recesses of his eyes and the curve of his mouth. Zhenguan knew that a joke was on the tip of his tongue. Daxin continued, "If children who were not aware of the custom came to the door to receive the sticky rice, would you and Yinchan order them to fill the platter with white rice?"

Zhenguan snapped him on the arm playfully. "Actually, I was thinking about how this custom came into being in the first place, and why it has survived to this day. Neighbors are not related to us like family, but we have alleys and lanes in common, and our forefathers felt an affinity with their forefathers. So when a family celebrates, it cannot but share its joy with its neighbors: the recipient of a gift reciprocates by giving rice and other food. So on the one hand, it is an exchange of courtesy; but on the other hand, it is also an act of extending congratulations on joyous occasions."

"If you go on, I'll have to cancel my plans to go to England!"

Daxin blurted out suddenly. Zhenguan knew that he had received a scholarship to attend the University of London, and that he would be leaving after his military service. They both felt uncomfortable during a moment of awkward silence. Zhenguan hesitated, then put on a smile. "Knowing what's good here shouldn't prevent you from finding out what's good about other cultures. As long as you remember what it's like to be Chinese, you will always be Chinese, even if you travel over distant mountains and seas."

Those were her words, but she was thinking: Two years from now, he will be in another country. That was still a long way off, and no one could tell where things would lead by then. And though the future was unpredictable, Daxin himself was trustworthy. Of course . . . trust doesn't always last forever. First Uncle was one example, wasn't he?

This alone prompted her to keep her distance. She didn't want vows or commitments, only a meeting of minds. As long as she was worthy, Daxin would return to her, no matter the time or distance. After all, only what came back could ultimately belong to her. But Zhenguan also wondered whether this was simply her womanly pride speaking. Don't men and women think differently? No! Zhenguan understood herself. She wasn't one to indulge in worries. When faced with serious matters, she would sulk and fret for a couple of days at the most, but the dark clouds would always lift.

Daxin couldn't come up with anything appropriate to say. "Let's not talk about this! It's still two years away. . . . I'll come up with an answer then, and we'll see which direction the wind blows."

"Fine. Whatever will be will be, right?"

"So you're going to come with me to the cottage and help

me finish the sticky rice, aren't you? There's a platter full of it."

Zhenguan trailed a couple of steps behind him, then stopped short and exclaimed, "It's almost lunchtime; we can't hide in a little corner and eat on our own!"

"What do you suggest?"

"I'll heat it up again in the kitchen. You can either share it with everyone else or eat it yourself."

"Okay!"

Back at the "arm's-length" cottage, Zhenguan fetched the sticky rice and was about to leave when Daxin said, "Come, sit for just a while." He pulled up a chair and turned to pour her a cup of tea.

"Please don't trouble yourself," Zhenguan said. "Tell me, who's the guest here?"

Daxin had already set the tea down in front of her. The two sat facing each other, wordless. There was a small square-shaped clock on the table with a milky white frame and a copper stand, a gift to Daxin from Fourth Aunt. As Zhenguan fiddled with it, a knob came off and fell to the floor, rolling over to Daxin's side of the table. Zhenguan stood up to fetch it, but Daxin had already bent over to pick it up. As he fastened it back onto the clock, he asked Zhenguan, "Have you read the poetry of Yuan Haowen?"

Zhenguan sat down in her chair and said, after some deliberation, "Yuan Haowen, one who likes to ask questions. His name suggests that he is nosy and querulous, but his poetry is refreshing and full of life."

"Do you know how he composed his most famous poem?"

Zhenguan shook her head. With a smile on his face, Daxin told her the story: "Yuan Haowen was on his way to take an exam when he met a hunter of geese. The hunter said he had just caught and killed a male goose, and that the female goose had somehow freed itself from the net but kept hovering and howling in the vicinity, refusing to leave. Finally she killed herself by plunging into the ground. The poet Yuan Haowen purchased the two geese from the hunter and buried both together by the river shore."

"The books never mention that the two geese were male and female! How come you know more than the hunter?"

Daxin laughed, "So you had heard the story before! Why did you pretend that you hadn't?"

Zhenguan was silent. Daxin extracted a piece of folded paper from his books and said, "I copied down the first half of the poem. Why don't you read it when you get home? Don't open it before then!"

"Whose rules are these? I'm going to read it right now!"

"Fine. Are you going to read it right here then?"

Zhenguan didn't reply. Instead, she took the paper from his hands and fled from the cottage like a whiff of smoke. She slid into her grandmother's room, checking to be sure that it was empty. She bolted the door and unfolded the piece of paper:

I ask the world, what is love
That drives one to live and die for it?
Two flying visitors traveling from north to south
Their old wings have weathered summers and winters
Happy are meetings and sad are departures
The world is full of devoted lovers
The answer lies
Among the layers of distant clouds
The thousand folds of misty mountains
Where is the solitary shadow flying to, where?

II

After dinner, Zhenguan followed her grandmother back into her room. Once they were seated, Zhenguan whispered into the old lady's ear, "Grandma, do you remember things from before?"

"Yes."

"Do you remember what I looked like when I was a little girl?"

"Let me think . . ." She wiped her face with a wet towel that Yinshan's wife had handed to her and said, "You had a very round face, and your eyes sparkled."

"No, what I meant was: was I good-looking or ugly?"

"Silly grandchild," the old lady chuckled. "We're all born of our mothers and fathers. Every child is a beautiful flower!"

"Grandma . . ." Zhenguan helped her grandmother remove her hair accessories and asked again, "Tell me, Grandma, won't you?"

"Okay, okay." She smiled, and her eyes crinkled at the corners. "You weren't really pretty, but you charmed people! We used to say that able mothers give birth to babies with charm. So intelligent women have a charm that is more important than a beautiful face."

"Why would you say that?"

Yinshan's wife answered for Grandma, "The elders used to say that charm and luck are better than beauty, because a beautiful woman without charm is destined to live a hard life. Haven't you heard that before?"

Her sister-in-law left the room with the basin full of water, and Zhenguan sat on the edge of her grandmother's bed, thinking. Yes, indeed it was true: a girl born with ravishing looks, but without charm and luck, would live a doomed life. So much wisdom was embodied in the sayings passed down through the ages! Perhaps these sayings had not been intended as legacies; and yet they had survived, no doubt because they had proven to be true, generation after generation!

"Zhenguan," Grandma was fixing up her hair and saying, "remember to switch on the radio when it's time!"

"Grandma, have you forgotten?" Zhenguan asked. "They've already broadcast the last episode of the radio play, *Husband and Wives for Seven Lifetimes*!' "

"I haven't forgotten. They're playing the first episode of a new play today!" Grandma was seventy years old already, but her eyebrows danced and eyes sparkled when she mentioned the new play, just like those of a thirteen-year-old girl on her way to the temple to watch an open-air performance.

"You're still going to listen to Taiwanese opera on the radio? But First Uncle bought you a color television set!"

"He doesn't know how to spend his money! What's the use of buying me a television set when I won't even watch it? I feel like a duck listening to thunder when I watch television!"

Thinking of First Uncle, Zhenguan remembered some unfinished business. Seeing that no one was around, she tugged at her grandmother's white shirt and whispered into her ear, "Grandma, do try to persuade First Aunt to go to Taipei with First Uncle. Husband and wife are husband and wife. They were torn apart by circumstance before, but they shouldn't have to live separate lives anymore. First Uncle's Japanese wife, Ruriko, is—"

Her grandmother interrupted. "You think I haven't tried to persuade her? I have blisters on my lips from trying to persuade her! I told her: Guofeng's business is in Taipei, you should join him there, mother and son, mother-in-law and daughter-in-law, so he doesn't have to travel back and forth. His Japanese wife is a generous and accommodating woman, you should be able to work things out!"

"What was First Aunt's response?"

"I've said it a million times, but she still refuses to budge."

Zhenguan stopped talking. Just thinking of First Aunt made her tongue-tied.

"It's all right, I'll continue trying to convince her. You and Yinchan, however—"

At that moment Yinchan came into the room. "Grandma, what are you saying about me?"

"That you're a busybody, sticking your nose into everything!" Zhenguan answered.

Yinchan wasn't offended at all by her words. She laughed. "So you're still talking about the same thing!"

"Yes, what else would we be talking about?"

Just then, returning to his room, Yincheng felt his son's diaper and found that it was wet. He reprimanded his wife, not knowing that she had just changed the diaper. She hurried to change it again without a word in her own defense. Having witnessed the event, Yinchan sought out Yincheng and gave him quite a scolding for giving his wife a hard time.

Yinchan told Zhenguan a little later, "I had to give him a piece of my mind, or else I would have seen myself scolding him in my dreams!" As she knelt down to light the mosquito-repellant incense coil, she added, "I haven't seen you in ages. Why don't you stay overnight? I'll let your mother know!"

"What will you tell her?"

"That Grandma wants you to stay over, of course!"

Actually, Daxin was scheduled to leave early the next morning, and Zhenguan had already thought of staying over at Grandma's in order to spend more time with him.

When Yinchan left the room, her grandmother said to her, "Zhenguan, you and Yinchan are going on twenty-three. Nowadays people get married later in life. In my opinion, you should see the world while you're still young. I have spoken to your First Uncle about arranging for a couple of positions for you two in his Taipei office. . . ."

"What about Yingui?" Zhenguan asked.

"She's getting married at the end of the year. You and Yinchan, on the other hand, are still young and unattached."

To Zhenguan, Taipei was a mysterious place. It was Daxin's city; he was born and raised there. It must be a good place, she reasoned, because it had shaped Daxin, with his big heart and gentle spirit. And anyway, matchmakers were bound to start knocking on their doors sooner of later if they continued living in this little town. Yinyue and Yingui were perfect examples.

"Grandma, when will First Uncle expect us to arrive in Taipei?"

"When would you like to go?"

"How about after Mid-Autumn Festival?"

As they talked, someone called out, "Grandma, are you in?"

Zhenguan poked her head out and was greeted by the sight of Daxin. "Grandma's here. Come in!"

"Daxin, it's you! Yes, do come in and take a seat!"

Zhenguan had gotten up to fetch Daxin a chair, but he walked straight over to Grandma's bed. "I've come to say goodbye. I'm leaving tomorrow."

"Why so soon? Can't you stay a few more days, at least stay until Mid-Autumn Festival?" Grandmother's sincere invitation made it very difficult for Daxin to respond. Seeing that he was looking to her for help, Zhenguan came to his rescue. "Grandma, he's serving in the military, like Azhong, and they have to report back to camp at designated times!"

"Oh, of course. When will you return?"

Daxin glanced at Zhenguan and said, "I'll come whenever I'm off duty!"

Grandma took a close look at Daxin. "You sound all stuffed up. Are you suffering from a cold?"

"It's no big deal, it will go away very soon!"

"You must have left your windows open while you slept! There's a draft down there at the cottage. You must take care." Turning to Zhenguan, Grandma said, "Go fix your cousin Daxin a bowl of pepper noodles, and make it really hot and spicy. That should chase the cold away!"

Zhenguan glanced at Daxin before leaving for the kitchen. She thought: Would this chemist believe in the healing properties of such an age-old remedy? Their eyes met; Daxin's were gentle and trusting, like those of a calf. . . . Escaping his gaze, Zhenguan headed toward the kitchen. Seeing the pots and pans there, she came to understand why women like her aunts could spend a lifetime cooking three meals a day for their husbands and families!

Five chili peppers were probably too much, and three were most likely not enough. Zhenguan tried to put just the right amount into the noodles. When she arrived at Daxin's door, she suddenly realized that she hadn't tasted the dish herself yet. She hurriedly took a little sip of the noodle broth and found that it was fiery hot! Daxin took the bowl from her at the door, and following Grandma's orders, got right down to business gulping the noodle soup. He emptied the big bowl in no time at all, exclaiming, "Wow, that tasted great!"

Both Grandma and Zhenguan laughed. The three talked a little bit more, and then Daxin walked Zhenguan to the door. "I'm taking the six o'clock train. When do you get up?"

"I usually sleep until seven-thirty," Zhenguan replied.

Daxin was quiet for a moment before he said, "Okay, it's up to you, but—"

"Actually—"

"I would hate to have to say good-bye to you anyway," Daxin concluded.

At these words, Zhenguan bit her lower lip and felt a tug at her heart.

He asked her, "When are you going to Taipei?"

"I'm not sure yet."

"I hope you'll like it there."

"Yeah . . ."

"Well . . . I'd better get back!"

"Okay."

"Good-bye then."

"Yes, good-bye. . . ."

But his feet didn't budge. Zhenguan looked up into his eyes.

"I guess Grandma's waiting for you," he said quietly.

"Umm, you take care of yourself. . . ."

Daxin nodded and looked at Zhenguan again before leaving. It was White Dew, the fifteenth solar term, when summer meets autumn, and the moon was a crescent hanging above the rooftops. Zhenguan stood at the door and looked out at the arm's-length cottage, which wasn't far away. She suddenly felt a tinge of sadness.

III

Zhenguan woke up at four o'clock in the morning. She wanted to go back to sleep but couldn't. She had slept fitfully anyway, waking every other hour throughout the night; she felt as if she hadn't slept a wink at all!

The morning train was to depart at six o'clock sharp. Daxin would probably have to leave at five-thirty to catch it, since the station was a ten-minute walk from home. Yincheng's wife would serve him breakfast beforehand, and Fourth Aunt would be there to see him off. Zhenguan certainly had no reason to accompany a young man to the train station at the break of dawn. What would people think if they saw the two of them together at that hour of the morning? So, had she gotten up just to quietly watch him leave the house?

She had come up with a host of reasons not to see him off. She might as well go back to bed until six or seven, and then she wouldn't have to face him at all. But it wasn't that easy. Somehow, she could not stay asleep. One's heart tends to have more control over the body than one's intellect and will.

Five-fifteen. Daxin must be eating breakfast or chatting with Fourth Aunt now. Maybe . . . Forget it! Forget it! At times like this, it was probably best not to say good-bye. Bidding farewell in person would only be embarrassing.

The stars faded with the twilight and then it was time for him to depart. Morning had broken, and the streets were slowly coming to life: commuting students, fishmongers with the day's catch, the pig castrator with his flute, the night watchman on his way home. . . .

Daxin must be leaving for the station now with his luggage

and knapsack. He must be making his way through the front hall, out the front door, into the courtyard. He . . .

Zhenguan buried her face in her pillow. She realized at that moment: All human suffering stems from attachment and longing. And it is so difficult to rid oneself of either, even when it is necessary to do so. In her angst, she finally dozed off again. And when she awoke, the world was already a flurry of sound and motion.

Yinshan's wife and Yinchuan's wife were handing towels and basins of water to their in-laws as they went through the morning rituals. They were greeted by Yincheng's wife, who was carrying a porcelain bowl. Zhenguan knew that it was filled with breast milk for Grandma.

Zhenguan sat down and put her arms around her sister-in-law, saying, "Azhan still needs to be held all the time. If you're busy with the baby, you can squeeze out the milk first and have someone else bring it to Grandma."

Yincheng's wife whispered into Zhenguan's ear, "Dear sister-in-law, there is something that you don't know. The milk gets cold if you don't drink it immediately. The elderly have weak digestive systems and should drink only warm milk." With these words, she started to unbutton her blouse. Zhenguan averted her eyes and saw Grandma sitting at her dressing table. She wore a traditional but elaborate coiffure, her hair braided up into a bun. It was a hairstyle that had not been passed down to the younger generation, and few knew how to create it anymore. Yinshan's wife could only stand by and watch Grandma do her own hair.

Zhenguan saw a jade hairpin, a bead ornament, and two fresh red blossoms in Yinshan's wife's hands. "Sister-in-law," she asked, "why didn't you pick fragrant magnolias?"

"Magnolias grow in trees and I couldn't reach them. Why don't you fetch a ladder and gather some for Grandma?"

After Grandma had finished putting up her hair and washing her hands, Zhenguan went to sit on the edge of her bed. Yincheng's wife was squeezing milk from her nipple. She only had half a bowl and now had to switch to her other breast. Zhenguan watched as she squeezed with her right hand and a milky white jet squirted out, and it reminded her of when she herself was a baby, of the deep love for her mother that went beyond words or memory.

After the milking session, Zhenguan's sister-in-law left the room. Zhenguan sat by her grandmother's side, watching her drink the milk. She finished most of it but left a little bit for Zhenguan. "This is for you!" she said.

Zhenguan took the bowl but glanced at it warily. "But Grandma . . ."

"This is the reason for Azhan's good health! You don't know how to appreciate this!"

So Zhenguan tilted her head and drank the milk.

"How was it?"

Zhenguan patted her chest and felt a warm current pass through her heart. "I can't describe it!"

When she returned to her grandmother's room after doing the dishes, she found the old lady sitting in front of the mirror, applying powder to her face. The fragrant powder was a product from Hsinchu. After pressing it on the skin, one had to even it out with the fingers. Zhenguan stood behind Grandma and watched. Something Daxin once said came to her mind: "I used to look down on girls who wear make-up. But after watching Grandma apply hers one day, I came to realize that women put on make-up as a courtesy to the world. . . ."

Her grandmother looked at Zhenguan's reflection in the mirror and asked, "What's on your mind? You seem to be in a trance!"

Startled from her reverie, Zhenguan embraced Grandma from behind and fell into her arms. Wrinkling her nose, she said teasingly, "I was thinking that I should get Grandpa to come and see you!"

The two of them were laughing as Yinshan's wife came back into the room. She had fragrant flowers in her hands, and she put them into Grandma's hair.

Zhenguan said jokingly to her sister-in-law, "Wow, you're being partial here—your heart and liver are not the same size. Don't I get flowers too?"

"Well, the heart and liver are in fact not the same size! And you shouldn't jump to conclusions: look what I have for you!"

She motioned for Zhenguan to sit down with her on the edge of the bed. At first Zhenguan did not understand why her sister-in-law had suddenly grabbed her hand, but she realized that there was something important to be said. As she pinned flowers onto Zhenguan's collar, Yinshan's wife whispered, "I thought you were going to help me pick magnolia flowers! I waited in the garden for you to come, but you didn't show up!"

Surprised, Zhenguan asked, "What has happened?"

Yinshan's wife's eyes suddenly filled up with tears, and she said, "First Aunt has been packing her things. We were curious but no one dared ask why. Last night I ran into her and she told me that she was making plans to move to a temple on the mountain—"

"What?"

"She said she wants to go to the Blue Cloud Temple to thank

the deities for answering her wish. She wants us to assume our filial duties and respect our elders."

"But why?"

"I don't know. I wanted to tell you last night, but you never left your room and we had guests over. You're the only person that I've told; the others don't know about this yet. You should tell Grandma about it, but in secret. If Grandma tries to stop First Aunt, she will surely oblige!"

No matter what other people thought, Zhenguan believed that she knew First Aunt quite well. A few days ago, before First Uncle and Ruriko left, she had seen First Aunt cooking rice noodles for the couple.

Zhenguan waited for a bit after Yinshan's wife left before saying to her grandmother, "Grandma, please summon First Aunt to ask her some questions."

"What kind of questions?"

"Sister-in-law tells me that First Aunt wants to go live in a temple. I don't know the details."

Hearing this, Grandma shouted, "Suyun, Suyun!"

First Aunt came almost immediately. Zhenguan heard her grandmother blurt out, "Why did you keep this from me? You must think I'm too old!"

First Aunt knelt in front of Grandma. Zhenguan felt very awkward and tried to make her aunt stand up, but she was rooted to the ground and would not budge. Zhenguan implored her grandmother, "Grandma, ask First Aunt to stand up, please!"

Her grandmother and her first aunt were both in tears. Zhenguan thought: She really must be Grandma's favorite daughter-in-law. Sometimes when people are advanced in age, they become children at heart. Right now, for example, Grandma was really acting like a spoiled child.

"Ma, you know that's not how I feel—"

"If it weren't—" Grandma stopped and then said, "Why is it that you're leaving me?"

"Mother . . ."

"If something is bothering you, why don't you just tell me?"

"If I do tell you, Mother, then you must let me have my way!"

"Tell me what's on your mind!"

First Aunt wiped her tears and said, "After the retrocession, those who were drafted by the Japanese army either returned or sent news of their whereabouts. But we didn't hear from Guofeng at all. All these years I have offered incense to the deities every day, making wishes, praying for Guofeng's safe return. I vowed that if he were to come back to me, I would enter the sacred grounds of the temple to live out my life as a nun, to honor Buddha as a vegetarian."

Zhenguan's eyes filled up, and Grandma's cheeks were wet with tears. First Aunt wiped them from Grandma's face and continued, "Now that Guofeng is back, I must fulfill my promise. I cannot go back on my own word, for it was a sacred vow made before all the deities of heaven and earth. My only regret is that I will not be able to fulfill my filial duties toward you. Mother, do forgive me!"

Grandma started to sob. She patted Suyun's hands, saying, "Oh, you silly, silly girl!"

The room filled up with people: Second Aunt, Third Aunt, Fourth Aunt, Fifth Aunt . . . they all tried to persuade First Aunt not to renounce the secular world. Grandma was just starting to recover a bit when she suddenly said, "No, you are not to go, no matter what! If you leave, it will only be over my dead body. At this moment in time, I would rather disown my son than lose my daughter-in-law, for you and I have been through the hardest of times together."

Zhenguan left the room. She walked to the yard outside the kitchen and turned on the faucet to rinse her face. People and events are tossed around on the waves of life, she thought; and yet, here was her aunt, whose heart was attached to one and one alone. Thinking about First Aunt as she stooped over the pool of water, Zhenguan felt a surge of tears.

twelve

I

The moon was already very beautiful by the twelfth day of the lunar cycle. But by the thirteenth or fourteenth day, the moon began to entice the eyes, and by the fifteenth day, Zhenguan no longer dared lift her head to meet its gaze!

Daxin had been gone for over ten days already. Zhenguan waited anxiously for a letter, but to no avail. Was he that busy? Had something happened? Or had he fallen ill? But that couldn't be, because she knew he was in good health. . . . What was wrong? Zhenguan's heart felt suspended in midair. It would be easier if her heart had in fact left her and flown up into the sky, because she wouldn't have had to be responsible for it any longer. But that wasn't the case. Her heart went here and there, up and around, refusing to settle down in her chest. And she suffered along with it.

At dusk, after supper, everyone scrambled to get ready for a trip to the beach to enjoy the sight of the full moon. Some of the elderly members of the family were less than enthusiastic, saying that the moon seen from their backyard was just the same. Most of the younger couples, though, as well as her fifth aunt and her cousins, were all excited to go to the beach. Zhenguan wanted to stay at home, but Yinchan managed to drag her out the door.

If Zhenguan hadn't gone along, she might never have come to understand, or at the very least it would have taken her much longer to realize: one's state of mind greatly influences how one perceives the outside world. As beautiful as the sky may be, with no one special to share it with, scenery is merely scenery, water is merely water, and the moon is merely the moon. And all are irrelevant. When Daxin was in her life, the world and its surroundings were imbued with meaning. Now, she could no longer reclaim that world; heaven and earth had left with him.

Zhenguan sulked for several days after the full moon festival. On the eighteenth, she finally received a letter. Feigning composure, Zhenguan searched for a pair of scissors. Maybe it was because she was in such a hurry, or maybe it was because the scissors were dull, but she had great difficulty opening the envelope. She finally tore the envelope open with her shaking hands.

Zhenguan:

I have settled in, and all is well. I have studied for sixteen years, and my chance to serve our country has finally arrived. Grandma's ancient remedy is very potent indeed! My nose was no longer congested when I awoke that day. I was very much surprised to find out that you were capable of making such delicious soup (you should open a restaurant) . . . !

Let me describe my surroundings to you: Penghu is a strange place. People say that winters are terrible here, and the gales are reportedly so strong that if you stick your head outside, you risk having it swept away by the wind. One has to grab hold of something secure to avoid being blown over; even the greatest poet would have trouble keeping hold of his muses here!

Probably because all its aggression is vented in the winter, the climate on the Penghu archipelago during the rest of the year is actually quite temperate. Other than the sound of the birds and the crashing of the waves, it is relatively quiet. The terrain is gentle and rolling, which is a pity, because it cannot capture the dew and rain; there are no black mountains, white waters, flying waterfalls, and shining pools of spring water. In Chinese landscape paintings, the abundance of vitality is often reflected by a body of clear water. This is what Penghu lacks.

When I arrived, I was very much fascinated by the short fences made of lava rock that are used to mark and delineate property. Rather than obstructing one's vision, they only enrich the appearance of the rolling fields.

The weather has been fine, even though the forecast on television often reports that it's cloudy and rainy. What a joke . . . !

Zhenguan managed to suppress a smile at first but could not help chuckling out loud as she read the end of Daxin's letter. Her laughter dispelled the shadows that had been lurking in her mind for the past few days. Until then, she had not been able to fully grasp the dramatic twists and turns of love that tormented the protagonist in the romantic story of the Peony

Pavilion; now she finally understood what the poet Gu Kuang meant: "Love is the most inscrutable of sentiments."

Is love so dazzling? Can love bring one back to life? A few minutes ago she was frozen, as if in an icebox. Now she felt as if she were basking in spring sunshine. All because of one letter from Daxin, which Zhenguan read over and over again. She was still immersed in the delirious joy of it when Yinxi suddenly appeared before her.

He had been troubled by a huge and malicious boil planted smack in the middle of his face. Fourth Aunt ran all over town seeking advice from Western and Chinese physicians. The practitioners of Western medicine prescribed injections, and the practitioners of Chinese medicine recommended herbal packs. But the boil just continued to grow. Looking at his swollen face, Zhenguan said, "Still running around? You should lie down and get some rest. You don't want Fourth Aunt to catch you up and about like this; she'll certainly reprimand you!"

Yinxi ground to a halt but said matter-of-factly, "No, she won't. Ma and Grandma are in the vegetable garden."

"The vegetable garden?"

"Yes." Yinxi leaped up like a frog and said, "They're catching toads!"

As she looked at Yinxi's boil, it suddenly occurred to Zhenguan that Grandma must be trying some ancient remedy, because toads were considered to be one of the five poisons. "Come on, Yinxi," she said. "Let's go to the garden."

Zhenguan was leading the patient to the doctor, but Yinxi thought they were going off to play, so he grabbed her hand and wouldn't let go. Holding his fingers in her palm, Zhenguan thought to herself: Yinxi's mother and Daxin's mother were cousins on the paternal side, and Yinxi's mother and her own mother were cousins on the maternal side. Yinxi and Daxin were cousins, and Zhenguan and Yinxi were cousins. So in this network of relations, Daxin wasn't just a bosom friend to her, he could also be considered a relative, her brother. . . .

In the vegetable garden, Fourth Aunt was bent over, hunting for toads, and Grandma was standing beside her with a tea-colored urn covered with a lid of red tiles.

"Grandma, how many toads have you caught?"

"Only two. Why don't you help us out?"

"Aren't two enough?"

"Have you seen his boil? It's as big as a teacup!"

Zhenguan squatted down and joined in the hunt. Before long she discovered a very ugly creature staring at her fixedly, wrinkled and covered with dirt. In fact, at first glance, it looked like a pile of mud. She would have missed it if it hadn't hopped.

"Hey! There's one over here."

Her grandmother and aunt asked, almost in unison, "Can you tell the difference between a frog and a toad?"

Zhenguan did not answer right away because she was in the process of nabbing her prey. As she snatched up the little creature, she heard Yinxi say, "Elder sister, a toad is uglier than a frog!"

Prize in hand, Zhenguan handed it over to Grandma, saying, "Frogs have white bellies, and this creature here has a spotted belly!"

Her fourth aunt identified the creature as a toad too. Grandma slit its stomach with a knife, and within seconds, all of its entrails were exposed: heart, lungs, gall bladder, liver. . . . Grandma found the lungs in the jumble of flesh and blood and cut off one lobe, then handed it to Fourth Aunt to place over Yinxi's boil. Zhenguan wanted to keep her eyes on Yinxi's boil and the strange creature at the same time. But her fourth aunt's hand was covering Yinxi's face to keep the lung in place, so she turned her attention to the toad with one remaining lung.

When her grandmother extracted needle and thread from her topknot, Zhenguan wondered: What is she up to? She isn't going to sew up the toad's belly, is she? Can the toad survive? Before her wide eyes and gaping mouth, she saw her old grandmother transformed into a surgeon as she started to sew the toad's bloody belly together again.

"Grandma!" Zhenguan exclaimed. "What's the use? The toad is going to—"

"Watch what you say. The toad is a creature born of heaven and earth. We have only borrowed a lobe of its lung; now we have to release it!"

"Can a severed lung regenerate itself? Will the toad survive?"

Her grandmother had just completed the last stitch. Zhenguan saw her tie a knot and solemnly place the toad back onto the ground. "Look, it's still conscious," she said. "It will revive when you put it in a cool and shady spot later."

Yinxi was moving around, and Grandma scolded him, "Look at you! Keep your hands off your face!"

Zhenguan saw that the toad's lung was still stuck to Yinxi's boil. "Grandma, who taught you this?"

The old lady laughed. "Human experience is passed down from one generation to the next."

"Shouldn't you leave a mark by tying a string around the toad or something?"

"If the toad bounces and hops about, Yinxi's boil will heal. You only need to look at Yinxi to know whether or not the toad is alive!"

Was this the way of the world? Was there really such a thing as symbiosis? Zhenguan looked for a spot to set down the remaining toads, thinking that they would be hopping all over the garden by the time Yinxi's boil healed. She felt an immediate urge to return to the cottage to write Daxin a letter. She did so after accompanying Grandma back to her room.

Daxin:

As you serve our country, you have my heartfelt admiration.

The *Women's Book of Virtues* says that a woman must possess culinary skills and be well versed in the art of brewing wine. All I did was to cook a bowl of noodles, an easy task; how could I mess up? I've helped my mother in the kitchen since I was ten years old, and once I spilled hot soup all over myself because I couldn't tell whether the rice was cooked or uncooked and had to use a spoon to ladle out the gruel to examine it up close.

Yinxi has a boil on his face, and Grandma treated it with an ancient remedy. She covered the boil with the lobe of a lung from a toad; it should heal in a few days' time (I helped Fourth Aunt catch the toads!). You must be concerned, as I was, that the toad had its lung cut out. Grandma says it will regenerate, though; do you believe it? I do! Human beings are at the top of the evolutionary ladder, but in terms of vitality, we cannot compare with the creatures in the lower ranks. When I was a child we used to catch crabs; I have seen them cut off their own legs with their claws in order to escape death. I also remember seeing earthworms continue to wriggle even after their bodies were cut in two by the spade of the gardener, for the severed parts of the earthworm are capable of regeneration and reproduction.

In comparison, human beings seem to be the most fragile and vulnerable creatures between heaven and earth.

Best wishes,
Zhenguan

II

Zhenguan:
Happy Mid-Autumn Festival!

Everyone here has been very hospitable. They sent us two dozen bottles of beer, enough to add two inches to our waistlines! It was only fitting for us to return the gift, so I stumbled out onto the streets to shop for one. And I can tell you that it was no easy feat!

In the evening I gorged on a feast with my brothers in arms until my stomach drooped!

It's a pity that I am so far away from home. The beautiful moon framed in my window hangs there in vain. How did you spend the moon festival?

Wishing you happiness,
Daxin

Zhenguan:
It was a joy to receive your letter.

I remember from biology class that the lungs of toads do possess the ability to regenerate. As you said, in the face of calamity human beings are the most frail of all; there is no exit for us, trapped between heaven and earth. But I still think that ours is the best kind of existence. The Buddhists say: Existence in the form of the human body is a hard-earned privilege. Hard-earned indeed!

I cannot picture you catching toads. Don't you girls all share a morbid fear of snakes, frogs, rats, and the like? My youngest sister is thirteen years old, and she is the fiercest of all the girls in my family. Even so, one day she started screaming when she was taking a bath, and we all ran to her rescue. She had been scared witless by a tiny little mouse drinking water in the tub. We said: "Open the door, we'll catch the mouse for you"; she didn't dare move, though, so I said I'd have to climb in through the window to help her. "No, big brother!" she screamed. "I'm stark naked!"

The wind and rain here have been highly unpredictable these past two days. Yesterday I planted a box full of flowers, but last night's raging storm has reduced them to green and red tatters soaking in mud; I'd been counting on the flowers to blossom and thrive, and to brighten up my windowpane.

It is early morning now. I can see the ocean outside my window. There is a huge drum in the ocean, and when the waves are tall, it starts to beat. The beating reverberates every night, pounding in my ears, numbing them. It seems as if the waves are going to come into my room at any moment. When they crash on the shore, the drum in my heart beats in harmony; I either fall asleep immediately or stay awake all night.

I'll write more tomorrow. . . .

Zhenguan:
The farmers have harvested the sweet potatoes. Now they will be sliced and dried under the sun. We have provided a neighbor with the water and electricity and space to lay out the snowy

white potato slices. The whole street is paved with them, and the air is thick with a sweet aroma that one can smell from miles away.

Have you any good books to recommend? Do send me some to read, okay?

Daxin

His last two letters arrived together. Zhenguan received them at dusk and read them in her room behind the closed door, again and again, until night fell. And still she couldn't get enough. The next day she sent him books and wrote him a simple note at the counter of the post office.

Daxin:
I am sending you some books on one condition: that you provide me with a book report after reading them!

The neighbor who dried her sweet potatoes in your compound must have a daughter . . . am I right?

Let me tell you an amazing but true story: the sister-in-law of one of my grade school classmates was the daughter of the owner of the 369 Hotel in Penghu. When she was a young girl, she emptied a basin of water by throwing it out her second-floor window. My classmate's brother just happened to be walking by, and he was soaked. He was going to curse the culprit but was surprised by the sight of the young girl at the window. She went downstairs to apologize to the young man, and that was how they met and eventually got married. Why don't you give it a try too, maybe walk around the neighborhood now and then?

Good luck!
Zhenguan

On the sixth day, Daxin's reply came.

Zhenguan:

I have received the books, thank you. Yes, I will send you a report. But how am I to enjoy them knowing that I'll have to write about them? Can't I just delight in the music without having to sound out the chords? Being lazy as I am, I like to read with a cup of tea and listen to the breezes caressing my ears. Your solemn assignment has made me quite nervous. Isn't that cruel of you?

It is time to harvest peanuts. We soldiers have been enlisted to help the farmers dig them from the ground. They have rewarded us with, of course, peanuts! It will be some time before we run out of peanuts to munch on. The harvest has stripped the land bare; fields that used to be green are now covered with yellow scars. It is a stark and alarming sight.

You were right. The neighbor does have a daughter, but unfortunately, she is only seven years old. Ha!

I just got a letter from my baby brother. He wrote: "How have you been, brother? I have not been getting good grades recently, but my teacher has praised me on my compositions and entered me in a writing contest." He is in fourth grade, and his only worries are unfinished homework and mother finding out that he has been outside playing. How lucky he is!

He told me something funny: His teacher asked the class to keep a diary. My brother copied my sister's diary entries and was mocked by his classmates. He had the audacity to retort: We are in the same family, therefore we live the same life. . . . I wonder if I was so impetuous when I was his age?

By the way, was the water-splashing story true?

Daxin

Zhenguan read the letter again and again, but found no mention of whether or not Daxin had gone walking near the 369 Hotel, as she had suggested. So she asked him specifically in her next letter.

Daxin:
I will be leaving for Taipei in ten days. I will be working at First Uncle's company, and Yinchan will accompany me. What kind of a city is Taipei? The *Book of Rites* states that one should be able to redistribute all of his possessions and be at ease with moving even when he has already settled down, but I hope that I will be able to get used to the customs and way of life in Taipei!

I have been packing my clothes and other miscellaneous items. I am not making much headway, though. Have you been to that place?

Zhenguan

Daxin's letter came six or seven days later.

Zhenguan:
It is October 10. The leafy vegetables that I planted have finally emerged. The sprouts are tiny, yellowish, and timid; they appear to be very fragile and tender (whereas the neighbors' turnips are very plump!). My vegetables refused to sprout at first, and I was frantic. I later found out it was because I did not cover the seeds with earth, and they were exposed to the air.

Life grows under these conditions: darkness, water, warmth, and love. Little plants cannot bear too much light! The hopes that I planted have begun to grow, and this makes me very happy. It would be even better if I could stir-fry such happiness and eat it!

I did go there, and I carried my umbrella!

Zhenguan smiled. He was perceptive and yet so mischievous!

So you are going to Taipei! How exciting! Taipei is full of smog, streets that never sleep, and a three-month-long rainy season. But you get addicted to Taipei after you live there for a while, because it is a place with such feeling!

Nevertheless, I must warn you that Taipei's weather can be biting, so do take care!

Best wishes,
Daxin

III

After dinner, Zhenguan walked down to the beach alone. She wanted to wander on the seashore and say good-bye to the sea. The sea reminded her of her mother's warm embrace. But starting tomorrow, she would be a visitor in an alien land. As of tomorrow, she would have to seek out the familiar sight of the sea and the glowing lights of the fishing vessels only in her dreams! She had lived in Jiayi and Tainan before. There was a sense of homesickness then too, but it was nothing like what she was feeling now.

She was going to Taipei, home of the man she loved. She felt as if she were about to embark upon a pilgrimage. How fortunate she was to have encountered a man such as Daxin. Taipei, oh Taipei! Taipei with its broad avenues and winding alleys, Taipei with its capricious climate. Taipei—so unfamiliar, and yet, because Daxin had grown up there, somehow strangely intimate.

At the dock where the fishing boats were moored, someone was fixing a broken power generator. The repairman had hung a small radio on the boat's mast, and in the darkness, Zhenguan could hear music coming from it. She caught glimpses of flickering light coming from the boat.

Dreams of youth shatter,
Happiness can melt into sadness,
Saying farewell at the harbor,
The stars shine like my tears. . . .

The man hummed along with the song. Zhenguan looked up into the night sky. Stars were indeed flickering! Could they really be tears of sorrow for her departure? Her owns tears fell onto her collar, and she thought: Wasn't she supposed to be filled with joy tonight? Why was she crying? Was she feeling a deep longing for the sea, or was she touched by the lyrics of the sorrowful song? Or perhaps these were tears of joy at the thought of Daxin. The suffering and torment inherent in life she now looked forward to with obsession, so in love with life was she.

By the time Zhenguan returned home, it was already nine o'clock in the evening. When she stepped into Grandma's room, she found that they had a visitor. It was Old Lady Huang, a longtime friend of her grandmother's who lived in the neighborhood. Zhenguan and Yinchan stood in a corner of the room listening for some time before they finally realized what the two old ladies were talking about. The visitor was complaining about her grandson's wife.

"You remember back when we had to walk great distances to fetch water, and every drop of water was like a drop of sweat? Nowadays water comes out of the faucet; people today are blessed. Even so, they should learn to be grateful for what they have. But she doesn't have any insight at all! Every time she turns on the faucet, she lets the water flow for more than ten minutes, even allowing the basin to overflow. I have taught her to turn off the faucet when she's soaping, and to turn it back on when she's done, but she gets upset at me."

"She's young, and she doesn't know any better," Grandma said. "You have to be patient with her."

"Does she have any ears for me? I only gave her a few words of advice, and she went back into her room, refusing to come out for dinner. My grandson, her husband, had to go in to persuade her to come out. I knew there was something not quite right about her when they were planning to get married. My husband even said that women with shrunken shoulders and frail backs do not make good wives. But Ayeh was in love with her, so we went along with the marriage. Now we have to bear the bitter consequences! I told him a long time ago that a good wife would bring good fortune for generations to come, but that a bad wife would bring generations of misfortune. He wouldn't listen. Ah, it's his fate!"

Grandma consoled Old Lady Huang for quite a while before she calmed down and finally reached for her walking cane. Zhenguan and Yinchan walked the old lady home and returned to their grandmother's room. When they got back, they said in unison, "So, Grandma, you have helped settle that family dispute!"

The old lady smiled. "There is a saying: You can go on a vegetarian diet for three years and still not accumulate enough good karma to know what's going on in other people's households. All I did was lend her an ear and allow her to vent her anger!" As she spoke, she took out a lacquered box from her closet. Zhenguan had caught glimpses of the box when she was a child but never knew what it contained. Seeing her grandmother in such a solemn and serious mood, she decided not to get ready for bed quite yet. Instead, she went up close to see what Grandma had to show them.

Zhenguan and Yinchan both peeked into the box and exclaimed at the same time. They had seen jade pendants hanging from their mothers' necklaces, and they also seen Aunt Ruriko's jade gourd pendant, but they had never seen a collection of so many jade ornaments, large and small, together all at once! There were jade buttons, jade lotuses, jade flowers, jade hairpins. . . .

The largest, only the size of a matchbox, was a carving of the golden boy and the jade girl. The golden boy was kicking a shuttlecock, and the jade girl was clapping her hands in joy. The smallest was a jade pomegranate carving; Zhenguan tried to imagine how even a craftsman with extraordinary skills could have managed to create such an intricate piece of artwork so many years ago. The carving of the pomegranate was the size of a peanut, and yet every detail from the tip to the stem was clearly rendered. One could not help but be amazed at seeing such a masterpiece. The other jade carvings of bottles, urns, peaches, and almonds were the size of one's pinkie, and each was a joy to behold.

"Grandma—" Zhenguan began.

Yinchan interrupted, "Why is this treasure chest here? How come we knew nothing about it?"

Grandma picked out two jade pendants from the box. One

was the carving of the golden boy and the jade girl, and the other was a carving of two mandarin ducks frolicking in the water. Both pieces were translucent emerald green and exquisitely carved. She placed them in her hands and looked at the two girls, saying, "I was going to give these to you as wedding gifts. But I think that this would be a good time too. You will be going to Taipei tomorrow, and you won't be at my side anymore."

Suddenly the atmosphere grew very heavy. Zhenguan looked at Yinchan, and Yinchan looked at Zhenguan. They tried to console their grandmother. "Grandma, you can visit us in Taipei! First Uncle has invited you to visit him in Taipei more than once!"

Grandmother broke into laughter. "Me, go to Taipei? I have no neighbors there, at alley's end and across the fence. No one knows me, and I don't know anyone; how lonely I would be!"

Zhenguan herself could imagine what it would be like, the sense of alienation. But she was willing to risk it for Daxin. For Daxin, it was worth any hardship and challenge.

"Okay now, don't try to persuade me. Take your pick here, one each. When you wear the jade pendants I will be with you."

Yinchan asked Zhenguan, "Which one do you like?"

Zhenguan said, "Why don't you choose first? The other will be mine."

"Yours or mine, it really doesn't make a difference. I'll pick one with my eyes closed." Yinchan selected the carving of the mandarin ducks. "Ah, you have the golden boy and the jade girl!" she said.

Zhenguan was wearing a gold chain already, so Yinchan helped her hang the pendant on it. As she was doing so, she whispered into Zhenguan's ear, "I knew you liked this one because I saw you eyeing it several times. Okay, there you go."

Yinchan's head was bent, her chin lowered. Zhenguan kept quiet; she studied Yinchan's curly hair and stately nose. Yinchan was Third Uncle's daughter indeed, the two so strongly resembled each other. Just then, Yinchan suddenly looked up and asked, "What are you staring at?"

"Your eyes. . . . Why are your eyes so big?"

The two girls exchanged smiles, and no words were necessary.

Even when she was lying in bed, Zhenguan did not feel at all sleepy. She fingered the jade pendant dangling at her chest and looked out the window. The lights were out, but in the darkness she could detect a faint glimmer outside the house. It was going to be a long night . . . when would day break?

thirteen

I

She had been in Taipei for three months now, but Zhenguan just had not grown to like the place. Daxin would ask her in his letters: "Have you fallen in love with Taipei yet?" She did not know what to say; it wasn't exactly yes or no.

Zhenguan:
When I was a student, I used to walk quite often past where you are living now because it was one of the many alleys across from campus. There is a Szechuan restaurant there that I frequented; and near Dr. Zhang's Dental Clinic lived an old painter. When the class bells rang, he would post a sign that read COME FOR LUNCH! at the entrance to the alley. I never went there, so to this day, I still don't know whether he meant it as an invitation or whether it was simply a clever way to attract customers to his restaurant.

If you turn right from Azhong's dormitory, you will arrive at the Chemistry Department. The third window on the second floor was my lab. And right outside the Evening Division, facing the track field, is a beautiful little path flanked by white birches. Have you discovered it yet?

Enclosed please find a tourist's guide of Taipei. I asked my sister to buy it and send it to me (she must think I'm really homesick!). I hope you will find it useful.

The postman is here, so that's all for now!

Daxin

Zhenguan:

I have sent you several letters in a row describing Taipei, and they have made me nostalgic; I've never been away from home for so long before! "Yesterday I went home in a dream"—I wonder who wrote that. And you know what? I did dream of returning to Taipei last night! I was very excited about visiting you but awoke just as I arrived at the alley where you live. Imagine my disappointment!

Dawn is about to break. Outside my window I can see thousands of lights sparkling on the ocean. They appear to be swaying with the waves, shining brightly and resolutely all along the bay, each latched to the next. The moon has set, and the ocean and the sky are one color. I cannot tell whether it is the lights of the fishing vessels at sea or the low-cast stars that attract the hordes of fish tonight.

How are you liking Taipei?

Daxin

When Zhenguan received letters like this one, she would

be at a loss as to how to respond; Daxin was a native of Taipei, and his father and elders were all in Taipei. Naturally he would feel a sense of loyalty to the place, and of course he would want Zhenguan to feel an affinity with his hometown as well! They hadn't made things clear between the two of them yet, and Zhenguan could appreciate what Daxin was trying to do. But the people that she had run into in Taipei were either cunning or aggressive; the poor were not content, and the rich knew no discipline. . . . Daxin's expectations made it difficult for Zhenguan to fully assess her impressions of Taipei. So she replied in her letter: "I have not come to a conclusion yet! Give me time, and I'll let you know."

With Yinchan it was a different story. The two of them lived in a small apartment that Azhong had helped them find. Whereas Zhenguan usually went home right after work, Yinchan loved to roam around town and would come back to tell Zhenguan about her adventures. On weekends and holidays, when Zhenguan cocooned herself in her room and slept, Yinchan would run off to the National Palace Museum or to the zoo, map in hand.

This Sunday, Zhenguan slept until nine o'clock in the morning. When she awoke, she found Yinchan still snuggled under her blankets on the top bunk. She kicked the mattress from below and asked, "Aren't you going to do any exploring today?"

It was December, and the day was cold and wintry. Yinchan was awake, but she did not want to leave the warm bed. With her blankets wrapped around her, she sat up. "First Uncle and Aunt Ruriko have invited us to move in with them," she said. "What do you think?"

What did she think? When the two of them were leaving for Taipei, Fourth Aunt had tried to convince them to stay with her parents in Taipei, at Daxin's home. But Grandma and the other elders thought that it would be more appropriate for the girls to stay with their First Uncle and Aunt. They finally ended up renting an apartment. This was actually Zhenguan's idea, her reason being that they would be just a stone's throw away from Azhong's school dormitory.

There were other reasons too. She didn't want to stay with First Uncle because she wished to avoid living with his Japanese wife, Ruriko. Ruriko had her heart set on playing matchmaker and had introduced Zhenguan to a doctor who had just returned from Japan. They had met twice already, and Zhenguan thought quite highly of the young man. Nevertheless, there was one tenet she had subscribed to ever since coming of age: that there were good people and good things, but they didn't necessarily have anything to do with her. Sometimes it's best to keep a distance, so that when people meet, there will be only civility and good will.

Out of sheer timidity, she decided not to stay at Daxin's house. She had anticipations about their future relationship that made her more cautious than ever. . . .

Yinchan could understand all her considerations and decided to stay with Zhenguan. After a good deal of thought, Zhenguan concluded, "We can't please everyone, so we might as well stay here. Here we live right around the corner from Azhong's university, and we can visit him anytime we want."

"That's just what I was thinking!" Yinchan replied. "Yesterday at work, First Uncle asked me again. Director Lai and his secretary were both there, so I couldn't really say much. I told him that I would talk it over with you. . . ."

Zhenguan smiled. "I'm not moving. So what are you going to tell him?"

"It's up to you; either way, I'll respect your decision. There's no point in us splitting up!"

Hearing these words, it occurred to Zhenguan that with Yingui's wedding at the end of the year, the sisters were getting married off one by one. Who knew where their lives would lead? Zhenguan suddenly felt extremely grateful for Yinchan's companionship.

Before leaving for Taipei, the two girls had visited Yinyue at Saltwater Town. She was holding her baby in her arms, looking very much like a young mother and wife. One moment she was unwrapping candy for them to eat, and another she was off to the kitchen to check the chicken soup on the stove. Her sisters-in-law came out to greet her one after the other, and there was no chance at all for the three of them to engage in intimate conversation.

"Zhenguan—"

"Yinyue—"

"So you are leaving for Taipei. When will we get together again?"

As Zhenguan pondered, Yinchan responded, "At Yingui's wedding!"

Yinyue had asked the question with joyful anticipation, but Yinchan's answer somehow cast a shadow over the three of them: another sister was leaving home to get married. . . .

Zhenguan was jolted back to the present by Yinchan. "Hey! Has someone cast a spell over you?"

Zhenguan adjusted her pillows and flopped down on the bed again, pulling the blanket up to her chin. "Have they decided yet on an auspicious date?" she asked.

Yinchan didn't quite understand what her cousin was talking about. "What did you say?"she asked.

Zhenguan shut her eyes momentarily, then said, "Have Yingui's in-laws decided yet?"

"Oh." Yinchan snuggled back into bed. "Yingui hasn't told me anything. She might write to us in two or three days."

"Are you going to sleep in today?"

"Well, there really isn't much left to do in Taipei. Don't you think I've seen all that there is to see?"

"Have you ever! Third Aunt says that you never get homesick because you're always busy running around here and there. She says you're like a bird let out of her cage."

"Well, when you're new to a place, you're curious. Now it's your turn to go looking around!"

"What?"

"Oh, I don't know. If Daxin finds out what we really think of Taipei, he'll be upset!" Suddenly Yinchan leaped out of bed. "I have a feeling that there's a letter in the mailbox. Let me go and check!"

When Yinchan reappeared, she had breakfast and two letters in her hand.

"Whose letters?"

"Guess!"

Zhenguan sat up to examine the letters. One was from Yingui and the other from Daxin. Yinchan asked her jokingly, "Which first—breakfast or mail?"

"Oh, you!" she exclaimed as she jumped out of bed.

"What a stupid question. Of course you're going to read the

letter first. It's going to fill you up so you won't even need breakfast!"

"Quiet, or I'll sew your mouth shut!" Zhenguan said laughingly.

And so they read one letter each.

"What did Yingui write?" Zhenguan asked.

"They set the date of the wedding for December 28, just a few days before the new year. Yingui wants us to get permission from First Uncle to go home two days in advance."

"Five days all together. Do you think First Uncle will say yes?"

"It's still a month away. We'll see. He has to let us go! Some things are cyclical, and if you miss one opportunity you'll have another. But other things happen only once. We may have free time some day in the future, but where are we going to find another Yingui who's getting married?"

"You're right, Yinchan. But First Uncle has his considerations too. If he gives us the time off, what is he going to tell others when they ask for leave?"

"Well . . ."

"But let's not worry yet; we'll see how it goes. I don't think Yingui or First Uncle will blame us whether we ask for leave or not."

II

Zhenguan received a call from Ruriko, First Uncle's wife, one day just as she was getting off work. Ruriko could speak Taiwanese fluently, having learned the language from her husband while they were still in Japan. From her words and tone,

Zhenguan could sense the bliss of a woman who had found the man of her life.

"Is this Zhenguan-ko?" Ruriko had the Japanese habit of adding an endearing "-ko" to women's names.

"Yes, Aunt Ruriko, this is Zhenguan speaking."

"Is Yinchan with you? Do you know what day it is?"

"No, is this a special day? Yinchan is here too; do you want to speak to her?"

"Let me tell you first, and then I'll talk to her. Today is your first uncle's birthday. I have prepared a feast, and I'm counting on you both to come. Do drive here with First Uncle after work; it's been a while since I last saw you!"

Zhenguan paused for a moment and then consented. Her aunt continued, "First Uncle loves rice dumplings wrapped in bamboo leaves, so I made some this morning. Do you girls like rice dumplings?"

"Yes! Where did you learn how to make them?"

"I went to the market and asked the old lady who sells them to teach me. Why don't you come and find out if my rice dumplings are tasty?"

Zhenguan passed the telephone to Yinchan. Yinchan kept erupting into laughter during her conversation with Ruriko.

"What was so funny? You were laughing nonstop!"

Yinchan said, "Aunt Ruriko was telling me how she spent seven days trying to master the technique of wrapping the rice into the bamboo leaves. She is making her debut today, but the first few that she wrapped this morning turned out rectangular rather than triangular, and she is wondering whether First Uncle will make fun of her!"

"That's no problem, we'll help her out by eating all the rectangular ones!"

"That's what I told her!"

As the girls were tidying up their desks, First Uncle walked in. The two girls stood up to greet him. "Uncle!"

"Ah, so your aunt has called you already. I'll wait for you outside."

The uncles at home were all bronzed and weather-beaten by the sun and wind. In contrast, First Uncle appeared younger, with his rosy complexion, and it was difficult to find traces of the hardship that he had endured while he was a soldier in the Japanese army. But brothers are brothers, and all the uncles resembled each other somehow in their eyes, noses, and mouths.

When they were getting into the car, First Uncle told Yinchan to take the front seat by the driver and asked Zhenguan to sit with him in the back. There beside her uncle, she was suddenly reminded of the time she rode in a car with Third Uncle. Her uncles were all very good to her because she was without her own father.

"How old are you, Zhenguan?"

"Twenty-three."

"So you were born in 1949. I had just arrived in Japan then without a penny in my pocket."

Zhenguan listened to her uncle, feeling as if every word were covered with blood and tears.

"At that time, Kyoto was not what it is today. It was ravaged by war, and I couldn't find a job. I had nothing to eat all day, and by night, I slept on people's doorsteps. On the sixth day, I was almost delirious when a young girl stepped outside her door and tripped over me. It was Ruriko. . . ."

Zhenguan thought about how Ruriko had saved her uncle's life, and how First Aunt at home had waited for her uncle to return for all those years. Theirs was such an intricate and closely woven relationship: who had forsaken whom, who owed whom? There didn't seem to be any easy answers.

"Ruriko was but a high school student then. Her decision to marry me brought her many beatings from her father and elder brothers. We were later banished from her home. If one of her teachers hadn't taken us in, I don't know what would have become of the two of us; we might have died of starvation. It was only recently that we got in touch with her family again."

Zhenguan's eyes were brimming with tears, but she had left her handkerchief at the office. She nudged Yinchan, who was sitting in front of her, and Yinchan passed her a hand towel; Zhenguan noticed that it was already tear-stained.

"Uncle, it's good that you have come back; everyone in the family is happy for you."

They drove past Renai Road and around Linyi Street, an area with a number of Japanese-style houses. Zhenguan was counting the numbers on the doors when she caught sight of Aunt Ruriko waiting to greet them. Standing beside her were Azhong and the skinny doctor.

"Zhenguan-ko, Yinchan-ko," Ruriko greeted the girls one after the other. Because of her loyalty to First Aunt, Zhenguan had not liked Ruriko at all the first time they met. Later, she'd decided to treat her with respect only because she was, if nothing else, First Uncle's wife and an elder. But now, after listening to First Uncle in the car, she saw Aunt Ruriko in a new light. She had saved First Uncle's life, so she deserved Zhenguan's respect, her whole family's respect.

"Aunt Ruriko . . ."

Zhenguan held onto her aunt's hand. Yinchan's attitude had also changed. Ruriko looked over Zhenguan from head to toe and said to her husband, "Zhenguan's dress is so beautiful!"

For a moment, all eyes were on Zhenguan. Yinchan said, "Mine is pretty too; don't I get any compliments, Aunt Ruriko?"

Ruriko laughed. "You have to line up for compliments. It's not your turn yet!" When she spoke these words, she seemed as innocent and pure as a little girl. Looking at her, Zhenguan felt a sudden affection for her aunt. She was family.

Once inside the house, Zhenguan asked her brother, "How did you get here?"

Azhong motioned to the doctor beside him. "Mr. Zheng picked me up."

"I asked Kaiyuan to bring Azhong here," Ruriko said. "Okay, won't everyone please take a seat?"

The dinner table was long and rectangular. The host and hostess sat at the two ends; Yinchan motioned for Azhong to sit beside his sister, and she took the seat facing Zhenguan. This kept Zheng Kaiyuan at a distance from Zhenguan.

With each dish that was served, Zhenguan saw her uncle's face light up; but when the rice dumplings wrapped in bamboo leaves were placed on the table, he frowned. Zhenguan looked the other way as he reprimanded Ruriko in Japanese. Zhenguan couldn't understand a word of what her uncle said, but she heard her aunt gently explain, "They're family, so there won't be any misunderstanding. . . . They can have more than one, and next time I'll make them bigger. . . . Don't get upset, please."

And so saying, she unwrapped the dumplings and served up

three in a dish for each guest. So her uncle was scolding her aunt for making the dumplings too small, because it might give an impression of stinginess!

"Uncle, Aunt Ruriko has just learned how to make the dumplings. The smaller ones are more easily cooked, and Taipei rice dumplings are smaller than those from southern Taiwan anyway: they weigh only 250 grams."

Azhong chimed in, "Yeah, Taipei rice dumplings are only 250 grams each. But I've had rice dumplings that weigh 500 grams too! Dragonboat Festival is my favorite festival, and I miss the rice dumplings from the south: just one is big enough to fill you up!"

Everyone, including First Uncle, laughed. After dinner, they all went to sit in the living room while Ruriko went to the kitchen to clean up. Zhenguan joined her there. Her aunt was standing in front of the water basin. She was still wearing her gray silk dress, but she had already taken off the red coral necklace that she'd been wearing and tied an apron around her waist. Zhenguan stood behind her aunt, noticing the gold hairpin and red flower in her aunt's topknot. The look was simple and elegant.

"Aunt—"

Ruriko was humming a Japanese tune when Zhenguan entered the kitchen. She turned and asked, "Why aren't you in the living room? The kitchen is wet and greasy!"

Zhenguan stepped closer to her aunt and asked, "When is Yindan coming back? We'd love to meet her!" Yindan was the daughter of Aunt Ruriko and First Uncle. She was seventeen years old. When her parents returned to Taiwan, she had stayed behind with her Japanese grandmother, who felt that she should finish school in Japan first.

"Yindan-ko? We planned to have her come in June, but now

I am worried that she might not pass the university entrance exam because her Chinese isn't good enough."

At that moment, Yinchan joined them in the kitchen. Zhenguan asked her, "Is Azhong still here? What were you talking about?"

"Mr. Zheng was asking about what gets wrapped into those 500-gram rice dumplings."

Ruriko was curious. "Are there really rice dumplings that big?"

"Yes, I've seen them in Tainan!"

"And what was Azhong's answer?" Ruriko asked.

"A chicken leg, two egg yolks, three chestnuts, four shitake mushrooms, five pieces of pork. . . . People from the south are really generous!"

When they all returned to the living room, Ruriko asked Mr. Zheng to drive the girls home. Zhenguan declined the offer politely, but Mr. Zheng urged, "We're going in the same direction, and anyway, Mr. Jian has already left!" Mr. Jian was First Uncle's driver.

Zhenguan knew she should probably not insist on taking the bus home, so they all got into his car. Azhong took the front seat, and the two girls sat in the back. The four of them did not exchange any words along the way. Mr. Zheng stopped the car when they reached Azhong's university. Azhong got out of the car, saying thank you and good-bye. When he left, the skinny doctor asked the two girls, "Do you ladies want to enjoy the sight of the city lights?"

Of course, Zhenguan thought to herself, one day she was going to visit all the streets and alleys of Taipei and really see its true face, but only with Daxin. She wanted to know Taipei the way that Daxin knew her hometown!

Zheng Kaiyuan turned to look at the girls, waiting for an answer. Zhenguan squeezed Yinchan's arm in the dark. Yinchan finally cleared her throat and replied, "No, we're too tired!"

III

Zhenguan:

Last night I went to a play, and this morning I woke up with a congested nose and a dizzy head. I cannot help but think of the hot chili noodles that you prepared for me the last time. I just received your letter, and it has not only brightened up my day but also relieved my nasal congestion. Don't believe me? Wanna bet? I would definitely win and you would lose! Luck is on my side because just ten minutes ago, I won at a game of chess.

Actually, my victory doesn't necessarily mean that I have a clear head. I remember playing once with an old professor who told me that the true winner doesn't really have his heart set on winning. The philosopher Zhuangzi espoused a similar notion: he said that the virtuous think not and worry not.

So, Azhong has gone sightseeing with you? I thought he only knew how to make the honor roll, all work and no play. I have received your photograph. There are so many people in it, it wasn't easy figuring out which one was you. Are the two people in the front row First Uncle and Aunt Ruriko? I've been to the spot in that picture before. I remember a suspension bridge that it would chill your blood to cross. I also remember a very narrow trail hugging the cliff along the precipice. Am I right?

Best wishes,
Daxin

Zhenguan:

I am feeling woozy from having had too much to drink tonight (I can drink without getting drunk, but I only drink occasionally!), and I think it's a good time to write you a letter, even though I sent you one just this morning.

I do have a few days off this month, and I've considered returning to Taipei. But on second thought, three or four days doesn't amount to much, and I might as well wait until I accumulate enough for ten days of leave at the end of the year. Then I'll be able to celebrate the new year by the sea. How does that sound? I've been wondering how you are spending your time in Taipei. Taipei has changed drastically in recent years. Tradition has not been well preserved there, unlike where you come from.

You told me that at home you still practice the custom of welcoming the broom spirit during Lantern Festival. I looked it up, and I found a description of the ritual. According to custom in central China, people believed that every year in the first Lunar Moon, during Lantern Festival, all plants were potent, which is why brooms made of straw and bamboo are used for divination. Such is the power of tradition for a heritage perpetuated by blood ties and geography. The custom actually originated in the Jiangsu region, but your ancestors, even having left central China generations before, experienced catastrophe and war, and they clung to ancient traditions from home. There seems to be a common denominator in the blood of the Chinese people, a noble and distinct trait.

Will you be going home for Chinese New Year? I am not sure when I will be returning yet, but it will be after you anyway. See you by the seashore.

Happy New Year,
Daxin

fourteen

I

Yinyue and the others arrived early in the morning. Zhenguan and Yinchan could sense the festive excitement in the air the moment that they stepped into the house. Yinyue, wearing a brightly colored *cheongsam* with a camel-hair cardigan, had her baby in her arms. The baby was watching the chicken and the ducks, his pink mouth dribbling, and when Zhenguan set down her bags to pick him up, she saw that his eyes were as clear as two pools of water. Zhenguan gave the baby a peck on his chubby cheek, then wiped the drool off his face with a towel. "I am your auntie," she said. "Call me Auntie!"

Yinyue laughed. "It's too early! He's only three months old; if you want to hear him call you anything, you'll have to wait until next year!"

The baby's eyes glowed bright and true, and Zhenguan saw

herself reflected in their depths. She kissed the face of this tiny baby reverently, this child born to both heaven and earth. . . .

"Yingui has been anxious to see you. If you'd taken any longer to come home, her neck would have been stretched out like a giraffe's. Is First Uncle returning the day after tomorrow?"

"That's what he said."

"You must be tired after all that time on the train. I've already been to the train station twice to find out whether you had arrived."

"Sorry, the train was behind schedule. Where's your husband?"

"He won't be here until tomorrow. Wait a minute, what about Yinchan?"

Yinchan had just gone into her room to put away her bags and returned now to the yard, wanting to hold the baby. "You've been with the baby long enough already, it's my turn! If you get to hold him all the time, he'll be deprived of the chance to meet me, his aunt. Oh, little baby, good little baby. . . ." The baby started to cry as soon as he changed hands. Yinchan desperately tried to calm him, patting him and rocking, "Don't cry, baby, Auntie will be nice to you!"

But Yinyue's baby wouldn't stop crying, so she had to take over. "Grandma told me before that people never fully appreciate their parents until they have their own children," she said. "How right she was! Dear baby, don't cry, don't cry, Mother's here to look after you!"

The two sisters entered the house to greet everyone else. Zhenguan's mother had also come over to help out. Mothers and daughters, cousins and friends, all chattered away from dinner until bedtime. That night, with the exception of Yinyue, who had to take care of her baby, all five cousins slept in one room. Since odd numbers were considered unlucky, they also invited Yinshan's daughter to join them. Yinxing was seventeen going on eighteen, a junior in high school. She was shy and reserved, and her responses to questions were always shorter than the questions themselves. They stayed up all night talking. During festivals people are not supposed to turn off the lights and go to bed, so the lights were left on; it is hard to imagine how they could even carry on their conversations with so little rest.

The second day at home was just as chaotic, and everyone was busy until midnight. Soon afterward, Zhenguan rubbed her sleepy eyes and returned to her grandmother's room with her blanket. She almost tripped over something at the door. It was a small bucket of burning coals, and the cinders cast a pale glow into the darkened room. Yinchan was busying herself in the doorway.

"What is this all about?"

"Grandma can't stand being cold, so she has a little stove under her blankets to warm her hands and feet," Yinchan said.

"Aren't you worried about the room becoming too warm and dry? I heard Grandma coughing this morning!"

Yinchan was bending over the stove. Flickers of flames danced as shadows on her face, which appeared serene in the soft light. Zhenguan caught sight of two mandarin oranges in her hand. "Hey, why didn't you tell me you were roasting oranges?" she asked.

"It was just a whim. I was already lying in bed, but my mouth was so dry that I had difficulty sleeping, and I suddenly had a craving for roasted mandarin oranges. I started peeling them but it occurred to me that I should start a fire burning first, so here I am."

Roasted oranges are said to be good for relieving coughs. Zhenguan had tried the remedy when she was a child, and her coughing did stop, either because the oranges were effective or because it was time for her to feel better anyway. The mandarin oranges had tasted delicious, and the thought of them made her mouth water even now. Yinchan buried the oranges in the glowing cinders, covering them with ashes. In no time at all, the room was warmed with a pungent and spicy aroma. Zhenguan stared into the burning charcoal, thinking about how the heritage of many generations comes to be preserved in the perpetuation of such traditions, and she no longer felt sleepy.

Just then Yinchan, who was sitting by her side, stood up to leave the room. "Where are you going?" Zhenguan asked. "Do you have any idea what time it is?"

"Two oranges aren't enough for us," Yinchan replied. "I'm going to get some more from the kitchen pantry."

By the time five or six mandarin oranges had been roasted, it was already morning, and the rooster was crowing. The two girls hadn't slept a wink all night, but they felt full of energy nonetheless. Looking at the piles of orange peels, Yinchan laughed. "If Grandma wakes up to find all these peels here, she's going to wonder how she managed to eat all those mandarin oranges!"

"Grandma is the one with the cough, and look at who ate most of them!"

As the two talked, they went about washing up and changing their clothes. The bridegroom and his family came for the bride at nine o'clock. Zhenguan and her cousins, along with her mother and aunts, accompanied Yingui all the way to the town of Xuejia for a wedding luncheon prepared by the bridegroom's family. By they time they got home it was already dusk. She didn't know whether it was exhaustion, an overload of emotions, or motion sickness from the drive, but Zhenguan headed straight for her grandmother's bed and was asleep in no time at all.

Yinchan came in later, her three-inch heels clicking on the floor. "Aren't you going to have dinner?" she asked. "They're putting out several large tables in the front garden and backyard. Even if you don't feel like eating much, you should still have some soup . . . I'll get you some if you like!"

Zhenguan covered her face with the blanket, groaning, "Let me sleep."

"If you fall asleep now, it will be morning before you know it," Yinchan replied.

"So what?"

"But—"

"Please, I'm just going to lie here for a while. If there's anything good to eat, save some for me."

Yinchan finally left, and Zhenguan fell into a blissful sleep. She dreamt that she was somewhere she had never been before. She saw Daxin wearing familiar clothes, sitting in a field, singing. Zhenguan asked him, "What are you singing?"

"The school anthem!" he answered, all sparkling white teeth.

"That's not true; weren't you singing the Taiwanese folk song, 'Waiting for the Spring Breezes?' "

" 'Waiting for the Spring Breezes' is the school anthem!"

And he stood up and started to run. Zhenguan started after him, but something tripped her, and as she fell down—she woke up. She opened her eyes and then shut them again after readjusting her mattress and pillow and shifting positions. Now she was really going to get some sleep! In her dreams, Daxin was always there, constantly on her mind. But—

Much later, to her disappointment, Zhenguan woke up. Her stomach was grumbling, and she looked at the clock. Three-thirty: no wonder she felt tired! Yinchan was lying beside her, sleeping soundly. Curious to see what Yinchan had saved for her to eat, Zhenguan headed to the kitchen. She saw the light on: someone else must be having a hunger attack in the middle of the night too!

She walked into the kitchen and almost lost her balance at the sight of Daxin. "Wha— it's you!" she sputtered. He was seated on a stool, eating rice noodles. Fourth Aunt was heating soup for him over the stove. Zhenguan felt decidedly awake all of a sudden.

"I didn't expect to see you here!"

Daxin himself was so surprised that he almost choked on his noodles. "I wasn't expecting to run into you either!"

Fourth Aunt had finished heating the soup but turned to busy herself at the sink, saying, "Zhenguan hadn't slept for two days, so she fell asleep before dinner today. What are you going to eat? Here, Yinchan must have set aside this big bowl full of vegetables for you."

Zhenguan sat down and took a sip of the hot soup. She asked Daxin, "When did you arrive? It's so cold outside. . . ."

"I took the night train. It was two-thirty by the time I got to Xinying City. The streets were deserted and there wasn't a soul around, so I hailed a cab and came here; otherwise I would have had to wait until daybreak."

"Who opened the door for you?"

"Uncle!"

"He must have been surprised to see you standing there!"

"Yes, but he didn't scream out loud like you did!"

They chatted together, not wanting to stop. There was only a tiny lamp in the kitchen, and Zhenguan thought it a wonder, the two of them sharing its glimmer of light. After their midnight snack, they went to bed. Zhenguan woke up in a daze the next morning, unable to tell whether what had happened the night before had been merely a dream. She sat facing the mirror for a long time, hairbrush frozen in her hand. Looking at her messy hair in the mirror, she didn't even know how to begin fixing it up.

All of a sudden, Yinchan appeared behind her and put a brush through her hair, saying, "Let me help you, Daxin is here." Her words spilled out in one quick breath. Zhenguan, turning to look at the bed, realized that Grandma had already left the room. So that's why Yinchan was so direct.

"Yes, I saw him early this morning—"

Yinchan's eyes lit up. "You saw him? You knew that he was here and just now got out of bed?"

Zhenguan didn't reply and Yinchan continued, "Oh, I see, this must be what it's like to be in love!"

"What are you talking about?" Zhenguan protested. "Don't you jump to conclusions—"

Yinchan giggled. "People who are fond of each other think the same things and even sneeze at the same time! They must awaken at the same time too!"

Zhenguan's hair was done and though she pretended to give Yinchan a smack on the hand, she was secretly tickled by what her cousin had said. She had to hide her feelings, though, so she quickly left the bedroom with her water basin.

And by sheer coincidence, or luck, she ran into Daxin at the well. They looked at each other. Daxin spoke first. "Good morning, little girl!"

"What do you mean?" Zhenguan retorted, splashing Daxin with water.

Daxin moved to avoid getting wet. "Weren't you all sleepy-eyed last night? The more I look at you, the more you resemble a little girl. You know, I just realized something. . . ."

Zhenguan feigned indifference.

"Your hairline dips down into your forehead, making your face look like a heart." Daxin laughed. "All the beautiful women depicted in Chinese paintings have foreheads like yours. I wonder why I hadn't noticed it before. . . ."

Zhenguan bent to fetch her water and did not respond. Silently, she thought to herself that Daxin must have been blind not to notice.

Daxin continued, "Really, did I surprise you last night?"

"It was more than a surprise," Zhenguan began. She turned to face Daxin. "I thought I was dreaming!"

Daxin said, "If I surprised you, you surprised me even more! I almost fainted at the sight of you in your nightgown."

Zhenguan's pail was already full, but she hardly noticed. All she wanted was to disappear from his sight. Setting down the water ladle, she ran away as fast as she could.

II

It was Chinese New Year's Eve.

Most of the women of the house were in the kitchen, preparing the rice cakes that are a custom for New Year's celebrations, while Zhenguan ran back and forth between her own house and her grandparents'. Zhenguan's mother asked Third Uncle to write auspicious lines of verse in Chinese calligraphy on strips of red paper. The red strips, known as Spring Festival scrolls, contained two lines of rhyming verse and were pasted on either side of a door frame or window to usher in the new year.

"We don't have to be so picky about the scrolls that are pasted inside the house," she said. "The spring couplet for the main entrance, however, is very important because it faces the street where people pass by every day. Spring scrolls on the front door represent the spirit of the family living behind it!"

Her mother was a person who was attentive to even the smallest of details. Zhenguan had noticed, in fact, that the women in her family all seemed to share that trait. They treated everything with reverence, and every task had to be done properly, from cutting a piece of paper to folding a shirt.

In the past, Azhong had usually taken care of the Spring Festival scrolls. Yesterday, however, Second Uncle had caught ten perch. So Zhenguan's mother, remembering a kind teacher who had taught both Zhenguan and her brother when they were children, asked Azhong to bring some fish over to the teacher as a New Year's gift.

Zhenguan ran into Third Uncle and Daxin in the main hall. They were pasting Spring Festival scrolls onto the wall. Pointing to a stack on the table, Third Uncle said, "The Spring Festival scrolls are ready. It's just like your mother . . . all the lines have to rhyme, the calligraphy has to be just right, the meaning has to be auspicious, and the ink has to be perfectly saturated. The store-bought Spring Festival scrolls simply will not do, because those calligraphers are interested only in how many they can sell. Tell your mother that I have thrown away countless reams of red paper just to satisfy her, and that she owes me a big fat red envelope of money for all my efforts!"

Zhenguan unfurled the red paper scroll to read her uncle's spring couplet, and she said, "Yes, you do deserve a big red envelope!"

As they were talking, Third Uncle's wife walked in with a bamboo basket. She said to Zhenguan, "You're just the person I wanted to see. I was going to ask Yinan to send this over to you, but I couldn't find him anywhere!"

Zhenguan's mother did not know how to make rice cakes for the new year. The rice cakes Zhenguan had been enjoying since childhood were always made by her aunts and grandmother. Third Uncle glanced at his wife's basket and said, "Those aren't enough! Why don't you give them one more basket? The children have all grown up. Yesterday Azhong stood by my side, and I discovered that he is almost as tall as me. If he could eat one rice cake when he was ten years old, imagine how many he can eat now that he's twenty!"

Third Aunt wanted to say something in response, but seeing that Daxin was there as well, she decided to let it drop. So Zhenguan came to her aunt's defense, saying, "Uncle, Auntie did ask Mother last night whether she wanted an extra basket, but Mother said no. She said that my brother and I aren't as fond of rice cakes as we used to be when we were children, and that if we got two baskets, she would end up eating rice cakes for two whole weeks until Lantern Festival. My mom is the only person in the family who simply cannot resist rice cakes!" Third Uncle stopped reprimanding his wife upon hearing Zhenguan's words.

Daxin then said to Third Aunt, "Yinan went out with a

friend, and I don't think he'll be returning right away. Let me be your errand boy. . . ." He glanced at Zhenguan and added, "I just heard Zhenguan say that she's giving out red envelopes of money!"

Zhenguan's aunt and uncle laughed; Zhenguan smiled but said nothing. She picked up the Spring Festival scrolls and followed Daxin. The two were walking down the street when Daxin suddenly turned to her and said, "Did you know that you carry yourself very well when you're walking?"

Zhenguan lowered her head. "I don't know what you're talking about!"

"Are you sure, or are you just reluctant to give me another red envelope?"

"Well, I'm not sure whether there are any more red envelopes, but I do know that there is plenty of red paper!"

Daxin was defeated by Zhenguan's quick response. So he decided to say what he was really thinking. "What I meant to say was: our ancestors used to say that nobles have a leisurely and unruffled gait. . . . That is how you walk, naturally and gracefully, like flowing water and floating clouds!"

Zhenguan smiled. "No matter how you try to flatter me, you're getting nothing but red paper."

When they arrived at Zhenguan's home, her mother was standing at the red table, cleaning the incense ashes scattered on Zhenguan's father's spiritual tablet. Seeing Daxin, she said, "I just peeked outside to see if you had arrived, and I'm happy that you're here. Azhong is visiting his teacher. I was waiting for him to come home so that he could invite you to join us for dinner to celebrate New Year's Eve."

Glancing at Zhenguan, Daxin said, "Well, I am already here without an invitation! Isn't this even better?"

Zhenguan's mother brought out plates of various sizes for the rice cakes and sticky rice dumplings wrapped in bamboo leaves. "Here's some glue," she said to her daughter. "Why don't you put up the Spring Festival scrolls, now that you have some time on your hands!"

The Spring Festival scrolls were pasted onto the gateposts and door panels. Smaller ones, with lucky characters such as "spring" and "happiness," were also pasted onto windows, rice urns, water urns, stoves, and closet doors. Zhenguan and her mother usually picked them out at stores, but the scrolls that they pasted on the panel of the front door were written by Third Uncle. Zhenguan got a chair and had Daxin stand on it. She brushed glue onto the scrolls and handed them to Daxin.

Zhenguan's mother paid great attention to detail. A few years ago she had pasted all the Spring Festival scrolls herself because Zhenguan and her brother were still young and not yet capable of doing a neat job. The task was finally passed on to Zhenguan two years ago, when Zhenguan's mother knew that she could trust her daughter to be conscientious about her work. In truth, Zhenguan knew that she resembled her mother closely in character. Likewise, although she had never seen Daxin paste paper before, she gave him the Spring Festival scrolls because she knew that she could trust him.

The doors and windows were done; next came the furniture. For the cupboard, Zhenguan chose a scroll with the characters, "brimming with gold"; for the water urn and stove, "spring." The last remaining scroll read "A hundred sons and a thousand grandchildren." Daxin asked, "Where are you going to paste that one?"

"The back door."

"I don't think the back door is the best choice."

"Then where do you think we should paste it?"

"On the door of the Family Planning Center!"

Zhenguan laughed. "Oh yeah? I think we should paste it on your mouth!"

Zhenguan's brother returned home after all the Spring Festival scrolls had been put up. Zhenguan asked, "What took you so long? And how is our teacher?"

Azhong said, "He's fine. He said he hasn't seen you for years, and that you should visit him when you have time!"

Daxin asked, "Wait a minute, you two aren't in the same grade; how could you have had the same teacher?"

"When I graduated Azhong was only in the fifth grade. So the same teacher that taught me also taught him," Zhenguan explained.

Azhong asked Zhenguan suddenly, "Hey, sis, do you remember the first time I delivered your lunchbox to you?"

"Of course!"

She had been in the fifth grade and he in the third. He'd delivered her lunchbox but did not know whether he should leave it on the windowsill or walk directly into the classroom. The entire class was busy taking an examination at the time, and Zhenguan was working on a math equation.

Azhong laughed. "The teacher was saying that I made quite an impression on him, because I walked in and put the lunchbox on your table and called out 'Sister!' You were sitting in the first row then. The teacher said he was surprised to see me walk out of the room totally at ease. He was a strict person, and all the students in the school feared him."

Azhong's story reminded Zhenguan of another episode. When Azhong graduated from kindergarten, the five graduating classes took a group photo. Azhong spent a long time trying to find himself standing amid two, three hundred people. After finally identifying himself in the crowd, he made a mark above his head in the picture for future reference.

Zhenguan asked her brother, "When you delivered my lunchbox, weren't you aware that you could leave it on the windowsill? Or were you afraid that it would get lost?"

"I saw stacks of lunchboxes on the windowsill, and I was worried that one more would topple all the others. I was also worried about you not being able to find it among all those other lunchboxes."

At that moment, Yinan and Yinding walked into the room. Yinan was quite tall and bulky—six feet four, with a back as strong as a tiger's and a waist as thick as a bear's. People could always identify him immediately because he looked exactly like his father.

"Ah, Daxin, you're still here, huh? Haven't you noticed Zhenguan's expression?"

Zhenguan looked at Daxin and asked Yinan, "What do you mean?"

Yinan didn't say anything. Instead, he put on a grim and droopy face. Then he laughed. "You look like you want us out of here! Yinding, am I right? We saw that expression on your face the moment we came in!"

Yinding was not as hefty as his father or brother. He looked more like his mother, especially in his facial features. Nevertheless, he had inherited his father's height. Yinding winced and said with a laugh, "I'd better keep my mouth shut; otherwise Zhenguan will give me a lashing!"

Smiling, Zhenguan replied, "Come on, I'm not that mean! You guys are vilifying me. What Grandma said is true: narrow alleys breed internal feuds . . . it's easy to tease people who are close to you."

Yinan's hand flew to his forehead in mock horror. "Oh my gosh, what an accusation! Yinding, aren't you going to call for help? Get Yinchan to bail us out!"

Yinding laughed. "Are you kidding? She's Zhenguan's closest ally. She won't help us at all!"

"Daxin, do you know why Zhenguan had that look in her eyes?" Yinan asked. "Because she has x-ray vision, and she could tell that we were coming to take her visitor away from her. We've been asked to fetch you home for New Year's Eve dinner. Now we're really going to be on her bad side. When I said she wanted to see someone leave, I was talking about us, not you!"

Daxin said, "Does it matter where I stay for dinner? I've said yes to Auntie already, how can I go back on my word?"

"You mean Zhenguan's mother? That's okay, I'll explain to her—"

Zhenguan's mother walked in before Yinan had finished his sentence. She asked, "What are you going to explain to me? You're not here to take our visitor away from us, are you?"

"Actually, that's exactly what we have in mind!"

"I'm afraid I can't allow that: I've already prepared his meal."

The two brothers finally had to go home without Daxin, failed in their mission. Zhenguan and the others sat down with her mother and second aunt. During dinner, everyone tried hard not to mention their cousin Huian's name. He had left for the United States two months ago to pursue graduate studies, and since then, Zhenguan's impression of him had grown quite negative. Seeing her aunt alone like this made her resent his decision to leave. After dinner, they all went back to the living room. Zhenguan stayed behind to help clear the dishes. She had just moved a stack of bowls to the kitchen sink and was rolling her sleeves up when Yinchan came in.

"Are you full?" Zhenguan asked her.

"I was, but I think that I'm already hungry again! How much longer do I have to wait for you?"

Zhenguan was washing the bowl that Daxin had just used, and as she swirled it under the water, she asked, "Why are you waiting for me?"

Yinchan flipped a page in her hand and said, "Because of this! Last year you won a hundred dollars. Today, I'm going to get it back, plus interest!"

"Flipping pages" was a game that they used to play as children. During Chinese New Year, the grown-ups would give out red envelopes of money to the children, and the girls would each extract five dollars in small bills. They would then insert the bills into the pages of a book at random and take turns flipping through it. Whoever flipped to a page with money got to keep it.

Zhenguan laughed. "So, you need a place to put your money, eh? Why didn't you just say so? You can deposit it with me or donate it to the family treasury."

Yinchan laughed too. "We don't know who the winners and losers are yet, so you can save your sermon for later. How about fifty dollars each? I'll go get the change!"

"Wait, wait, wait!" Zhenguan protested. "Don't you see all these dishes? We can play the game, but first help me out here."

Later the two girls were walking out to the living room when First Uncle came in with Ruriko.

"Uncle, Aunt!"

"Brother, sister-in-law!"

Everyone present could address the visitors directly as relatives except Daxin. So he just chimed in, "Uncle and Aunt!"

First Uncle looked at Zhenguan's mother and aunt, saying, "I thought you would be going home for dinner tonight, but since you didn't show up, I decided to come visit you with Ruriko. I'm excited because it has been so many years since I celebrated the new year at home."

Her mother and aunt agreed.

First Uncle took out several red envelopes from his pocket and handed them to Aunt Ruriko for distribution. Yinchan had already received her red envelope, but there was one each for Zhenguan, her two brothers, and Daxin as well. When Ruriko handed red envelopes to Zhenguan's mother and aunt, the two sisters laughed. "For us? We're too old to receive red envelopes!" Ruriko wouldn't take no for an answer, though, and stuffed one into each of their hands. She said, "Red envelopes are for children and adults alike. The Japanese say that one should never refuse the good will of others."

First Uncle again reached into his pockets, and out came a set of dice. He summoned Azhong, saying, "Why don't you place your bets and see if you can win all the money in my pocket! Who's going to get a bowl to throw the dice in?"

Zhenguan went to the kitchen to fetch a big bowl, and everyone gathered around the table, trying their luck. New Year's Eve was a time for family reunions. For an eighteen-year-old boy like Zhenguan's brother, who commuted to school every day, reunions were commonplace; but for her uncle, who had experienced war, separation, and thirty years away from home, the opportunity to sit at the same table with all of his family was a great blessing indeed.

As they were gambling, Zhenguan noticed that First Uncle's

hollering and yelps resembled those of a young teenage boy. Daxin and Azhong were on one team, and Zhenguan paired up with Yinchan. The girls won two rounds in a row.

Yinchan asked, "Who invented dice?"

"I'm not sure. Maybe it was Han Xin, the Han dynasty military general. He invented all kinds of gambling games to keep his soldiers entertained."

Daxin chimed in with a grin, "Han Xin did invent many gambling games, but not this one. It was Cao Zhi, a general from the Period of the Three Kingdoms, who invented dice."

Just then, Yincheng and Yinan entered the room; they had come to invite Zhenguan's mother and aunt to join Grandma in her room for a game of cards.

"Ruriko, why don't you join your sisters-in-law," First Uncle proposed. "Mother likes company!"

Once the three women had left, Zhenguan and Yinchan also got up from the table to start a game of page-flipping, giving their seats to Yinan and his brother. They had finished two rounds when Yincheng and Daxin came to join them.

"Wow, Daxin, Zhenguan must have prayed to the goddess of wealth. She's up to her nose in money! I think we should just watch."

Zhenguan laughed. "Yeah, you'd better not risk it. I have a manual by Han Xin here!"

And they resumed the game.

"Do you want to hear some of Zhenguan's childhood stories?" Yincheng asked Daxin.

"Sure!"

"When she was small, little Uncle fed her—oh, wait, you know about the seven fishballs already, let me tell you something else. . . ."

Zhenguan could see a glimmer of red from a ten-dollar bill. Her hand was in midair, ready to flip the page. She said to Yincheng, "Aren't your lips sore from talking so much?"

But Yinchan laughed. "No, do tell us more!"

"Don't get carried away, you're in the story that I'm going to tell too!"

This attracted everyone's attention. Yincheng continued, "When Zhenguan was five, she saw someone carrying a baby on her back. So when she came home, she found a pillow and asked Third Aunt to tie it onto her back—"

Zhenguan stood up to stop Yincheng from continuing, but he had already moved out of her way.

"—Yinchan then started to imitate Zhenguan, and for a while the house was filled with little girls carrying pillows on their backs, pretending to be mothers with little babies—"

Yinchan was already pounding Yincheng with her fists. Zhenguan cheered Yinchan on, "Get him, Yinchan, get him!" Daxin was watching the whole scene. Zhenguan put her shoes on and got ready to run after Yincheng; but first, she looked back at Daxin, only to find him laughing so hard that he was doubled over, his eyebrows knitted together.

III

Daxin returned to Taipei on the second day of the first lunar month. Zhenguan stayed at home until the ninth. On the night of the seventh, she was sitting in her grandmother's room. It was already ten o'clock, but the old lady wasn't sleepy at all.

"Grandma, aren't you tired?" Zhenguan asked.

Grandma looked at Zhenguan and Yinchan and said, "You'll

be leaving in a day; I want to sit here and talk with you a bit more." She held their hands to her face as she spoke. Zhenguan caressed her grandmother's weathered cheeks and asked, "Grandma, are you hungry?"

Before Grandma could answer, Yinchan nudged her, saying, "Of course, why don't you go to the kitchen to fix something? I think there's some fried flour batter in the cupboard."

Grandma said, "Actually, I am a bit hungry; let's snack on some fried flour paste!"

Zhenguan went to the kitchen and soon returned with three bowls, one in each hand and the third balanced between her two forearms. As they sat down to eat, Yinchan said, "Grandma, do tell a story!"

Grandma laughed. "Well, I guess we can't go to sleep right after eating, so I'll tell you a short story. . . . Fan Lihua of Cold River was betrothed to the Yang family when she was a little girl. It was her father's decision to marry her to the son of his good friend. But when Lihua grew up she came to dread her fate because Yang Fan, her husband-to-be, had a face as black as coal and was ugly as ugly could be. When she saw Xue Dingshan on the battlefield, she said to herself: That's the kind of man that I'm going to marry. So in order to do so, she moved mountains and emptied seas. Xue Dingshan killed his father and brother for her sake and regretted marrying her three times over."

"What happened then?"

"Later, the emperor ordered him to marry her, and the general Cheng Yaojin brought them together. When she led the army to fight in the west, she came across Yang Fan, her former husband-to-be, at the White Tiger Pass. Fan Lihua was armed with all sorts of magical instruments and eighteen different kung fu moves. She cut off Yang Fan's head, and when it fell to the ground, a drop of his blood landed on her. Soon after, the woman warrior gave birth to a black-faced baby in the barracks. His name was Xue Gang."

"Was he the one who wreaked havoc on the Lantern Festival?"

"Yes, Xue Gang was the reincarnation of Yang Fan, who had returned to seek revenge. When Xue Gang grew up he got into a brawl on the eve of the Lantern Festival and killed the emperor. Empress Wu ordered everyone in the Xue family killed, all three hundred of them."

The night was cold and chilly. What was Daxin doing in Taipei? Was he reading or engraving chops? On the day he left, he told Zhenguan that he was going to engrave a chop for her. What a pity that Daxin wasn't here to hear Grandma's story about karma. . . .

Every household was busy the next day with preparations for the ritual celebration of the Jade Emperor's birthday. Zhenguan didn't go back home until late at night, but she would have stayed at Grandma's even longer if she hadn't had to leave for Taipei early in the morning.

When the clock struck twelve, marking the new day, the celebrations in honor of the Jade Emperor's birthday began. Zhenguan heard the distant popping of firecrackers, but in her dreams, they sounded like cannonballs, going off one at a time, not like the rapid fire of machine guns. For her, tonight was a solemn occasion, not a frivolous one. Half awake, she heard her mother washing up and conducting a ritual in the main hall. Soon her brother joined in.

Zhenguan knew that Azhong had gotten up to help Mother light the firecrackers. Mother was timid and had to cover her ears when they went off. When Father was alive, he used to light the firecrackers, but now the duty had been passed on to Azhong, the man of the household. Did Daxin wake up at midnight on the Jade Emperor's birthday to help his mother with the firecrackers?

Zhenguan thought: ten, twenty years from now, she would be running a household, and like her grandmother and mother, she planned to observe the rituals and customs that accompanied all the seasons and the days of the year. She would pay respect to their ancestors and honor the past. Chinese proverbs say that though one's ancestors are far away, one must honor them sincerely. Everyone must read the classics, no matter what. . . .

Someday she would wake up in the middle of the night to pay homage to the sky and the earth and the gods. And she would be nervous about lighting the firecrackers. How she hoped that there would be someone like Daxin to help her send her wishes to the Jade Emperor on his heavenly throne!

fifteen

1

The seventh day of the seventh moon of 1972 fell on August 15. Zhenguan was busy at the office that morning when the phone rang. Yinchan answered, muttered a quick greeting, then handed the receiver to Zhenguan.

"Hello?"

"Zhenguan, this is Daxin."

"Oh, hello!"

"I got home yesterday evening. What are you doing after work?"

"Why do you ask?"

"Can I visit you tonight?"

"Isn't there a typhoon coming our way?"

"Yeah, my mother said I brought the typhoon back with me," Daxin said, and they both laughed. "But weather permitting, I'll pick you up at seven-thirty sharp."

Zhenguan hung up the phone and spent the rest of the day looking out the window, hoping that the wind and rain wouldn't pick up. When they got home, the two girls had dinner. Afterward, Zhenguan took a shower, and by the time she had finished, Yinchan had already made herself scarce. Actually, there was no reason for her to disappear, for Zhenguan and Daxin had nothing to hide, and they certainly didn't mind the company.

Zhenguan was comfortable with the status quo: still waters run deep, she thought. Her relationship with Daxin might not match the intensity of his relationship with Liao Qinger, but then those two young lovers had spent every day together, and theirs was a kind of puppy love, an infatuation based as much on curiosity as it was on attraction. Furthermore, Zhenguan didn't want to rush into a relationship with someone with Daxin's romantic history. She wanted to distinguish herself from Liao Qinger; and she wanted him to genuinely sense the difference before they became more intimate.

Daxin knew how Zhenguan felt, but he also wanted her to understand: "My relationship with you now is different from my relationship with her; ours is based on an affinity of mind and spirit."

Both were thinking along the same lines, and much was left unsaid. But Daxin also had his own reasons for holding back. For one thing, he didn't have a penny to his name. Although his family was well off, he believed that he should be able to support himself rather than depend on his inheritance. He was a man of ambition, with plans to pursue his studies abroad. Zhenguan had come unexpectedly into his life. Now he had so many important decisions to face all at once.

Zhenguan had started to regret not going to college. If she

had, then she might be able to study abroad as well. Daxin was a proud man, someone who would not get married until he had made something of himself. He could not promise her anything now, because who knew what might happen in four years' time? And yet, not committing to something soon would make it appear as though he lacked sincerity. Zhenguan knew him well, and it was against his nature to be evasive. Given his personality, there was no way that he would leave a wife and children at home to go abroad on his own. But the only alternative appeared to be a five-year-long courtship! It's not too late for men to get married at thirty, but at twenty-eight going on twenty-nine, Zhenguan would be an old maid.

The world is full of uncertainty, and Daxin didn't want Zhenguan to live in anxiety, waiting for him. Zhenguan understood Daxin's hesitation; but she also knew that, ultimately, a romantic relationship cannot withstand the test of too many burdens and obstacles. After much deliberation, Zhenguan came to a conclusion: If she was worthy, then Daxin would always return to her, no matter how much time and space might separate them, even if he had to come back crawling. He had already returned tonight despite a raging storm. Their meeting would be like the reunion of the spinner-girl and the cow herder across the Milky Way: Daxin was born on the celestial seventh day of the seventh lunar month; it also happened to be the day that Zhenguan and Daxin first met.

When the doorbell rang, Zhenguan's heart fluttered. She hadn't seen Daxin for six whole months. She rushed to the door, not even pausing to check herself in the mirror, but she did straighten her skirt quickly. There he was, radiant. How she had missed the sight of his friendly face!

"Come in," she said. But Daxin did not move. He smiled. "Isn't Yinchan here to greet me too?"

"Sorry, she's gone out," Zhenguan said, feigning a serious expression. "But I'll fetch you a chair if you like, and you can wait here all night until she comes home."

Zhenguan turned around, and Daxin invited himself in. The two sat down in the living room. Daxin looked out the window and said, "We used to eat right across from here. So much has changed."

Placing a cup of tea in front of Daxin, Zhenguan said, "If you want to get sentimental, there are plenty of other reasons!"

"Such as . . . ?"

Zhenguan faced him, twisting her fingers together nervously. "You should know!"

Daxin grinned. "Yeah, I was just thinking, why didn't you move to Taipei sooner? If you had been living here before . . ."

"What?"

"I would have come to visit you every day!"

They talked for some time, and then Daxin suggested that they take a stroll around the campus. Zhenguan went into her room and changed into a red and white gingham dress, all the while thinking how much she appreciated Daxin's candor. Remembering that it was raining, she grabbed an umbrella before the two of them stepped outside. The campus was right across the street, and Zhenguan had visited with Yinchan several times when they went to see Azhong. But it felt nothing like seeing it now, with Daxin by her side!

A steady flow of people streamed in and out of the campus gates. "Even though I've already graduated, I feel as if I never left the place," Daxin said. "I keep coming back here in my dreams!"

"The campus is full of memories for you, so you cannot tear your soul away from it. My grandmother says that one's soul can always find its own way. When people fall asleep, their souls go to places that they like and wander about. They don't return until it is time to wake up."

Daxin laughed. "Ah, so I have graduated in person but not in soul!"

When the two passed by the large school bell, Daxin said, "I've always wanted to ring that bell just once."

"You could throw a stone at it to make it ring!"

"That wouldn't be—proper!"

As they walked down the avenue lined with palm trees, Daxin stopped abruptly. "Look at those trees!" he exclaimed. "I came during the day and saw gardeners perched on ladders, trimming the leaves. I envied those gardeners, who can stay on campus all their lives, while we students have to leave after four years."

The nipping typhoon gusts were like tiny knives, scraping the skin, making the blood rush to the surface. In this kind of weather one felt fresh and cool and almost transparent. The two arrived at the sports ground and watched the track team jogging by. "Do you hear them singing?" Daxin asked. "If I were younger, I would sing along with them!"

Zhenguan laughed. "If you were younger? You're not exactly old now!" Daxin had already started to hum a tune.

Zhenguan said, "I was going to give you an album, thinking that you might be desperate for music, stranded on that lonely island."

"Good! I only brought one album with me, and I listen to it all the time."

And then, simultaneously:

"Which album were you going to send me?"

"Which album did you take with you?"

And the answer to both questions was like rain pattering on the windowpane, or wind flapping one's clothing: "Taiwanese folk melodies from the past."

A long pause followed, and neither of them spoke. Joggers kept running past. As they walked on quietly, Zhenguan felt the rain falling again. In typhoon weather, the rain comes and goes. She put her umbrella up; Daxin was having trouble opening his, a black automatic that was not cooperating. It started to rain harder, but the umbrella in Daxin's hand remained tightly folded.

Zhenguan quietly held her umbrella over his head. It was too small for both of them, exposing her right shoulder and his left to the rain. Though they had known each other for many years, they had never stood so close together before.

Under the street lamp, Zhenguan studied Daxin's face. His brows were furrowed as he tried to fix his umbrella. She suddenly remembered several lines from a book that he'd sent her recently. On the last page he had written a few words from the *Book of Rites*: "One should respect one's partner first before becoming intimate." And he added his own footnote: "True courtesy is to love her intimately after a solemn, respectful, and open wedding ceremony."

She didn't think that Daxin had written in the book simply because he needed a place to jot down a few thoughts. Zhenguan believed that from this night on, life would never be the same for either of them!

II

The next day the typhoon was still raging, and it turned out to be a very windy day. Yinchan looked out the window and said, "With this kind of weather, we might have the day off!"

When Zhenguan returned the night before at around ten o'clock, Yinchan had already gone to bed. Naturally Zhenguan asked her first thing in the morning, "Where were you last night? With the typhoon and all!"

"I was out with Cheng Kaiyuan. He's a nice guy, but he keeps appearing at the wrong moment!"

"When did he arrive? How come I had no idea when he came in?"

"You were in the bathroom. I lied to him, saying that you were out with a friend. He was going to sit for a while, so I had to pretend that I had a headache to make him go back to his clinic for some medicine. See, this is what he gave me." Yinchan showed Zhenguan some packets of medicine wrapped in green paper before throwing them into the wastebasket. She continued, "He's really nice; but the world works in strange ways! I just don't see the two of you together."

Zhenguan replied, "The situation isn't as complicated as you think. He's a friend of First Uncle and Aunt, so he's our friend as well. It is natural for friends to come and visit once in a while, so please don't make a big deal out of nothing!"

"If that's the case, then don't use me to fend him off the next time he comes!"

"We have nothing in common. I smile when he speaks to me, but only to spare him any embarrassment."

Her Japanese aunt seemed to have observed that something special was going on between her and Daxin over Chinese New

Year. Since then, Zhenguan had stopped running into Cheng Kaiyuan all the time. Nevertheless, the young doctor still dropped in occasionally, and he even said to Zhenguan once, "I am thirty years old already. I have been to many places and met many people, but of all the girls that I've met, none are like you."

Yinchan asked, "I know that you are open-minded about this; but what about him? Do you know what he's thinking?"

"He is an honest and upright person. We have nothing to worry about."

Zhenguan got dressed after breakfast, but Yinchan hadn't budged an inch. "You're still here?" she asked, surprised. "We're going to be late!"

Yinchan was reading the paper with one leg tucked under the other. "I'm sure we don't have to work today," she said, "but let me call First Uncle just to check."

But then Yinchan saw the look on Zhenguan's face and immediately changed her mind. "Okay, okay, I'll go get dressed. I'll be ready in three minutes."

Zhenguan's eyes said it all. Other people might get the day off because of a typhoon, but we're family and cannot just sit at home idly. Since we'll only worry ourselves anyway, we might as well go to the office and find out if the files are soaked in water. . . .

It was quite an ordeal for the girls to get to work. They had to stand in the wind and rain for almost half an hour to hail a cab because none of the city buses were running, and they were almost hit by a flying street sign. Then their taxi drove through large puddles, and when they alighted, a passing vehicle splattered mud all over Yinchan's skirt.

The power was out, and there was no electricity from the

first floor to the third at the office. Zhenguan climbed up and down the stairs but could not find her uncle. She was told that he had gone to the business department to check on damages. Despite everything, the phone calls kept coming in. Only two of the five operators had made it to work, so Zhenguan and Yinchan had to help out. At noon, Aunt Ruriko came into the office with homemade sushi; she also had to make an important international call of her own. Chaos finally gave way to calm at around three o'clock in the afternoon, and everyone pitched in to clean up the office before going home for the day.

Zhenguan was persuaded by Aunt Ruriko to go to her uncle's for dinner, but Yinchan declined, saying, "I have to go home. I'm filthy all over, and I desperately need a shower and change of clothes."

Aunt Ruriko said, "You can shower at our place!"

"Yes, but a shower is not a shower without a clean change of clothes; and your clothes won't fit me!"

The two girls convinced their aunt that they would come for dinner the next day after work. Their Japanese aunt finally let them go home, where Yinchan collapsed into bed the minute she took off her sandals. Zhenguan washed her face, and the two girls fell asleep without bothering even to change or to eat.

A few hours later, Zhenguan woke up suddenly from a dream, feeling like a zombie. Some unknown force drew her toward the door in a daze. There she stopped, still suspended in a state of stupor and waking sleep. The door was the color of unpolished wood because the landlord had not bothered to paint it. Zhenguan stared at it like a drunkard trying to focus on something; and strangely enough, the copper-plated door knob started to turn slowly. She grabbed it and flung the door open.

And what she saw was enough to shock a drunkard into sobriety. There, standing before her, was Daxin!

"Oh! It's you!"

Both were rendered momentarily speechless.

"You—"

Zhenguan laughed. "Why didn't you ring the doorbell?"

"I was just about to when you opened the door for me!"

Zhenguan realized at this moment that what her grandmother said was true! One's soul can defy the limitations of space and time. Just before a momentous occasion, one's soul sends out a precursor to meet the soul of the intimate other, knocking on the door to her heart. . . . Just now she had been deep in slumber, but his soul had flown before him to awaken her; his soul, like a headstrong child, was determined to fly where it wished, and it had found its way to hers. Were Zhenguan and Daxin really so intimate in mind and spirit? She had dreamed of his military post and his home in Taipei without actually visiting either place. But her soul did not know its way and had to make many detours to locate him.

"You . . . you look different! What's going on?"

"I just got up a minute ago, and I am still disoriented. I don't even know how I came to open the door!"

Daxin looked at his wristwatch. "It's seven-thirty; you haven't eaten yet, have you? Let's go, I'll treat you to a glass of lemonade."

"Well, I have to take a shower first."

"Okay, I'll just stand here and bask in the moonlight."

There was a distance of about ten feet between the bathroom and the courtyard. Zhenguan fetched her change of clothes and quickly ducked into the bathroom, apologizing. "Sorry to leave you standing out here; Yinchan is still sleeping inside. I'll be ready in no time at all."

When Zhenguan came out of the bathroom ten minutes later, Daxin was standing there expectantly. She had changed into a purple dress with white polka dots. Walking toward Daxin, she smiled. "Have I kept you waiting for long?"

"Yes!"

"How can I make it up to you?"

"You will have to eat three bowls of rice for dinner as punishment!"

As they left the house, Daxin told her not to skip meals and to eat more. "Skipping meals is very bad for your stomach. There are so many restaurants nearby, you can eat regularly at one of them!" Walking beside Daxin, Zhenguan's heart brimmed with contentment. She did not feel that Daxin was nagging her. She knew that he had the best intentions.

After dinner, the two headed for the snack shop a block away, walking briskly. "You don't have a record player where you live, do you?" Daxin asked. "Why don't you ask Azhong to put one together for you? It should be a piece of cake for an electrical engineering student! Also, there are a lot of concerts at the student activity center. You girls should check them out when you have time."

Since when had Daxin become so talkative? Zhenguan followed him to a table on the second floor of the snack shop. She realized then: this must be what happens to people when they begin to feel intimate with each other. Walking behind Daxin and admiring his broad shoulders and strong back, Zhenguan suddenly felt as if she could depend on him completely. He was wearing dark blue trousers and a green shirt, a combination that she couldn't decide whether she quite liked or not. Daxin clearly had little patience for shopping, least of all for clothes.

The two of them sat facing each other, sipping fruit juice.

Daxin opened the large manila envelope that he had been carrying and took out two binders, one large and one small. He laid them both squarely before her.

"What is this?"

"See for yourself!"

Zhenguan opened the binders to find that they were filled with printings of chops and seals that he had engraved himself.

"I started engraving chops and seals when I was in high school; they are all in this big binder. The smaller one is a graduation souvenir. It contains my engravings of poetry, and everyone in my graduating class has a copy. What do you think?"

Zhenguan nodded slowly as she flipped through the pages. Then she suddenly stopped and closed the binder.

"What's the matter?" Daxin asked.

Zhenguan looked up at him with mixed feelings of happiness and sorrow. "I cannot look anymore."

"Why?"

"Because if I do, I will not want to return the binder to you."

Daxin seemed very pleased as he said, "Well, good, because I was going to give it to you as a gift!"

Zhenguan's heart stopped beating for a moment and the blood rushed to her head. She was quiet, and then asked, "But what about yourself? If you give it to me—"

"I have my own copy."

Zhenguan lowered her eyes and said softly, "It's wonderful. How can I thank you?"

"There's no way to thank me, so you might as well not try at all!" Daxin smiled. He looked at her fixedly, and their gazes locked for several seconds. In that brief moment, Zhenguan came to understand why poets exalt and immortalize everlasting love. Even when she wasn't looking at Daxin, his image always filled her mind: his nose was so firm, his eyes like two pools of crystal-clear water.

The sky cannot do without the sun and the moon. Fortune-tellers say that the eyes are the sun and the moon of the face, and that both must be bright. Eyes that lack luster or eyes that flicker indicate personality flaws. A person with evil intentions will be betrayed by his eyes. The gaze of an upright person, on the other hand, will be clear and unclouded, bright but not dazzling. And his mouth, yes, his mouth will be very big indeed. A mouthful of food for him would be three for others. Zhenguan smiled at this thought. When she got home she was going to draw a caricature of a boy with a very big mouth and send it to Daxin in Penghu.

"What are you thinking about?"

"I can't tell you!"

"A gentleman or a lady has nothing to hide. I know what you're thinking about because your eyes reveal all; they're sparkling clear!"

"Uh-oh!" Zhenguan covered her eyes and laughed. "I'd better hide them from you then."

But Daxin chuckled. "Of course, I can still see your nose and your mouth. You have such a tiny mouth; how did you ever manage to swallow seven fishballs?"

Zhenguan removed her hands from her eyes. "Swallowing seven fishballs is nothing!" She winked at him. "Some people can stuff a whole chicken into their mouths!"

"Oh? Are there really people with mouths that big?" Daxin asked. He knew that Zhenguan was talking about him, and he could not help but smile. "Have you been to the National Palace Museum before?"

"No, not yet."

"There's an exhibition on ancient jade artifacts this month that I've been wanting to see. Would you like to go too?"

"Of course, I'd love to! After all, a gentleman resembles jade in character!"

Daxin smiled. "Then I'll pick you up on Sunday morning; what time do you get up?"

"Five o'clock."

"Five?" Daxin was surprised. "The roosters haven't even started to crow yet at that time of day. The roosters of Taipei get up later in the morning, just like its people."

"No, I don't really get up that early, I was just kidding—"

"I knew it!" Daxin said, laughing.

Zhenguan had a bunch of keys in her hands—keys to the front door, her room, the office, the filing cabinets. She playfully flung them all at the back of Daxin's hand. Daxin withdrew his hand and pretended to be hurt. But when he looked at Zhenguan's face, he broke into a broad grin.

III

Sunday, August 20. It was eight o'clock in the morning, and Zhenguan was almost ready to go, except that she hadn't gotten dressed yet. She sat on her bed, so lost in thought that she didn't even hear Daxin knocking at the door. The bus ride from Daxin's house in the West District to where she lived took about twenty minutes, she calculated. And she had to figure in some time waiting at the bus stop. When must Daxin have gotten up? Would he be late? The buses didn't always run on schedule because the drivers tried to pick up as many passengers as possible.

Zhenguan jumped up with a start when Daxin knocked on her door for the second time. She poked her head out, saying, "Oh, you're early!"

"And I even walked around the block once before coming up!"

"Did you run into Yinchan?"

"Yes, she let me in."

"Please take a seat, I'll be ready in a minute."

Ten minutes later, when Zhenguan appeared before Daxin, she was a vision in white: white dress, white socks, white shoes. Aunt Ruriko had given Zhenguan the white dress and six pairs of stockings when she came back from Japan last month. Zhenguan was wearing the dress for the first time today, for Daxin. A jade pendant hung from her neck: it was the carving of the golden boy and jade girl from Grandma.

And from his shining eyes she detected a sheen, like the glow of a fireplace when new firewood has just been added.

"I hardly recognized you," said Daxin, shy and somewhat timid.

"What do you mean?" Zhenguan asked.

Daxin paused for a moment before responding, "Well, don't you sometimes feel as if you're meeting life straight on for the first time?"

Zhenguan was quiet, and Daxin continued, "When confronted with life, sometimes I just become bewildered and can't tell head from tail!"

Not knowing whether to feel embarrassed or overjoyed, Zhenguan could only pretend to be looking for Yinchan. Where was she? Was she in the bathroom, kitchen, or bedroom? She was nowhere to be found.

"When did you last see Yinchan?"

"Just a few minutes ago."

So she must have left the apartment already. Zhenguan and Daxin locked up and walked out onto the street to catch the bus. They crossed at the crosswalk and stopped at The Ph.D. stationery store so Daxin could buy a pen.

When he came out, Zhenguan asked, "Did the saleslady still recognize you?"

"Which one?"

"You used to buy a lot of rubber erasers from her, and she thought—"

"Oh," Daxin chuckled. "She probably doesn't work there anymore. I only recognized the store manager."

As he put away the pen, Zhenguan saw several pieces of folded paper in his jacket pocket. Wherever they went, he always carried pen and paper with him, often writing things down by way of explanation, and whenever Zhenguan wrote something, he would always fold the paper carefully and tuck it away in his pocket.

When they got to the bus station, Daxin said he would purchase the tickets.

"Wait—" Zhenguan stopped him and took out Azhong's student bus pass. "You two look alike, why don't you use Azhong's bus pass?"

Daxin said solemnly, "It's okay to cheat a little when you're a student. But I am a soldier serving my country now, and I can't possibly . . ."

Zhenguan, mortified, wished that the earth would open up and swallow her whole. Why had she spoken without thinking first? Her face was still red when Daxin returned with the bus tickets. She ventured timidly, "Daxin, I am so sorry, I shouldn't have—"

Daxin laughed. "Actually, I could just as well have used my sister's bus pass for you! Don't worry about it."

They boarded an old, creaky bus. During the bumpy ride, Zhenguan occasionally glanced at Daxin's profile. He was wearing a white shirt and checkered trousers that day. He loomed large before her, as if she didn't have eyes for anything else.

Seated across from them was a woman carrying books in her arms. She was resting, with her eyes closed. Daxin whispered into Zhenguan's ear, "She is a professor in my department. Thank goodness she hasn't seen me."

"Of course she hasn't, her eyes are closed! Why are you afraid of your teachers?"

"I can't help it, she preaches to us whenever she can. So we always try to hide when we see her."

Zhenguan giggled, and the woman suddenly opened her eyes. Zhenguan didn't dare meet her gaze, so she looked down. When she peeked at Daxin, she found him perfectly composed and at ease. "Did she see you?" she asked in a little voice.

"No, I don't think so."

The bus swung around the South Gate, and it was time for them to get off. Daxin rang the bell, and the two alighted at the front of the bus.

"Whew, that was a close call!"

Laughing, they crossed the railway tracks and hailed another bus on Chunghua Road. Zhenguan boarded first, and Daxin followed. He had a colored guidebook with him and pointed out to her the different sights along the way. "Let me introduce Taipei to you," he said. "This is the circular intersection, these are the old houses on Yenping North Road, and this is Keelung River. . . ."

Zhenguan helped him turn the pages. Their fingers sometimes touched, and they would both quickly withdraw their hands.

"Do you like Taipei so far?" Daxin asked.

"It's too early to tell. . . ."

Daxin was quiet for a moment and then asked, "Thirty years from now, when you write about Taipei, what will you write?"

Zhenguan didn't say anything. She thought: Don't you know, Daxin? Do you even have to ask? I will remember this moment in time forever and ever. And it suddenly occurred to her: it wasn't that he didn't know how she was feeling; perhaps he was really asking himself, as if looking at his own reflection in the water.

"So you're not going to say anything?" he said.

"No, a hundred times, no!"

The bus turned a corner and the National Palace Museum appeared before them.

"Do you see it?" Daxin asked. "What does it remind you of?"

"The Forbidden City!"

When they got off the bus, Daxin held Zhenguan's beaded purse with gold threads for her. He looked at it closely and remarked, "You girls always have all these props. This is very pretty, though; where did you buy it?"

Opening her pink parasol with embroidered flowers, Zhenguan replied, "I didn't buy it anywhere. I crocheted it myself, bead by bead, thread by thread. It took me two months to make."

They climbed up the stairs. Daxin did not help Zhenguan with her parasol, and she wiped the perspiration off her forehead. When they arrived at the entrance, Daxin went to buy the admission tickets and pointed out to her, "Look, there's a sign there that says no cameras and umbrellas!"

Zhenguan leaned forward to read the inscription on the copper sign. Before she knew it, Daxin had grabbed her parasol and slipped through the entrance; by the time she could react, he was already standing inside, smiling at her. He was so quick! She did not miss the thoughtfulness in this small act: he spared her from asking him directly to help her with the parasol.

The museum housed five thousand years of Chinese history, artifacts that spanned the centuries; from the reign of the Yellow Emperor through the different dynasties to the present day, from times of peace and prosperity to times of chaos and hardship, all were brought together under one roof. Zhenguan scrutinized the displays in every cabinet and on every shelf. With the parasol tucked under his arm, Daxin took notes and made sketches in his notebook.

"Do you see that?" he said. "There's a carp jumping through the dragon gate. Its upper body has already transformed into a dragon, but its lower half is still the tail of a fish."

"Yeah, the tail is still flipping and flapping."

"And that's a jade cabbage!"

"How do you suppose the craftsman came up with such an idea?"

"And this jade carving resembles a slab of fatty meat. Doesn't it make your mouth water?"

"No, I never touch fatty meat!"

After looking at the crystal balls, they arrived at the glass cabinet where an instrument known as the *ruyi,* meaning "as you wish," was displayed. Daxin asked Zhenguan, "Pop quiz: What is that for?"

"It's a staff that government officials would carry in their hands when attending assemblies presided over by the emperor!" Zhenguan replied with confidence.

"No." Daxin grinned. "The ruyi is a back-scratcher!"

Zhenguan exclaimed, "You must be kidding; that's too far-fetched! Are you trying to fool me?"

"Why would I lie?" Daxin smiled. "Just look at it; isn't its function apparent?"

Zhenguan thought it made sense, but she still harbored some suspicion. "It's difficult for me to imagine," she said. "Meeting the emperor is a serious matter, but you tell me that it is used for back-scratching!"

"Back-scratching is also a serious matter."

Daxin failed to convince her, so Zhenguan said, "Okay, let's allow the matter to rest. I'll do some research on it!"

They headed out of the museum at one o'clock in the afternoon. "What did you think of your first visit?" Daxin asked as they both looked back.

Zhenguan said, "I used to feel a sense of affinity only with the Han Chinese, but now I believe that I am also closely related to the other ethnic groups that have reigned over China in the course of our civilization."

They had noodles for lunch nearby before boarding the bus for Taipei. On the bus, Daxin hummed one song after another; Zhenguan sat next to him and studied the right side of his face. His eyebrows were just the right shape, not too faint, and not too bushy. His eyes were clear and bright, flecked faintly with brown highlights. He was kind, handsome, intelligent, and steadfast; but these qualities alone did not sufficiently describe Daxin. Zhenguan was most impressed by his simplicity, despite the sophisticated environment that he had grown up in. He was always genuine and sincere. Zhenguan noted that he was wearing a simple shirt, his sleeves rolled up to reveal a peculiar watch on his wrist.

"Do you think it's ugly?" he asked, noticing that she was looking at it curiously.

"I guess you could say that!"

Daxin brought his hand to his forehead. "Oh no, not you too! It's the first thing I ever bought for myself, but all my sisters tell me that it's the ugliest watch that they've ever seen!"

"Actually, it's not that bad," she said quickly, smiling.

"That's all right," Daxin said. "Have you ever been to Zhinan Temple?"

"Yes, just at the beginning of this month Yinchan and I went there with Aunt Ruriko. She had never attended a vegetarian banquet hosted by a temple, so we took her there to experience one!"

"I went to Zhinan Temple with someone once to pray and offer incense."

Zhenguan didn't say anything for a moment. Then she asked, "Don't you know that relationships are wrecked if you go to the temple with your lover? How could you have taken her there? No wonder you split up!"

Daxin broke into a fit of laughter. "The woman I went to the temple with was my grandmother!"

"Oh, you—!" Zhenguan yelped and made boxing motions with her fists. Her face was red. Daxin smiled and said, "Okay, okay, no more joking."

They changed buses in the West District. It was three-fifteen by the time they arrived back in Zhenguan's neighborhood. "Are you tired?" Daxin asked. "Do you need a rest?"

"I'm all right."

"Let's go get some fruit! I won't be able to come out again at night. My plane leaves at eight o'clock in the morning, and I haven't even packed yet."

Zhenguan, numb, followed him into the snack shop. There wasn't much business on a Sunday afternoon. A noisy score of gongs and drums was playing on the radio, and the waitress, busy shaving ice, was humming a song:

At dusk
My lover will go out to sea
My heart aches
And black clouds cover my eyes
I want to say something
But the words catch in my throat
Love is a burden
Why is that so?
The ship is waiting
My lover is at the docks
Don't want to leave him
My eyes follow him. . . .

Zhenguan had finished her plate of watermelon by the time the song came to an end. Daxin, facing her, was pushing watermelon seeds around with his knife and fork.

"This was the worst-tasting watermelon that I've ever had; how was yours?"

"Not much better!"

"Okay, why don't we order two glasses of lemonade then?"

Neither spoke as they sipped their drinks. The lemonade passed through their straws and disappeared from their glasses bit by bit. Still, neither spoke.

Daxin finally broke the silence. "Have you ever thought about how engravers have to carve the mirror images of characters?"

"That is true indeed! Otherwise the print would be backward."

Daxin took out the paper and pen from his pocket and wrote the reflection of his name. "It's easy to engrave my name, and yours too," he said. He wrote Zhenguan's name backward as well. Looking at the six characters written side by side, Zhenguan felt as if someone had just squeezed her heart. Twenty-four years ago, in the south and in the north, two men had just become fathers. They named their newborns Zhenguan and Daxin. The two names were related: "Zhenguan" refers to the chastity of women, and "Daxin" to the fidelity of men. Both names stand for virtues that are constant and true.

The *Book of Rites* states that one must never change one's name after one's father passes away. At this moment, Zhenguan thought about the respect and gratitude she felt toward her father. He had not known Daxin's father, but now the two were meeting through their children, because Zhenguan had found a bosom friend in Daxin.

As Daxin folded the piece of paper and put it away in his pocket, Zhenguan quietly wiped away a tear from her eye with a corner of her handkerchief.

sixteen

1

Zhenguan:

I went to the airport early in the morning and, as usual, it was packed with people. Airports are always so crowded, you'd think that plane rides were free. Before I left, my grandmother asked me when I would been coming back. I said maybe next month, and that was enough to make her happy. Of course, if I were actually to return to Taipei so frequently, I might as well forward my paycheck directly to Far-Eastern Air Transit each month.

Breakfast was served on the plane, but since the acronym of the airline is FAT, many of the lady passengers decided not to eat the food.

All is well. The postman's here, so I'd better conclude this letter. Have you conducted any research on the function of the ruyi?

Daxin

At the end of the letter, he drew a bulky airplane that looked as if it were having difficulty staying afloat. The minute she finished reading the letter, Zhenguan picked up her pen to write back.

Daxin:

The following description is for your reference: the ruyi originated in India. Its tip often resembles a finger but sometimes takes the shape of a heart. It is usually made of bone or horn, bamboo or wood, jade or rock, copper or iron. It is three feet long and often bears inscriptions. In China, the ruyi is used either as a back-scratcher or as a staff that officials carry when meeting the emperor.

How's that? We had debated over the function of the ruyi without reaching a conclusion. Who's right now? I'll leave it up to you to decide, as I'd rather not be bothered with it.

All the best,
Zhenguan

P.S. Daxin, I have a sudden urge to leave this world for a while.

The last sentence seemed out of place. What Zhenguan really meant was: Now that you're not here, I have a sudden urge to leave everything behind so that I can go and visit you. She certainly didn't expect that this sentence would cause Daxin to send two letters in a row, both by express mail.

Zhenguan:
This morning I went digging for clams down at the beach, and we had fried clams for lunch. I just received your letter. I thought we shared a common trait: the more difficult the situation, the more reluctant we are to take a final bow and go into hiding. Why are you so pessimistic all of a sudden? Write back to me as soon as you can; a few short lines will do. I just want to know that you are all right.

As for the function of the ruyi, or "as you wish," the answer was just what I expected. I had a feeling that both of us were right. Isn't that great?

I anxiously await your reply.

Wishing you happiness,
Daxin

With no reply from Zhenguan, the second letter came two days later.

Zhenguan:
I have a very good book with me here. Do you want to read it? I'm sure you'd like it. I will lend it to you under one condition: you have to write back first!

Yesterday I watched the live broadcast of a baseball game. The Taipei team won the World Series for Little League Baseball. I was so proud, I wanted to walk down the street shouting: I am from Taipei!

I just received letters from two classmates studying in the United States. What a mysterious place! English must be like the language that people in northern and southern China were so eager to learn when the Northern Tribe took over China.

And the Chinese people living in the United States are a funny breed, for they have made an alien land their home. They are like the floating duckweed and grass that take root wherever their seeds land. . . . They seem to be torn between their native and adopted homelands. I cannot help but think: Did they have to leave in the first place?

There is a Test of English as a Foreign Language exam at the end of October. Maybe it doesn't matter whether I take it or not, though, because if I can find a good reason, I will decide not to study abroad!

Daxin

Upon receiving the letter, Zhenguan immediately replied:

Daxin:

How can you not take the test? Giving up this opportunity would mean more than simply wasting a few hundred dollars on the registration fee; you would also be forsaking the expectations of so many people.

Aunt Ruriko once said that we must not renounce the good will of others. Think about it: someone has written the exam for you, someone has prepared a place for you, someone has mailed the examination identification card to you, and a postman has delivered it to you. Many people have made it possible for you to take the test. How can you allow all that effort to go to waste?

Prepare for the exam and study hard; your country depends on you. For the time being, I will stop writing!

Good luck,
Zhenguan

At the end of the letter she had added: "I am reminded that

a gentleman possesses virtues like that of jade," but after some consideration she crossed it out. The words were still visible, though, so she got a pair of scissors and cut them out. This made a hole in the stationery, but she mailed it anyway. Zhenguan had planned to wait until the end of October to write to Daxin again, but another letter came from him four days later:

Zhenguan:
This morning as I lay in bed, my muses paid me a visit, and I came up with this couplet:

A year glides by before you know it
So if your chance comes, grab it.

My first year of military service is already over, and I hope the second year will pass just as quickly. In the journey of life, that which seems the most distant is often that which is right in front of you. I have started to think about many things since I met you.

I should send you the books I promised. But do you know what they are? Only a few chemistry textbooks, none of which would probably appeal to you. It was just an excuse because I was so anxious to hear from you. So please forgive me!

It's been cloudy here in Penghu, with little sunshine. Someone told me that the weather in Taipei is very stormy. I can tell by the crazy pounding of the waves that it is true.

Wishing you happiness,
Daxin

P.S. I am disturbed that you always cut out the best parts of your letters for yourself!

11

On October 29, Daxin returned to Taipei to take his exams. The next day he called Zhenguan and asked her to meet him at the Twin Leaf Bookshop. Zhenguan arrived for the date dressed in a gray skirt, gray socks, gray shoes, and a red shirt with white collar. Daxin was browsing through the store when she arrived. She studied him from behind: pale yellow corduroy pants, the sleeves of his white shirt rolled up to his elbows. Zhenguan thought: a marked improvement!

It was his father's birthday that day, and Daxin had to return home, so they only talked until nine o'clock. Walking Zhenguan to her door, he said to her, "As soon as I get back, I'll write." Under the warm glow of the street lamp, Daxin looked sincere. But for some strange reason, Zhenguan had an icy premonition that she wasn't going to see him again for a very long time.

Indeed, in the two months that followed, Zhenguan received no word from Daxin at all. Every day, she wondered how she could withstand the torment. From morning to night, she suffered. It felt as if her heart were being grilled, roasted over a slow fire.

January tenth, and still no word from Daxin. . . . She finally decided to release herself from such torturous waiting. Zhenguan started to tear his letters into pieces, page after page. In the twenty-four years of her life, those letters had been among her most precious belongings because they touched her soul so deeply. But she tore them into shreds. How could anything in life remain constant, when one was capable of destroying her most cherished possessions in a fit of passion?

Daxin must be feeling regret, she thought. He wasn't supposed to have moved in her direction on his life journey. They just happened to have crossed paths; and although they had a great deal in common and much to talk about, they still had to follow their own courses. . . . To love means having no regrets. Zhenguan was still young and hot-headed. She thought: If her love ever became a burden, then she would put an end to it! But was love so simple? Daxin and Zhenguan had already proved to each other how deeply they felt for each other.

The torn letters lay in heaps, like little hills on Zhenguan's desk. Three or four bundles of letters remained intact, but her heart and hands were already exhausted and weak, her eyes sore from crying. With glue and tape she started to piece the torn letters together. Her tears stained the pages, and the watermarks spread out layer by layer, fold by fold. In spite of her misery, Zhenguan still noticed all the signs of Daxin's strength: the paper that he used was brought from home, and he had cut it himself. He always said that store-bought paper was too coarse. Zhenguan found her shell-shaped purse made of lambskin and satin. She put the mismatched fragments of paper into the purse—the purse that Daxin had held, that his hands had touched. . . .

So let it be! Let him decide for himself! Daxin was an intelligent man, with his own reasons and rationale, and she would accept his decision. She had no doubts that he would find the best way to handle all the important matters in his life.

At this time, a strange letter came from Kaohsiung:

Miss Xiao:

I have just retired from military service. Daxin asked me to write you a letter on his behalf as soon as I returned to Taiwan. He wants to make sure that there is no misunderstanding between the two of you. . . .

While he was on leave, there was a case of theft in the military compound, and an investigation had to be conducted. Since this is confidential, I am not at liberty to disclose the details; but the truth has been revealed recently. Daxin, however, has fallen ill and is still recuperating. He will return to Taiwan when he is well, and he will be able to tell you everything then. For the time being, please don't worry about him.

Sincerely yours,
Ruiguo Zhang

Zhenguan let out a sigh of relief when she first started reading the letter but was overcome with worry by the time she had reached the end. She felt as if her heart were suspended in midair. . . . What had happened to Daxin? He was ill in a place where there was no family to take care of him!

One day passed, and others followed. Zhenguan had nightmare after nightmare. On the sixth day, she couldn't stand it anymore; she finally summoned enough courage to call Daxin's mother, after finding her telephone number on an envelope that Daxin had left with her. Of course, if she had received no word from Daxin either, she would no doubt be of little reassurance. Nevertheless, a mother knows when her son is in trouble. Zhenguan was going through torture and torment herself and could only imagine how Daxin's mother must be feeling.

For several nights, Zhenguan dreamt of her anxious face. Daxin's mother had to withstand all the uncertainty, if only to put up a brave front for her seventy-year-old mother-in-law. But how could she take the terrible suffering in private? As for the old grandmother. . . . Daxin, the oldest grandchild of the Liu family, was like a piece of her heart. Throughout his childhood and even into his adulthood, she had visited countless temples, offering incense and praying for the health of her grandson. Zhenguan could see her trudging along with her tiny bound feet, wishing for nothing but Daxin's well-being.

Zhenguan simply wanted to find out a bit more from Daxin. If he didn't want his family to worry about him, then she could tell a white lie for him and say that he'd had his appendix taken out. A little bit of information was all that it would take to bring some solace to both sides; and it would certainly be better than not knowing anything at all. Zhenguan just wanted to do her part for Daxin, her bosom friend.

After an extended telephone conversation with Zhenguan, Daxin's mother decided to fly to Penghu to visit Daxin. It was best to go and find out what was wrong with him, she thought, lest both their hearts remain wracked with anxiety. If it weren't for the fact that she was nothing to Daxin in name yet, Zhenguan would have flown to Penghu herself, in the middle of the night if necessary. A mother's love for her child knows no bounds; and when Zhenguan hung up the phone, she came to understand what Mencius meant when he said that one who is not filial to one's parents does not deserve to be a human being.

Of course, Daxin's grandmother was kept in the dark. Daxin's mother left everything at home and flew all the way to Penghu on her own even though she was prone to motion sickness. Zhenguan visited Dragon Mountain Temple every morning to pray for Daxin. Kneeling before the goddess of mercy, Zhenguan wished fervently for Daxin to be well. Three days passed, and as Zhenguan counted the hours until his mother's return, a letter arrived, and the words contained in it cut into her heart like a sharp dagger: "I cannot forgive you for what you have done."

She did not know what to do with the letter in her hand. Her hands shook, and her tears fell on the paper. There was nothing on the page but those words. He didn't even address her by name! She could hardly believe her eyes. She had tried only to do what was right for him. But in return he had come to hate her. Did he really think she was a busybody or, worse yet, a gossip? Didn't he understand how she felt? Fifty years hence, when she thought back on what had happened, would she forgive herself for sitting paralyzed in his moment of need?

How does one distinguish between an insider and an outsider? Was she supposed to just stand by and watch? She would rather that he blamed her than to feel that she had not tried everything in her power to help him. If one does not do what must be done, he will be forever plagued by remorse and guilt, and the hurt will last a lifetime; after all, we only have one life to live. If one makes a mistake in this lifetime, he will have to wait many more lifetimes to make amends; but if one is wronged, he will suffer only through this life.

Daxin was a sensitive man; how could he react like this? Given how she cherished and understood him, how could he respond with such hurtful words? Zhenguan's tears gushed as if a dam inside her had burst. Suddenly, everything in life seemed regrettable. Zhenguan packed up all the letters Daxin had written to her, all the gifts he had given her, including the binders with printings of his chops and seals that he gave her the night of the typhoon.

Daxin:
I have no right to keep them for you any longer. . . .

Zhenguan was sobbing so hard that she had to stop writing. She cradled her head in her arms and hunched over the desk. Pain tore through her heart, and she knew then that for the rest of her life, thoughts of this moment would bring forth an ache that knew no relief.

I am returning the two binders to you. I apologize for not returning your letters, but they are already torn up. I will be indebted to you all my life.

Zhenguan

She had actually patched together and saved most of the letters that she had ripped up, but she wanted to get under his skin. She wrote in his binder:

When the clouds disperse in the wind
Remember Huang Zixing. . . .

Huang was a colleague of hers. She wrote his name down because she wanted to make Daxin jealous. Love makes fools of us all. Swept up by the intensity of her devastation, she sent everything to Daxin. She knew perfectly well how he would react, but she did it anyway, disregarding the inevitable consequences. She figured that eventually the storm would pass and all would return to normal. . . .

There was no reply from Daxin for two weeks. Zhenguan knew he would be upset, and she continued to go to Dragon Mountain Temple every day. Now she knew what it must have been like for First Aunt when she prayed to the gods to protect her husband while he was away at war. And now she knew how grateful her aunt must have felt when she found out that he was alive and well; her greatest priority was for the grandparents to see their son again, and her own feelings had been set aside. First Aunt hadn't received much of an education; women in her day could barely read. But she was capable of grasping the essence of true love, and she loved so selflessly. . . . Compared to other people, her aunt was quite remarkable.

During Chinese New Year, Zhenguan went home, as was customary, and then returned to Taipei. The five-day holiday was the worst Zhenguan had ever experienced. When she went back to work on the sixth day of the Chinese New Year, Yinchan saw how distraught she was. Nevertheless, she asked Zhenguan, "Has it occurred to you that you might be wrong?"

"Me, in the wrong? Of course! How could I be right?"

Yinchan looked at her and said evenly, "You are to blame. You really hurt him by doing what you did." Seeing that Zhenguan was speechless, Yinchan continued, "Daxin is an educated and sensible person. You should know that better than anyone!"

Zhenguan started to tremble, as if struck by lightning. With her back to Yinchan, she wiped her tears. Yes, I have wronged my old friend, she thought. I have hurt Daxin; even Yinchan knows him better than I. . . .

Yinchan went on, "And you must take into account the fact that you caught him at a very bad time. How could he take another blow from you? You should write him a letter of apology! If you don't, I'll do it for you!"

"No—" Zhenguan cried out. "It wouldn't do any good! He's upset with me—"

The phone rang and Yinchan answered it. She motioned for Zhenguan to take the receiver, whispering, "It's his mother!"

Zhenguan picked up the phone timidly. "Auntie . . ."

"Zhenguan, has Daxin written to you?" Daxin's mother asked.

Zhenguan shook her head as tears streamed down her face. Daxin's mother repeated the question, and Zhenguan remembered that she was on the phone. "No," she said aloud, but softly.

"This boy—" Daxin's mother started to blame her own son. "Sometimes he's like a little child. He hasn't experienced hard times, which is why he's being so obstinate."

Zhenguan wiped away her tears. "Maybe he's too busy to write. . . . He'll be completing his military service soon."

"Yes, there are but a hundred more days to go, and he'll be back in June. When he returns, I will have to talk some sense into him."

The minute Zhenguan hung up the phone, she started wishing for the days to fly by. She could only believe that once she saw Daxin in person, everything would be as it should be.

seventeen

1

At the end of June, Zhenguan learned from Daxin's mother that Daxin had returned to Taipei. Every day she tore a page off her calendar: from the first of July to the second, eighth, tenth, then the fifteenth. . . . Zhenguan wasn't sure whether she was still alive, because if the two of them were both in Taipei, why did it feel as if he were so far, far away from her? She felt as if they were separated by a vast mountainous expanse.

She hadn't been able to eat, let alone sleep, for days. She didn't blame him, of course, because she was responsible for what had become of them today. But he was leaving on the nineteenth; he'd be gone in four days and three nights. Didn't he want to see her before he left? He would be deserting her in this big, empty city; how she was supposed to live her life alone from now on?

At two o'clock in the morning, Zhenguan was still tossing and turning. The radio by her bedside was playing a song:

The park is dark
Only a few stars dot the sky
Keeping me company as I cry
Alone, looking up into the sky. . . .

Tears flowed from Zhenguan's eyes, down her nose, cheeks, ears, the back of her neck. Her pillow was soaked, but the tears kept coming. She got up and quietly left the room, taking care not to wake Yinchan. Standing in the courtyard, she looked up at the moon, shining brightly. A year ago, Daxin had stood at this very spot, under the same moonlight, waiting for her. Then . . . Zhenguan stood crying in the moonlight. Tears wet her face, and the wind dried it.

"Why aren't you in bed? What are you doing here?" Yinchan had gotten up. Zhenguan answered without meeting her eyes, "It's so hot inside, I came out to get some fresh air."

Yinchan did not say a word. Instead, she came and took Zhenguan by the hand and, half-pushing half-shoving, moved her back to the bedroom. There, the two girls sat side by side in silence. After quite some time, Yinchan heaved a big sigh. "If it's too hot inside, you can turn on the fan. Why are you doing this to yourself?"

Zhenguan fell into Yinchan's arms and cried and cried.

The next morning, Zhenguan woke up with swollen eyes and couldn't stop coughing and retching. Yinchan was worried sick. "Look at you," she said.

"I'm okay, I just need to lie down for a while."

"If lying down could make you well, then doctors would be out of business. Who's going to feed their wives?"

"I—"

"From now on, I'm in charge. Stay in bed, I'll be right back!"

Yinchan dressed quickly, then ran out to find a doctor. She was soon back with an old doctor, who proceeded to examine Zhenguan with his stethoscope. Yinchan helped Zhenguan roll up her sleeves and undress. Zhenguan could not remember the last time she had seen a doctor. She was born with the strong constitution of a girl whose people lived by the sea. Her illness made her realize that human beings were as fragile as porcelain dolls.

The doctor gave Zhenguan an injection, and Yinchan went with him to his clinic for medicine. When she came back, Zhenguan urged her, "I'll take the medicine, but you'd better get to work."

"Work?" Yinchan rolled her eyes and brought Zhenguan a glass of milk, saying, "I called First Uncle and asked for leave. Uncle told me to take care of you, so that's my business now. Drink up, Aunt Ruriko will be here soon."

At ten o'clock sharp, Aunt Ruriko arrived, bringing Zheng Kaiyuan with her. Zheng Kaiyuan felt Zhenguan's forehead and asked, "How are you feeling?"

"I'm okay."

He picked up the medicine by her bedside and examined it carefully. "This medication is too mild; the doctor who came to see you must have been an old doctor . . . ?"

Zhenguan nodded. He continued to talk to her. At first Zhenguan responded, but soon she closed her eyes and feigned weariness. Before long, she had actually fallen asleep.

It was already one o'clock in the afternoon when she awoke. The guests had gone, and Yinchan had dozed off with her head cradled in her arms. There were flowers and fruit on the table.

Where was Daxin? Wasn't he going to visit her? Didn't he care if she were dead or alive? Did he even know that she had fallen ill? Had she committed such a terrible mistake? Why was he so angry with her? If he were to leave without a word, she would surely go mad!

When she woke up the next day, Zhenguan started to get ready for work. Yinchan pushed her back into bed, saying, "Are you out of your mind? Go back to bed and behave!"

"But . . ."

"No buts. You're not well, just look at yourself!" she said, handing Zhenguan a small mirror. Zhenguan hesitated for a moment before taking it. She hardly recognized her own face! Was this the daughter of the Xiao family who had grown up by the sea? She never knew that love could incapacitate a person like this. During her childhood, she, Yinchan, and Grandma used to attend the folk opera performances that were staged in the temple square. The protagonists in the plays would always fall ill when they were lovesick. It seemed the performances hadn't been so dramatic after all. . . .

"Okay, I will stay in bed for another day, but under one condition."

Yinchan laughed. "You're ill, and you still want to bargain? What's the condition?"

"I'm not going to work today, but you must. There's no reason for two people to stay at home when only one is ill."

"You're sick and weak. If I stay at home, you'll at least have someone to talk to," Yinchan replied.

Zhenguan covered her face with a towel and moaned, "I just need sleep . . . who'd talk to you?"

So Yinchan assented and went off to work, leaving Zhenguan to lie in bed alone. Her mind was racing: Why wasn't the phone ringing? Was the doorbell out of order? If it was broken, she thought, how would Daxin let her know when he arrived? He couldn't really be angry at her, could he? He must be playing a joke on her. When she had teased him about his past with Liao Qinger, hadn't he written her saying, "I have received your letter. I was angry, a little bit; why did you have to drive me into a corner?" And at the end of the letter, he wrote, "—actually I am not angry; on the contrary, I am touched! Sorry, sorry, I will engrave a chop that says SORRY, and stamp it all over the letter. . . ."

The phone rang suddenly, and Zhenguan felt her chest tighten. Good, at least her heart was still beating. She put on her slippers and went to answer the phone. "Hello?"

"Zhenguan, this is Zheng Kaiyuan."

"Oh, Dr. Zheng . . ."

"Are you feeling better?"

"Yes, thank you."

"Can I drop by to visit you?"

"Oh, I'm sorry, but I'm getting ready to go to work—"

"Oh, in that case, do take good care of yourself."

"Thank you."

When she hung up the phone, it suddenly occurred to Zhenguan that she should wash her face and get dressed. He hadn't called, but he might drop by to see her! She could not meet him in this sorry state. After all, she had always been the cheerful and lively Zhenguan. . . . She was putting on lipstick when the doorbell rang. Everyone in the family always told her that she had beautiful lips. She wanted them to be beautiful for Daxin! Now that Daxin was here, everything in the past was suddenly bearable, even the tears and the torment. He had finally come and was no longer upset at her—

But it was Zheng Kaiyuan who stood outside her door. Zhenguan suddenly understood what it must feel like to be born mute.

"I had to come and find out if you were really feeling better."

Zhenguan swallowed and said, "I was just on my way out! There's no one at home, so please excuse me for not inviting you in."

"Let me accompany you to your office then. Some of the cabs are not air-conditioned, and it is very hot outside."

On their way to Zhenguan's office, neither spoke. Zhenguan thanked him as she got out of the car. On the second floor of the office, in front of the elevator, Zhenguan ran into Yinchan, who was so surprised to see her that she dropped all the documents in her hands. "Can't you stay put so I don't have to worry about you?" she demanded.

Zhenguan explained what had just happened, and Yinchan said, "That man is really determined!"

"No," Zhenguan said. "I don't think that's his intention. He was just showing his concern. On the one hand, Aunt Ruriko has asked him to take care of me, and on the other hand, he is my doctor. If I were a doctor, I would treat my patients the same way."

Yinchan said, "You're right. But what kind of doctor would force his patients to leave their beds?"

"I'm better, anyway."

"I guess I'll have to take your word for it."

By three o'clock in the afternoon, however, Zhenguan's face was pale, and she fainted at her desk. There was commotion in the office. Some of her colleagues called a taxi and some went to find medicine. Finally, Yinchan accompanied her home. When Zhenguan was back in her bed, she thought: I might as well lie down now and never get up again; let the days fly by, and soon it will be the twentieth. Daxin wasn't going to come. She should give up hope. Once her heart lost hope, she wouldn't have to think about anything at all!

Zhenguan could tell from Yinchan's expression that Daxin wasn't coming. Yinchan must have called him; he knew that she was ill, and yet he had hardened his heart and decided not to see her. Yinchan suddenly blurted out, "I'll call him again!"

"No! No!" Zhenguan grabbed her hand and said, "He's not going to come, no matter how many times you call!"

Yinchan burst into tears. "But however wrong you may have been, he still shouldn't treat you like this—let me ask him why he's doing this to you!"

"I am to blame for everything! It's not his fault," Zhenguan murmured.

Biting her lower lip, Yinchan said, "I'll call his mother!"

"Yinchan . . . I know Daxin, and if he doesn't want to come, no one can make him. If you forced him at knifepoint, you'd only end up killing me instead."

"But—"

"He thinks he's right, and you must let him be. If you call his mother, Yinchan, I will never forgive you."

Both girls broke down. Tears can scorch the skin like melting candle wax. Wiping her eyes, Zhenguan thought, Okay, Daxin, you're not coming to me, so I shall have to go to you; at this point, stubbornness and pride no longer mean anything.

Actually, I wasn't trying to act haughty; I simply thought: regardless of how wrong I've been, you should be able to read my mind. . . . We've shared our thoughts. Don't they count? I know that I was wrong. You didn't want your family to worry about you. But do you know that I couldn't stand for you to suffer alone, to bear all the weight on your shoulders?

She couldn't afford to be sick any longer. Daxin was leaving the day after tomorrow. She had to get well so she could visit him the next day. It was the eighteenth. Zhenguan stayed in bed all day, and Aunt Ruriko stayed with her until dusk. She left with Zheng Kaiyuan in the evening, knowing that Yinchan would soon return. Zhenguan looked at her watch: it was ten minutes to six, and Yinchan would be home any minute. If she didn't leave now, Yinchan would never let her go later. Zhenguan left a note saying she was going for a walk on campus. The campus was huge, and Yinchan would not be able to find her there. It was six-fifteen when she left home. Daxin was probably having dinner. . . .

She really did walk around the campus. It was summer vacation, and the area was practically deserted. Azhong had gone home a few days before but would be returning in ten days or so to help his professor with a research project. It was already seven-thirty by the time she got to the main entrance of the campus. What should I do now? she wondered. If she took a taxi, she would arrive in ten minutes, appearing before him abruptly. That wouldn't give her enough time to think things through. She would take the bus, then; she needed time to quiet her mind. She walked to the bus stop.

A long time ago, she had stood at this very spot with Daxin, waiting for the bus. . . . After Daxin left for England, how would she be able to live in this city? Memories of him would leap out at her at every step. Their shadows and footprints were reflected and imprinted all over Taipei. Unless she locked herself indoors, memories would jump up and touch her, hurt her; and even if she were to shut her door, she wouldn't be able to shut out memories of Daxin, because he had once sat on her chair, his feet were once perched on her desk. . . .

When the bus arrived at the South Gate, it was already ten past eight. Nevertheless, Zhenguan got off the bus two stops in advance and decided to walk the rest of the way. Daxin had grown up here, so she felt a sense of reverence. She should still be able to reach his house by eight-thirty, which seemed to her like a good time, not too early, not too late.

Zhenguan walked down Chunghua Road and turned onto Chengdu Road. When she got to Kunming Road, she discovered that her palms were wet with perspiration. She had never visited his house before, but now she was almost there. Should she venture in? The front of the house was lit up; it was also a storefront. She decided to take the back alley. What was she going to say if someone asked her what she was doing there?

As Zhenguan walked down the dark alley, which led directly to his back door, she was reminded of a line from Daxin's letter: "I like to walk by myself down lonely alleys. As I climb the stairs, the moon seems like a crescent in the sky, and my heart is as still as water, water in an old well."

So this was the alley that he was referring to! Standing under the eaves of a neighbor's roof, Zhenguan looked up to find Daxin's bedroom window. His grandparents and parents lived on the second floor, his brothers on the third, and his sisters on the fourth. His uncle's family lived in the adjoining building. Daxin's window was the one facing west on the third floor. The moonlight shone into his room. So, that was his room! The lights were on. How are you, my dear friend?

From nine o'clock to midnight, Zhenguan stood under his window, her feet firmly rooted to the ground. The lights from Daxin's room burned on. On the eve of his departure, was he just sitting there under his lamp?

We need not meet, she said to him silently. You have decided. And if you can live with it, what more can I say? To stand here like this is good enough for me. To have known you at all was enough to make my life meaningful. . . .

It started to drizzle. When Zhenguan left, Daxin's lights were still on. Was he going to stay up all night? Or maybe he had forgotten to turn them off.

The clock struck one just as she arrived home. Yinchan opened the door for her. At the sight of her, Zhenguan felt a tightness in her chest, and then darkness descended upon her. She managed to walk only a few steps before collapsing into Yinchan's arms.

II

Zhenguan stayed in bed for two weeks. Yinchan wanted to call home several times, but Zhenguan forbade her.

Daxin had left for England. The day of his departure, Zhenguan had an intravenous needle stuck in her arm. She wouldn't eat, so Zheng Kaiyuan had to give her injections of saline solution. She answered when people spoke to her, but nothing really registered. There was only one thing on her mind: How will I ever find him? London was so far away. She could barely survive away from home; how would she leave Taiwan and venture into a strange and foreign land? It was a dangerous world out there, and she didn't even know if she had enough money in the bank.

In the Ming Dynasty novel, Fan Juqing and Zhang Wenbo were two bosom friends. They made a pact to reunite on the Double Ninth Festival. After they went their separate ways, Fan got caught up in the hustle and bustle of making a living and did not take heed of the passing days. On the morning of the Double Ninth Festival, neighbors came and presented him with the cornel flower, reminding him of the pact he'd made with his friend. They were separated by thousands of miles, and traveling to their meeting place would take over a day. One's soul, however, could travel thousands of miles overnight; and since Zhang was a man of honor, Fan could not forsake him. So he slit his throat to release his soul so that it could fly off to meet his friend. . . .

Zhenguan thought of dying. If she couldn't be with Daxin in person, then maybe her soul could fly to his side! She wanted to seek him out, to ask him why he had taken her so far away and then abandoned her, why he had left her in despair. For fifteen days, the thought of death filled her mind. It was Azhong and Yinchan who finally pulled her back to the world of the living.

She had still been running a high fever, though. Azhong returned to Taipei to find her sick in bed. He stayed by her side, grinding ginger, while Yinchan knelt by her bed, spooning rice gruel and slices of pickled cucumber into her mouth. Seeing the faces of her loved ones before her, Zhenguan shed tears that dripped into the bowl Yinchan was holding.

"Don't be silly, don't be silly," Yinchan murmured. Zhenguan scrutinized her cousin's face. Her eyes and eyebrows resembled Third Aunt's, her nose and mouth resembled Third Uncle's, and the shape of her face resembled both Grandpa's and Grandma's. . . . All the dear, familiar faces of home appeared before her—faces of her grandfather, her grandmother, her mother and cousins, all the people who truly loved her.

She remembered the plays that she used to watch as a child. When the characters stepped on stage, they would always proclaim: "My father and my mother loved each other and gave birth to me. Life is a precious thing that must not be taken lightly." Yes, life was indeed full of blessings, and yet Zhenguan had made herself miserable, all because of Daxin.

During her illness, Zheng Kaiyuan made many house calls. As he sat quietly by her side, Zhenguan would think: no matter how Daxin treated her, she would always feel as if she had spent a lifetime with him. She would never be able to love in the same way again, even if she tried . . . even if the other person had unparalleled looks and outstanding talent, she would only end up forsaking him.

She couldn't do anything to change her state of mind. In her childhood, she had liked to watch people dig wells. When the iron pestle hit the deepest part of the well, sweet water would gush out. But one's heart can accommodate only one well. If the terrain of the heart is arid, and if the well-digger lacks instinct, then years may pass, and still the well of one's heart will remain empty. Daxin had dug deep into the well of Zhenguan's heart. Daxin, only Daxin.

Eventually Zhenguan went back to work. Every morning, for six or seven days, she left at seven-thirty and got home at six. Yinchan was heartened. One night, just before bedtime, she asked Zhenguan, "How are you doing?"

"What do you mean?"

"Are you feeling better?"

"I'm okay, as you can see. I'm sitting here right in front of you, aren't I?"

"I mean inside, your heart!"

Zhenguan was at a loss for words. Does a broken heart ever heal?

On Aunt Ruriko's birthday, the two girls had gone to their uncle's for lunch. Aunt Ruriko was baking a cake in the kitchen and humming a tune, "My Heart Broke on Mount Fuji." Zhenguan remembered that she had felt a new sense of respect for her aunt after her uncle told her how the two of them had met. Nevertheless, she couldn't help but think of First Aunt, who was left alone back home.

In the old days, women loved wholeheartedly. If her capacity for love matched First Aunt's, she would not be in so much pain today. Daxin did wrong her in the beginning, but she shouldn't have made the gigantic mistake of returning all his letters and presents to him in one impulsive move. Her fury wreaked havoc on the two of them. Proud as he was, Daxin would never allow anyone to hurt him that way; and so, they broke each other's hearts.

Zhenguan felt she had aged overnight. But compared to her first aunt, Daxin and Zhenguan were so young and immature. It was only because of their youth that they could amplify a minor misunderstanding into something with the magnitude of the sky.

Getting no response from Zhenguan, Yinchan continued, "I know that you are suffering. But if you don't tell me anything, I can only guess. If you are feeling even a little bit better, please let me know so I can worry a little less!"

Zhenguan stroked Yinchan's hair and said softly, "Don't

worry about me. I really just want to go home. I want to see First Aunt, and I miss Mother and Grandma. Yinchan, let's go home, all right?" Yinchan's eyes brimmed with tears. Holding Zhenguan's hands, she did not know what to say.

The next day after work, the girls agreed that one of them should go to the train station to buy their tickets, and that the other should go home to start packing. Zhenguan got off the bus and started toward home. Walking down the sidewalk paved with red bricks, she began to bid farewell to Taipei City. To her, Taipei was filled with memories of love as well as pain. Taipei was the hometown of her beloved.

Suddenly Zhenguan heard a child's voice singing behind her:

Bowl after bowl of rice,
The bowl that Mom filled for me tastes the best,
Shirt collar after shirt collar,
The shirt that Mom has sewn for me fits the best. . . .

A little girl going home from kindergarten was singing the song. Zhenguan stopped and watched her skipping by.

Road after road,
I love best the road that leads to Mother. . . .

Tears finally fell. The child's song opened a floodgate. How she wanted to fly back into her mother's arms, how she wanted to be in the presence of her dear mother back home! In the spring, Zhenguan's mother liked to stir-fry Chinese chives and bean sprouts. In the summer, she would make soup with tender bamboo shoots. In August and September, she would buy water chestnuts and cook them with pork chops, and when the stew was ready, she would add a handful of chopped coriander. When doing the laundry, she would separate Zhenguan's clothing from her brother's. Zhenguan learned from the *Book of Rites* that men were superior to women; however, her mother had received only a few years of Japanese education, and even she took care to observe Chinese etiquette. Zhenguan was not allowed to step over her brothers' shoes; she had to make a detour to walk past them.

Zhenguan's father had passed away many years ago. Her mother still lit incense every morning and every evening in his memory. She preserved all the things that he had left behind, including every little piece of clothing. She honored him in death as much as she had honored him when he was alive. Zhenguan's mother also taught Zhenguan to know her own worth and place. What is meant to be yours will always be yours. You should accept what is yours calmly and with reverence.

The phone was ringing when Zhenguan arrived home. She picked up the receiver and heard the operator ask, "Miss Xiao?"

"Yes."

"You have a long-distance call."

"Is this Zhenguan or Yinchan?"

"Third Uncle, this is Zhenguan speaking—"

"I couldn't get through to your first uncle, so do notify him immediately: Grandma has just taken a bad fall and is unconscious. You'd better come home as soon as you can."

III

The night train swayed and rattled on the tracks, taking them back home. First Uncle could have asked the chauffeur to drive them, but he later decided against it because the roads were dangerous at night. Zhenguan and Yinchan held hands as they gazed up at the sky. First Uncle and Aunt Ruriko sat in front, also looking dazed and dismal.

Stars glimmered faintly in the midnight sky, reminding Zhenguan of the glitter of Daxin's clear and shiny eyes. In a letter, he had once described his experience of taking the express train at night:

> When I have trouble sleeping, I look up into the night sky and watch the darkness turn into day. I lack the words to describe the sight of daybreak; but the moment when the sun shows itself, Mother Nature puts on a spectacular show of color and light. The traveler is rendered speechless and can do nothing but be touched to the deepest core of his being. . . .

How was Daxin?

In two more days it would be the seventh day of the seventh lunar month. They didn't follow the lunar calendar in England. Would he know that his lunar birthday had arrived? Last year in March, Zhenguan had run into a high school classmate. Her classmate had stayed in the same dormitory as Daxin's university sweetheart, Liao Qinger. Zhenguan asked her whether she remembered Liao's boyfriend, and her classmate replied, "Oh, do you mean that chemistry major whose hair stood on his head like bulls' horns?" She raised her index fingers to her head, mimicking two horns.

When Zhenguan parted with her classmate, she'd gone to Yenping North Road and bought a comb made of horn, which she sent to Daxin with a letter recounting the classmate's words. Within a few days, Daxin wrote back, saying, "Is this a hint? Am I that ugly? I have received the comb, and I will comb my hair every day."

Why did he matter so much to her? Zhenguan pondered the question over and over. She decided that it was because he was so much like her, almost her alter ego. He could always pick up any thought where she left off and capture her sentiments exactly. Once she told him about the incident in her childhood when her cousins pushed her into the fishpond and a crab had clamped onto her pant leg when she climbed to shore. He immediately said, "Ha ha, you used yourself as bait to catch the crab."

When they'd gone to visit the National Palace Museum, they sat on the bus humming songs. Zhenguan sang, "the sea breezes laughed at my silliness," and Daxin joined in with matching lyrics from another song: "and now the moon laughs at mine."

If it weren't for all this, their almost cosmic understanding of each other, she wouldn't be feeling the way she did now. . . .

Some passengers were snoring away while others sat with their eyes wide open. A young man sitting in the back turned on his tape player, and a sad melody filled the train.

The moon shines on the mountaintop
And the stars glitter
I am not guilty of any crime
Why has my man treated me so cruelly. . . .

Zhenguan turned her head and tried hard to hold back the tears.

When they arrived at the station, her first uncle hailed a taxi, and the four of them hurried home. They arrived at dusk;

in the faint glow of early evening, the air felt fresh and cool. Zhenguan was reminded of the days when she had to wake up at the break of dawn to prepare for school examinations. Those were good times. She hadn't come to know Daxin yet. The pain and joy came later, after Daxin entered her life. Before that, her heart only trembled lightly, like teardrops on eyelashes.

Zhenguan finally arrived home in the twilight. Here were the people she loved, the people who loved her. Why does anyone ever leave home to wander? The wounds we are afflicted with when we are away from home can only be healed when we return to our place of origin. Lucky are those who never have to leave home. They are the people who can talk about happiness. . . . When the taxi stopped in front of their house, Zhenguan looked up and practically stumbled out of the car.

The four of them knelt down and crawled toward the door. Dressed in blue and black, Zhenguan's mother and first aunt greeted them, sobbing loudly; crying, Zhenguan clung to them. A wail of anguish and unbearable pain rose from her gut.

eighteen

1

The oil lamp flickered in the wind, which occasionally made its way through cracks around the windows and door. The flame, jumping and bouncing, filled the room with shadows. This was Zhenguan's fifth night keeping vigil by her grandmother's coffin. Everything was white: the candles, the tablecloth, Zhenguan's gown, even her face. A straw mat covered the floor, where Zhenguan knelt with her uncles and cousins. Yinshan was the oldest grandchild in the family, and according to custom, he was like the youngest son; so, like his uncles, he wore a mourning robe made of hemp. When Zhenguan touched the robe, its coarseness stung her heart, which felt raw, as if it had been rubbed with sandpaper.

On the third night, the womenfolk had started taking turns sleeping. Zhenguan was Grandma's granddaughter on the maternal side, and custom did not dictate that she stay by her grandmother all night. Nevertheless, she remained there, without rest or sleep, observing the mourning ritual with the closest of kin among her uncles and cousins.

When Zhenguan was three, her mother gave birth to her younger brother. From then on, Zhenguan had been weaned and sent to Grandma's. She could not vividly recall details of her early childhood, but when she was around four or five she would sleep with her grandmother, and in the winter, when everything between heaven and earth froze, Grandma would get up early in the morning to make porridge. She fed Zhenguan, spoonful by spoonful.

Zhenguan stayed with her grandmother throughout her years in elementary school. Knowing that Zhenguan liked mung bean soup, Grandma would make it all summer, from May to July. Zhenguan would stand in line after school and wait for Grandma to pick her up. Grandma could always spot her right away among the rows of students, and they would go home to have mung bean soup. She would be indebted to her grandmother forever and ever. The memories made Zhenguan's eyes, already dry from so much crying, brim with tears once again. The Chinese have always believed in reincarnation and karma. The reason for such a belief is sentimental: if we don't go on to live another life, how are we to repay our debts from this one?

The last time she was home for Chinese New Year, she had helped Grandma and First Aunt make red rice cakes in molds engraved with turtles, the symbol for longevity. They made thousands of red turtle rice cakes and laid them out on the table. Third Aunt cut out cabbage leaves in the shape of the cakes and brushed them with oil. Yinchan squatted on the floor and ground fried peanuts into powder with mortar and pestle.

The peanut powder was later mixed with minced meat and chopped vegetables and used as stuffing for the vegetable buns and red rice cakes. The peanuts bounced around in the mortar during the grinding process, and some even jumped out; Yinchan would have to grind with one hand while picking up stray peanuts with the other. Before long, she ended up pounding her own hand! So Zhenguan took over, and as she ground the peanuts, she felt as if it were her heart in the mortar, being crushed to powder.

That year was the worst. Daxin stayed away, and there was no news from him at all. On the fifth day of the new year, she was scheduled to return to Taipei. Yinchan was in Third Aunt's room, and mother and daughter chatted away. Zhenguan's mother had come over to Grandma's to spend the night with Zhenguan. While she was talking to Third Uncle, Zhenguan went into her grandmother's room.

Grandma sat up in bed when she saw Zhenguan enter. She pulled Zhenguan into bed, saying, "It's freezing cold outside, you're not dressed warmly enough."

"I just took off my overcoat, Grandma; I'm not cold at all."

Little did she know that would be the last time she would ever see her grandmother. The two of them sat together under one blanket, which was warmed by a heater underneath. Zhenguan hoped that she would never have to leave.

"When are you coming back?"

"I'm not sure. I'll return whenever there is a holiday."

"Good, come back and let me see you. Oh, you are so far away from home. . . . You will be in Taipei tomorrow at this time; you are all like birds now, flying here and there. Zhenguan, my girl, you are so far away, and I cannot have you by my side every day, so remember this—"

"Grandma, I will remember—"

"Talent isn't enough, and beauty is fleeting; you must be kind and capable, a strong woman with good virtues."

That was their last meeting, and those heartfelt words of wisdom had become her last to her granddaughter. Now, recalling that night with Grandma, Zhenguan was unable to contain her tears. She cried out of guilt and a deep sense of regret. It was right of Daxin to treat her the way he had. The way she'd behaved, she certainly did not deserve such an honorable gentleman. That she had given him a hard time when he most needed a friend was not only inconsiderate, it went against everything she had ever been taught. After all, she had been raised to observe the rules of etiquette and to follow the family tradition of making virtue an integral aspect of one's life. All the elders in her family always took care to serve as good examples. She had betrayed her own upbringing. She had shamed her parents and her family and, even worse, betrayed the person whom she cared for more than any other. . . .

Let the tears flow until they become blood, she thought. It was only then that her grandmother and her father would understand her confession.

II

A week after the funeral, Zhenguan's first uncle and first aunt left, one after the other. Zhenguan knew that she could no longer spend her days in Taipei. Taipei was for the brave and intrepid! No, she decided, she would never leave home again. Like the old farmers living by her elementary school, she was home to stay forever.

Yinchan decided to stay at home too. Azhong helped them take care of their rented apartment in Taipei. Zhenguan spent the days with her mother and aunt, and she gradually regained her peace of mind. Forty-nine days passed. One hundred. Aunt Ruriko came to attend the memorial rituals, then returned to Taipei. Seeing her aunt come and go, Zhenguan felt that Taipei was far, far away.

Before her aunt left, she had tried to persuade Zhenguan to return with her. Zhenguan promised that she would think about it. Taking her uncle and aunt to the station, Zhenguan suddenly remembered: First Aunt had once told her she intended to retire to the mountains, but Grandma had held her back. Now that Grandma was gone, no one in the family could stop her! No matter what, I will see her off, Zhenguan thought.

Compared with First Aunt's suffering, the pain she was going through suddenly seemed inconsequential. She remembered the chop engraving prints that Daxin, braving typhoon winds and rains, had given her. How could she have returned them to him, lied to him about tearing up his letters, mentioned the name of another man just to spite him? He had all the reason in the world to turn his back on her!

Zhenguan anxiously located the torn letters she had pasted together and read them, one by one. They brought tears to her eyes. Daxin had written so many letters to her, and on those pages, he held nothing back. He told her everything, things that he would never even tell his mother and sister. "This morning I woke up with a stuffy nose," he wrote. Even that he shared with her! "When a book is thicker than three inches, I use it as a pillow. . . ." A comment that anyone else might have laughed at, but that she understood completely. "The crickets have been impetuous, chirping in unison and making such a racket. . . ."

Daxin knew her so well, and how lucky they were to have found each other. Zhenguan finally realized that it was she who had wronged him! Bosom friends never complain about each other, like Baoyu and Daiyu in *Dream of the Red Chamber*. He had wanted her to quietly wait for news; she shouldn't have allowed her impatience to get the better of her. He was only angry because he wanted nothing less than perfection; could she blame him? She should have known better! Why did she act so rashly, returning all his things, stabbing him at his weakest moment?

She'd found the shreds of paper still in the shell-shaped purse. Now she understood why Daxin had left without saying good-bye. What could he have said? They had no commitment to each other, and both their hearts were broken. Wracked by heartache, each would have been at a loss for words. The paper shreds were damp and soggy. Zhenguan fetched a little basin and spread the pieces out to dry in a drafty spot with sunlight. She decided that from that day forth, she would lay the shreds of paper out under the sun whenever the seasons changed, just as Grandma used to lay out her beautifully embroidered chemises in the open air. . . .

Suddenly a gust of air lifted the little scraps, and they danced in the wind like white butterflies. Zhenguan dropped everything to run after the flying pieces of paper. Just then Yinchan arrived and asked, "What's that?"

Zhenguan did not answer. Yinchan caught a few scraps in her hand and, deciphering the writing on the paper, said, "You, you . . . this man is going to ruin you!"

Without a word, Zhenguan snatched the pieces of paper from Yinchan's hand and stuffed them into her purse. The purse had a strange clasp, and none of the boys had ever managed to open it—not Yincheng, not Yinan, not even Azhong; but, strangely enough, Daxin was always able to open it with just a tap and a snap!

Yinchan thought Zhenguan would be angry, so she mumbled, "I'm sorry, I shouldn't have said that."

Zhenguan hadn't even been much perturbed at first, but now Yinchan's words kindled her wrath. "I wouldn't be upset if you didn't know anything about this. But you know everything, so why did you have to bring it up? You, of all people! Scold me as much as you want, but not him!"

"All right, it's my fault!" Yinchan looked so much like Grandma with her head bent like that. Zhenguan suddenly thought of how Yinchan had taken care of her, fed her, looked after her when she was ill. . . .

"No, Yinchan, I am to blame too. I am in a terrible mood, and the words just came out! Please, let's just forget about it. I know that you know me better than I know myself."

nineteen

1

Zhenguan was going up Guanziling Mountain for the second time. She was accompanying First Aunt.

She had gone up Guanziling Mountain once before, when she was in fifth grade. Her whole class went, all forty-seven of them. They took up five tables when they feasted on vegetarian food served by the temple. And they stayed overnight on top of the mountain: all the boys at the Temple of the Grand Immortal, and all the girls at the Temple of the Blue Clouds. When one is only twelve years old, some things are clear, others ambiguous. When the girls touched the boys by accident, they would blow on the spot—their elbow, shoe, sleeve, or even a corner of their desk—to sterilize it. But up in the mountains, the girls and boys willingly helped each other out by carrying each other's water bottles and sharpening each other's bamboo cane tips.

Zhenguan could no longer remember what she had been like when she was twelve. On her way up the mountain this time, she stopped some little girls and boys who were collecting firewood and asked them how old they were. She would question First Aunt about whether she had been anything like these children when she was young.

Of all the women in the family, her first aunt was the only one who had never permed her hair. When everyone else tried to persuade her to get a perm, she would say: "I am used to my hairstyle." She wore a tight bun at the back of her head that was shaped like a banana. When First Uncle returned from Japan, even Zhenguan thought her aunt should get a new hairstyle, because she looked older than her age. Second Aunt, for instance, had a head full of curls that made her look more youthful. But First Aunt insisted on keeping her hair the way it was. Zhenguan knew that her aunt was really keeping her hairstyle for Grandma's sake. Grandma needed a hair extension to tuck into her hair in order to tie it into a bun. Her old ones were thinning, and First Aunt wanted to keep her hair long so she could cut it off later and make new ones for Grandma when she needed them.

As First Aunt turned toward her, the bun that was so familiar to Zhenguan disappeared from view. "Yes, there is a resemblance, especially to the one wearing red. Do you remember the red dress that you used to wear?"

Indeed. Zhenguan remembered that it had puffy sleeves, a collar shaped like a lotus leaf, and three buttons. Her second aunt had made the dress for her on New Year's Eve so she would have something new to wear on New Year's Day. Children take such things very seriously. As a little girl, Zhenguan not only felt that she had to wear a new dress on New Year's Day, she even took a few pennies out of her bamboo piggy bank to buy herself some red flowers made of straw. Scarlet and crimson, they were pinned in her hair, and she wore them from the first day of the new year until the tenth. When the celebrations were over, she reluctantly removed the flowers and kept them in her mother's and grandmother's drawers for safekeeping. The next year, however, when she retrieved the flowers, they were broken and torn, and she ended up having to buy new ones anyway.

For her, wearing a red flower in her hair during the first days of the new year was as important a ritual as wearing a fragrant sachet for Dragonboat Festival. She finally stopped when she turned twelve, for fear of running into boy classmates on the streets. If they saw her with flowers in her hair, they would draw pictures of her on the blackboard and tease her endlessly at school.

What had Daxin been like when he was twelve?

Last winter in Taipei, Zhenguan, Yinchan, and First Aunt had visited Dragon Mountain Temple several times. Little boys with book bags slung over their shoulders at Laosung Elementary School reminded her of Daxin. He must have been a well-mannered young boy. Why did Daxin invade every thought that crossed her mind?

The three of them walked for over twenty minutes after they got off the bus. The Temple of the Blue Clouds finally appeared in the distance, and First Aunt was already starting to fall behind Zhenguan. Zhenguan looked back and saw Yinchan and her aunt walking up the slope slowly. Yinchan was thirsty, and she paused at the drinking fountain provided by the temple for passersby at the side of the road. She poured a cup of water for First Aunt and then another for herself. Before taking a sip, she called out to Zhenguan, "Aren't you thirsty?"

Zhenguan shook her head. As she watched them drink the water, she let her mind wander. When they were all children, Yinchuan and the boys used to raise silkworms. Everyone would gather around when the worms were spitting silk to watch them spinning and hiding themselves in cocoons. Wasn't she like a silkworm on a mulberry leaf in spring?

There was no way that she could recuperate in this lifetime. She knew that Daxin had always had trouble making decisions. He had led a comfortable life, which made it difficult for him to stand up for himself. Furthermore, he was as stubborn as a mule and rarely listened to the advice of other people. If they had just had one more year together, they would never have gotten into such a squabble. When she first got to know him, he had just ended his catastrophic relationship with Liao Qinger and was still hurt by the failure. Even though he got along so well with Zhenguan, he must not have been sure: was he ready to dive into the kiln of love again? After all, he had just climbed out of the fire, badly scorched. The misunderstanding between the two of them happened at this most fragile moment, before he'd had the chance to sort things out for himself. Having never gone through anything like it before, he certainly did not know the right thing to do. . . .

Yet the path of true love never runs smooth. Zhenguan was different from Daxin. She had been steadfast and scrupulous since childhood. She understood the bright side of Daxin's nature. She knew that she was right about him. She had no regrets. Most important, Zhenguan believed that one's spirit is the only thing that prevails between heaven and earth, and she revered her own spirituality.

As she walked, she thought, I might as well stay at the temple with First Aunt when we arrive—First Aunt, an abiding presence between heaven and earth. The impetuous and wild at heart often consider people with self-control to be repressed and bound. Little do they know that such people are simply being true to their own natures. And Yinchan? Of course Zhenguan was going to persuade Yinchan to return home even if she wanted to stay. How could one who has never weathered the ravages of love seek enlightenment in seclusion?

Thoughts raced through her mind. She reached the Temple of the Blue Clouds and turned to wait for her aunt and cousin. She looked back on the path that she had taken and suddenly felt as if she had left all her pain behind her, beneath her feet. The mountaintop was pristine, devoid of all the suffering that afflicted the masses down below.

This was First Aunt's third trip to the temple. She had already visited the place twice to make all the necessary arrangements with the temple staff. As soon as Zhenguan stepped over the threshold, two young Buddhist nuns led them all to a room on the west side of the temple. The chamber was large, almost as large as Grandma's bedroom. But except for a mattress on the floor, it was completely empty, obviously a room for reclusive meditation. First Aunt went to see the abbess, and Zhenguan opened the window.

"Wow, this is great," she said. "Yinchan, I'm going to stay here. . . ."

Yinchan poked her head out the window too. They did indeed have a good view. From their window, they could see the kitchen, the storage hut for firewood, and a nun chopping wood. On the other side, they could see mountains and acres and acres of orchards. Yinchan asked, "See that person walking toward us? Strange, aren't nuns supposed to shave their heads?"

"Take a better look to make sure that she hasn't!"

Yinchan continued, "Maybe Auntie won't have to shave her head after all—"

At that moment, a young nun walked in, lighting an incense coil. She said, almost cheerfully, "There are quite a lot of mosquitoes here in the mountains."

Yinchan asked her, "Are all nuns required to shave their heads? We just saw someone—"

The young nun smiled. "It is up to each nun to decide. If you shave your head, you are referred to as *shih,* and if you keep your hair, you are referred to as *gu*. That's about the only difference!"

The two girls nodded. Then they asked where the bathroom was and headed there, down the stairs, clothes tucked under their arms. Outside the bathroom was a big pool of water where Zhenguan and Yinchan filled their buckets. Inside, the nuns gave them soap and towels and pointed toward a number of tiny rooms paved with rocks, each so small that it could barely accommodate one person.

"There you are. Just close the door when you go in."

Life was so simple. There were about twenty stone chambers. Nuns came and went, each carrying only a bucket of water and a towel. Yinchan went into the chamber next to Zhenguan's. Separated by a stone wall, the two girls washed themselves to the music of the splashing water.

"Zhenguan—"

"Yes?"

"This must be water from the mountain springs!"

"How do you know?"

"I took a sip, and it tastes really sweet!"

After bathing, they did their laundry and went to hang their clothes out to dry in their room. But when they entered, they discovered that First Aunt's things were gone.

"What happened?"

"She probably took everything with her! She must have her own meditation room, because this room is just for visitors who have come to pray."

The two looked at each other in silence. A bell rang, and the young nun who lit the incense for them came in, saying, "It is time for dinner. The dining room is behind the altar of the Goddess of Mercy. You'll find it if you walk down the stairs."

Zhenguan looked at her watch. It was only four-thirty, far too early for dinner! "Do you know where my aunt is?" she asked.

"She is still with the abbess. She took her clothes with her. After dinner, you can find her three doors away from the restaurant. There will be two flights of stairs there and the sweet smell of flower blossoms. But don't knock on the wrong door!"

"What about you? Are you having dinner with us?"

"No, you will eat first. This is the rule here. We'll eat after you have eaten."

There were four dishes and soup, all vegetarian. Zhenguan and Yinchan were seated at a long table with wooden benches. They used bowls and spoons made of coarse clay that to Zhenguan seemed both simple and rich.

When Yinchan got up for a second bowl of rice, Zhenguan asked her, "Miss, how many bowls are you planning to have?"

"Three bowls are not too many, nor are five bowls too few. Will you be quiet? Everyone is looking at me now!"

They finished eating dinner, but it was still only five o'clock. Yinchan said, "Dinner was served so early, I'm sure we'll have to be in bed by eight o'clock. Where shall we go now? I wonder if First Aunt has returned?"

The two girls walked up the stairs to the main hallway and then took a shortcut that led to a side door.

"Why are there so many steps paved with rocks?"

"We are deep in the mountains. The nuns have transported sand and gravel to pave each step."

A nun was straightening earthen urns on the balcony. Zhenguan took a look and saw pickled vegetables in the urns. They made their way to their aunt's room, but the door was locked.

"What are we going to do now?"

"We could just sit here and wait!"

Yinchan looked around and said excitedly, "Do you smell the flowers? I think it's jasmine. Hey, that's our meditation room back there. I can see the yellow shirt that you hung by the window."

Zhenguan did not respond.

"What's wrong?" Yinchan asked.

Zhenguan pointed at the door, saying, "Read the lines!" These words were inscribed in elegant calligraphy:

When your heart is open and your desires are none
The moon will appear on the surface of the cold lake
Seeking enlightenment and self-discipline
One can find unparalleled harmony

The two girls stood at the door, waiting, but still there was no sign of First Aunt. Yinchan wanted to stay, but Zhenguan said, "No, First Aunt might be looking for us back there."

So they returned to their room. But they knew that there

was no one there because it was not lit. Yinchan exclaimed, "Is First Aunt lost, or are we lost?"

"There is probably unfinished business. Going into seclusion and becoming a nun is no easy feat."

"What should we do now?"

"Why don't we go to the back of the mountain? There are rocks there that we can sit on."

When the two girls stepped onto the mountain trail, the moon was already bright enough to light their way. Zhenguan walked briskly. Yinchan asked, "Do you think we should leave Auntie here? Everyone at home really wants us to convince her to go back."

Zhenguan said, "Almost a dozen people have tried to convince her to stay at home, and none has succeeded. What more can we say? Besides, we all know that First Aunt vowed to become a nun if First Uncle were to return to Taiwan alive. She has to fulfill her promise to Buddha. You know that she is determined, so why force her?"

"But we don't want to lose her."

"Don't you think that First Aunt has suffered enough?"

"I—I don't know how to put it."

"Yinchan, we know First Aunt better than anyone else because we drink from the same well. She hasn't set everything aside. On the contrary, she is doing this out of love! For thirty years, she prayed to see First Uncle come back alive. She knows that her husband must have made a wish to return home when he was wandering an alien land, fighting a war, and suffering from illness. Now his wish has been fulfilled, and someone has to pay the debt for having it come true. Aunt Ruriko saved First Uncle; and although First Aunt would never say it out loud, she means to sacrifice her life so that her husband can stay with his Japanese wife."

Under the moonlight, the rocks glistened with a silvery sheen. The two girls sat side by side, talking. Their hearts were lucid and transparent, like a sparkling bronze mirror.

"Yinchan, look! What's that?"

Yinchan stood up to take a closer look. "It's a couplet flanking the back door of the temple. Do you want me to read it?"

"Yes, please!"

At that moment, bells began to chime. Zhenguan stood up and walked to where Yinchan was standing, and they read the couplet together:

The bells awaken one from an illusory dream
The moonlight on the mountain bathes one in zen. . . .

II

Zhenguan stayed up in the mountains for more than ten days.

Every morning Zhenguan and Yinchan would pick flowers in the garden. They also helped the nuns water the vegetables; the temple grounds were filled with vegetable patches. Luckily the temple had a constant supply of water. The nuns had hollowed out mature bamboo shoots and cut them into segments of equal length, which they then tied with lead wire, making bamboo pipes that could channel water from the mountain spring into several large water tanks for the temple.

As Zhenguan watered the vegetables with the shell of a hollow gourd, she remembered what Daxin had written in a letter:

The leafy vegetables that I planted have finally emerged. The sprouts are tiny, yellowish, and timid; they appear to be very fragile and tender (whereas the neighbors' turnips are very plump!). My vegetables refused to sprout at first, and I was frantic. I later found out it was because I did not cover the seeds with earth, and they were exposed to the air.

Life grows under these conditions: darkness, water, warmth, and love. Little plants cannot bear too much light! The hopes that I planted have begun to grow, and this makes me very happy.

Zhenguan and Yinchan would attend lectures every evening. The Buddhist scriptures were read in Sanskrit, which was beyond their understanding. Fortunately, that was always followed by thirty minutes of explanation. The nuns who read would teach the other nuns to read. The two girls always chose unobtrusive seats at the back of the classroom.

"There are a hundred different kinds of suffering. Only the wise can shun suffering."

"Those who get angry are deprived, and those who complain taste bitterness."

"The wise do not get angry; only fools get angry."

"Don't get into fights even if reason is on your side; don't seek revenge even when you are wronged; don't get angry even if you are provoked."

"Character is fate. Suffering stems from one's character. To avoid suffering, one must transform one's character, polish one's character, and allow one's character to shine and sparkle!"

First Aunt sat in the first row. Her fifty-year-old eyes were as bright as the eyes of a five-year-old child. The light on the altar glows like the heart of a lotus, Zhenguan thought, like her first aunt's character. She will shine into her next life, and she will still be beautiful!

In the two weeks that followed, First Uncle visited Guanziling Mountain three times. The first time he came with Yinshan, the second time he came alone, and the last time he brought Aunt Ruriko. First Aunt received them in her meditation room. Zhenguan didn't know what the three of them talked about, but when they emerged from the room, First Uncle's and Aunt Ruriko's eyes were rimmed with red. First Aunt, however, seemed quite unaffected. Those who love the most deeply sometimes appear to be the most unfeeling!

It was Zhenguan's last night in the mountain temple, her last lecture. Time never stops for anyone. Sitting on the bench, Zhenguan suddenly felt deeply attached to the place. As the teacher recited, the class followed:

To save all creatures
Before attaining enlightenment
I will persist
Until hell is empty. . . .

Zhenguan's heart beamed, as if it had just been polished to a sheen. She felt inspired by the deep and dedicated love of the Dizang Bodhisattva, who is devoted to saving all creatures between the Nirvana of Sakyamuni and the advent of Maitreya. After the evening lectures, the two girls returned to their room to rest. The autumn mountain air was chilly, and Yinchan spread out her blanket to sit down, yawning like a child. Zhenguan did not move a muscle. Yinchan asked her, "Are you going to meditate all night?"

"I'm not sleepy yet."

"You don't want to leave this place, do you?"

"Maybe yes and maybe no. Why?"

"Either way, I'm going to drag you home with me!"

Zhenguan laughed. "I can walk on my own two feet. What are you, a gangster?"

The two girls lay down to sleep but heard the door creaking. Yinchan opened it to find First Aunt standing there. "Auntie, you're still up!" she exclaimed.

"Yes, I came to visit you two. I know you're leaving tomorrow. Do tell Grandpa and the others that I'm fine here, tell them not to worry about me."

"We will."

Zhenguan sat on her bed studying First Aunt, who, with her long hair, seemed nothing like a Buddhist nun. She looked as she did in the secular world. And though she had the magnanimity of those who have renounced secular life, her affectionate nature remained as worldly as ever.

"What else would you like for us to do?"

"I've said all there is to say at home."

"Auntie, you take good care of yourself here."

"I will."

Zhenguan walked her aunt to the door. First Aunt stopped her and said, "Stay inside, it's chilly out there. And there's something that I've wanted to tell you all this time: You're not a little girl anymore, you've got to think ahead about your life. Don't be too headstrong and obstinate. Don't let your mother worry about you."

"I know."

Later, Zhenguan went to bed without saying anything to her cousin. Yinchan asked, "What's wrong with you?"

"Nothing."

She switched off the light and lay quietly. She waited until Yinchan was asleep before sitting up. She pushed the window open to look at the moon. The night air was chilly and, as Daxin had said once, night can be as cold as water.

The night drags on and on, where can I go?
The door to my room is shut
With furrowed brows I watch the moon sink in the sky
I hold myself back and refrain from seeking you out
Lonely is my pillow
And my heart belongs to you
My longing for you plunges me into endless sorrow. . . .

Alas, Zhenguan failed in her attempt to hold back tears. . . .

twenty

The swallows had flown away, and the cicadas were chirping all day long. Once again, the sweltering heat of summer was here. This was Zhenguan's third trip up to the Temple of the Blue Clouds. Before, she had always been accompanied by someone, and she would go up the mountain on the main road. This time, alone, she was happy to try an unfamiliar route.

First Aunt had been in the temple for over a year. She went home only once, when Grandpa was ill. She did not even attend the weddings of Yinan and Yinding. Zhenguan's mission was to bring her aunt some summer clothes prepared for her by her daughter-in-law, Yinshan's wife. Yinshan's wife had wanted to come herself, but her three young children made it difficult to leave home. Yinchan also was supposed to join Zhenguan, but she had slipped in the bathroom two days before and sprained her ankle. Zhenguan decided to make the trip alone, thinking, I'll go and come right back, and if I can't return the same day, I'll just stay there for one night.

On her way up to the temple, she encountered a number of little boys catching cicadas. Some were perched in a tree, and others were waiting beneath it with nets in their hands. She stopped to watch, curious. Two of the boys looked like brothers. The elder of the two had just caught a cicada in the palm of his hand. He placed it inside a plastic bag and gave it to his little brother, who clutched it as if he were afraid the cicada would fly away. Zhenguan said to him, "Little boy, if you hold the bag too tightly, the cicada will suffocate!"

He was about six years old. He looked at Zhenguan, and then at his brother, not knowing what to do.

"Yeah, it's true," his brother confirmed. "If you hold the bag like that, the cicada won't survive, and we will have caught it in vain!" The older brother, about eleven or twelve, was wearing a T-shirt with his school logo. He took the plastic bag from his brother and showed him how to hold it properly. Zhenguan looked at his ruddy face and asked, "What are you going to do with it now that you've caught it?"

The boy wiped his brow. "I can listen to its chirping at home—it sings beautifully," he answered. "It was clamoring for me to capture it!" He lunged forward suddenly with his net, tied to the end of a long and slender bamboo rod. "Wow, I just caught another one!"

"Brother, is it male or female?"

"Male, male!"

"Then the one in the bag has a mate. Will they bear little cicadas?"

"I don't know!"

Zhenguan looked at the cicada trapped in the net. "How do you know it's a male?" she asked.

The boy laughed but answered seriously, "Because it chirps. Only male cicadas chirp, the females don't." He lunged again. Grabbing his little brother's hand, he ran toward the prey.

Zhenguan continued on her way up the trail. She arrived at a house where an old woman was collecting the vegetable leaves she had laid out in the sun to dry. A young boy stood beside her with a bamboo basket. The child spotted Zhenguan and called out to the old lady, who stopped working to greet Zhenguan. "Hello, it's so hot out here under the sun; why don't you come in and have a cup of tea before you go on?"

"Thank you, madam, but I am in a hurry to get to the temple."

"Good for you! May Buddha protect you and your family! Do you know the way? I can ask my grandson to lead you."

"I do know the way, but that's very kind of you."

The old lady said something to her grandson. He put down the basket and ran into the house, returning a moment later with a glass of water.

"Come, take a drink. One can get dizzy from the heat even staying at home, but you're out here walking under the hot sun."

The boy brought her the water, and his gaze and his gait tugged at Zhenguan's heart. They touched her deeply, the old woman's kindness and the little boy's solemnity. She drank every drop of the water and returned the glass to the little boy, who disappeared back into the house like a wisp of smoke. He looked so much like Yinxi.

"Granny, I'll be on my way now," she said.

"All right; do visit us on your way down."

Zhenguan arrived at the temple gate at sunset and set about trying to locate First Aunt's room. She realized all of a sudden that she had not warned First Aunt of her visit. She couldn't be away, could she? It was probably needless worry, though. After all, her first aunt was a quiet person who rarely ever left home. What reason would she have to leave her place of meditation? Even if she were not in her room, she would probably be in the nearby mountains, and Zhenguan could page her over the Blue Cloud loudspeakers.

Zhenguan was certain that she would find her aunt if she just looked around. Her aunt's room was locked, and Zhenguan stopped at the door, contemplating what she should do next. A nun passed by, and Zhenguan asked, "Excuse me, do you—"

The nun seemed to recognize her vaguely and said, "Are you looking for Suyun? She has gone into seclusion and will be away for some time."

"Oh, how long must I wait to see her?"

"Seven days."

Zhenguan was speechless. The nun continued, "Since you're here, though, why not just stay with us while you wait? I can show you to a room if you'd like."

Zhenguan followed her. They arrived at the room she remembered staying in last time with Yinchan. The nun lit a coil of insect-repellant incense before leaving, adding, "Let us know if we can help you in any way." Zhenguan thanked her and took out a fresh change of clothes. She went to the little stone chamber to bathe herself and then washed her clothing before going to the dining room for dinner. It was seven by the time she returned to her room.

Surrounded by quiet, she was finally forced to face herself. It was the moment she had dreaded. Daxin had been gone for two years now. In that time, Zhenguan had thought of getting in touch with him. The seasons had changed from winter to spring, spring to summer, summer to autumn. Zhenguan waited and waited, but there came not a word. With whom can I share my loneliness? she had asked herself over and over. The past? It didn't count anymore. . . . Such thoughts would have brought tears to Zhenguan's eyes before. But now she felt that all her frustrations had been exhausted in this battle of emotions. She knew that Daxin needed to collect himself. Both of them needed to regain peace of mind and allow their thoughts to settle, and neither would make any more moves until then. But how long was it going to take?

Zhenguan decided to walk toward the classroom, where she heard the chanting of mantras. She must learn to stand on her own two feet! The chanting took place at the west end of the temple now, because the number of people attending class had increased, exceeding the capacity of the old facilities. Zhenguan followed the lights. The mountains were quiet, and the stillness of the night made the temple seem calmer and darker.

Once inside the classroom, she felt herself becoming serene. The first line that she heard clearly was: "Greed, obsession, and infatuation bring about suffering." The words filled her heart like a net full of fish.

"Don't feel wronged. Even if the people of the world do not acknowledge you, heaven will."

"If you indulge in feeling wronged, worms will eat into your heart."

"Character is fate, and fate is character."

"Your conscience is the field that breeds your offspring. Good offspring come from good hearts."

"There is this life, and there is the next. One must live one's life in the context of both this world and the others to come."

"To hear the truth and not listen is foolishness."

Zhenguan ruminated over these words for the next two days and nights. And yet her thoughts continued to overwhelm her. At dusk on the third day, she sat on the rock that she had once shared with Yinchan. Reading the sutra behind the temple, she felt a sudden sense of urgency. All at once, she just wanted to leave the place. She returned to her room, packed her belongings, and turned her aunt's clothes over to a nun. "Why are you leaving now?" the nun asked.

"I did not tell my family that I would be staying here for so long. They will be worried if I don't get home soon."

"If that's the case, I won't try to keep you. Don't worry, I will give these to Suyun."

Zhenguan thanked her, then walked out of the temple into the gentle breezes of early evening. The trip down the mountain would take forty or fifty minutes, and she thought to herself, I should enjoy these soft winds as I walk; then I'll take the six-thirty bus home. Zhenguan realized why she'd felt so anxious a few minutes before. Her cousin, Yindan, had just returned to Taipei from Japan ten days ago, and today she was going to return with First Uncle and Aunt Ruriko to their ancestral home. Second Aunt was leaving for the United States tomorrow. Zhenguan's cousin Huian had started a family and was fulfilling his promise to take care of his widowed mother.

Events and people were all falling into place . . . with the exception of Daxin. Why was she still thinking of him? The sky darkened into night. Zhenguan looked at the sparkling lights in the distance, and a song drifted toward her:

I am not disturbed by love that has gone askew
As long as there's a road there will be traffic
The maple leaves fall off without dying
Because come springtime they will live again. . . .

Zhenguan trembled at the words. She ran after the singing voice.

The sun sinks into the western horizon without a trace
The water flows into the ocean without looking back. . . .

"Granny—!" Zhenguan recognized the old woman whom she had met three days ago. "Granny . . . was it you who was singing just now?"

She was shy, like a new bride. "Young lady, you are . . . ?"

"You gave me a glass of water on my way up the mountain."

"Oh, yes, of course! Have you finished your prayers?"

"Granny, I—were you singing just now?"

"Yes, that was me. Please don't laugh at my voice!"

"No, not at all. It was beautiful."

"I've known that song since I was a little girl. Sit with me for a while, won't you?"

Zhenguan sat down, her heart still aflutter from the song. "Granny, could you please sing it one more time for me?"

"No, no, I can't sing with someone listening," she demurred, smiling and covering her mouth with her fan.

"Where is the little boy that I saw last time? Your grandchild—"

"Oh, he is in the house. He's busy with the silkworms that he keeps in my sewing box. He picks mulberry leaves for them every day and doesn't seem to have much interest in studying. Oh, that boy!"

"Are there just the two of you?"

"Oh no, his parents are away visiting my daughter-in-law's parents. They will return tomorrow. Atong has a younger sister as well—"

"Granny, you have such a beautiful voice. Won't you sing the song again? Please!"

"My voice may be healthy, but my eyesight is failing. Yesterday while I was cleaning Atong's room, I threw away his box of silkworms by mistake. He was so upset that he cried for hours."

"Just like that?"

"The silkworms had already spun their cocoons. He had been raising them since they were baby worms, watched them shed their skins and spit silk. . . . I have suffered from bad eyesight for a long time. I cried my eyes out for his grandfather when I was younger."

"What happened? Did you find the box?"

"Yes, eventually, and nothing was missing. The silkworms were wrapped in their cocoons, though, so we couldn't tell if they were still alive. He couldn't even eat his dinner last night. I felt so bad for him! I tried to console him all morning, thinking that little children are easily cheered. But who knows, he is hiding in his room again. Let me go check on him."

The old woman stood up and Zhenguan followed. Just then,

the little boy started shouting, "Grandma, Grandma! Come quickly!"

"What's going on?"

The little boy rushed out of the house. Holding a box in his hands, he announced with shining eyes, "Grandma, they're still alive!"

"How do you know?" The old woman bent to look into the box and then said, "Yes, they are moving. Wait, is something different? They—"

The boy continued excitedly, "They're changing into moths! They're making their way out of the cocoons and preparing to fly away!"

Zhenguan's feeling at that moment was beyond words. It was as if her wounds had finally healed.

The child suddenly noticed her presence and became a little shy.

"Do you remember me?" she asked him.

"Yes . . . you're the auntie who was thirsty. Do you want to see my moths?"

"Yes, please show them to me!"

Zhenguan walked close to him and peeked into the box to see one moth after another flapping its wings. Her eyes filled up with tears, for in them she saw herself! She had been trapped for so long in a lonely cocoon. And now, this ten-year-old boy and his moths had brought her enlightenment.

The old woman asked her grandchild, "Atong, you are in fourth grade already. Do you know why silkworms spit silk and hide themselves in their cocoons?"

The child laughed. "Of course! Silkworms only hide in their cocoons for a short time. But then they transform themselves into moths that can fly away!"

Daxin had once told her that children are as genuine as genuine can be. Zhenguan's thoughts had been going around and around in circles before they finally found peace in this young child's words. The suffering, the spitting of silk, the self-captivity . . . these were nature's phases of transformation. But finally, the moth breaks through its cocoon to live its life!

Zhenguan nodded and bade them farewell, saying, "Granny, I'd better get going if I'm to catch the bus."

"It's almost eight o'clock, and the trail leading down the mountain can be treacherous. Why don't you stay overnight and leave in the morning?"

"Thank you, but if I hurry, I'll be able to catch the eight-thirty. If I don't get home tonight, my family will worry."

"You're right. I'll have Atong walk you down the mountain then!"

"But he's just a child—"

"Don't worry, he runs up and down that trail a dozen times a day. He can show you a shortcut that will take you to the bus stop in ten minutes."

The child walked her toward the bus stop, holding his box in his arms all the way. Zhenguan looked at him and thought of herself. She had been so obsessed with love, and it had brought her so much suffering. If it weren't for this little boy and his silkworms. . . .

"Atong, I don't know how to thank you!"

"It's nothing! Will you come visit us again?"

"Yes, I will."

Zhenguan felt as if she were returning to the world anew. Lights glittered at the bus stop. "Atong, we're almost there," she said. "I can make it on my own. Why don't you hurry home?"

"But Grandma wants me to see you off."

"The bus won't be arriving for another twenty minutes. You shouldn't let your grandmother worry."

"Okay, I'll be on my way then."

"Walk safely. And Atong, thank you."

The child disappeared like a nimble rabbit, and Zhenguan looked up at the moon in the sky.

Thousands of mountains bask in the same moonlight
Millions of households enjoy the same springtime
A thousand rivers reflect a thousand moons
And the clear, clean sky stretches for millions of miles.

She wanted to get back as fast as she could to the moonlight of her hometown by the sea. She was still Zhenguan, darling of her dear family. . . .

As for the pain that Daxin had brought her, she would return it all to heaven and earth, and to the deities between and beyond. This she would do on her way down the moonlit path that led her back home.

notes

CHAPTER ONE

1. In the traditional Chinese calendar, the year is divided into twenty-four terms, or *jieqi*. Great Snow is the twenty-first solar term, and it falls on December 7–8. Winter Solstice falls on December 21–22.
2. In the cycle of twelve years that comprises the Chinese zodiac, each year is assigned an animal. The sequence is as follows: mouse, ox, tiger, rabbit, dragon, snake, horse, sheep, monkey, rooster, dog, and pig.
3. The *Thousand-Word Classic, qianzi wen,* is a primer for Chinese children comprised of moral teachings and historical allusions. The text contains rhymed verses that facilitate memorization.
4. *The Women's Duties at Home* and *Words of Advice,* a guide to virtuous living.
5. During World War II, Taiwan was still under Japan's colonial rule. Many Taiwanese were forcibly drafted into the Japanese army, and many never returned.

6. The *Three-Character Classic, sanzi jing,* is a primer for school children. Rhyming lines embody wisdom in a series of three words.
7. Xu Maokung was a famous military advisor who assisted the emperor, Li Shimin, in founding the Zhen-guan reign (627–649) during the Tang Dynasty. The Zheng-guan reign is considered to be one of the most thriving and prosperous in Chinese history. Li Shimin, however, had to kill two of his brothers in a bloody *coup d'état* to become emperor.
8. Qin Shubao was a well-known general who fought by the side of Li Shimin.
9. Cheng Yaojin was also a famous general in Li Shimin's camp.
10. Yu Chigong was a loyal general to the Tang emperor.
11. Qi-xing Niang-niang was a fairy who fell in love with a cow herder. She and her lover were doomed to meet only once a year, on the eve of July 7 of the lunar calendar. According to popular belief, Qi-xing Niang-niang, also known as Qi-niang Ma, is the guardian goddess of little children and young women.

CHAPTER TWO

1. The ovary and digestive organs of the crab, considered by many Chinese to be delicious and nutritious.

Modern Chinese Literature from Taiwan

Wang Chen-ho, *Rose, Rose, I Love You*
Cheng Ch'ing-wen, *Three-Legged Horse*
Chu T'ien-wen, *Notes of a Desolate Man*